WICKED AS SIN

SHAYLA BLACK

WICKED AS Sin

ONE-MILE & BREA: PART ONE
WICKED & DEVOTED

New York Times
Bestselling Author

SHAYLA BLACK

Steamy. Emotional. Forever.

WICKED AS SIN
Written by Shayla Black

This book is an original publication by Shayla Black.

Copyright 2020 Shelley Bradley LLC

Cover Design by: Rachel Connolly

Edited by: Amy Knupp of Blue Otter

Proofread by: Fedora Chen & Kasi Alexander

Excerpt from *Wicked Ever After* © 2020 by Shelley Bradley LLC

ISBN: 978-1936596669

ABOUT WICKED AS SIN

**He's ruthless. She's off-limits. But he's just met his one weakness...
Now nothing will stop him from making her his.**

Pierce "One-Mile" Walker has always kept his heart under wraps and his head behind his sniper's scope. Nothing about buttoned-up Brea Bell should appeal to him. But after a single glance at the pretty preacher's daughter, he doesn't care that his past is less than shiny, that he gets paid to end lives...or that she's his teammate's woman. He'll do whatever it takes to steal her heart.

Brea has always been a dutiful daughter and a good girl...until she meets the dangerous warrior. He's everything she shouldn't want, especially after her best friend introduces her to his fellow operative as his girlfriend—to protect her from Pierce. But he's a forbidden temptation she's finding impossible to resist.

Then fate strikes, forcing Brea to beg Pierce to help solve a crisis. But his skills come at a price. When her innocent flirtations run headlong into his obsession, they cross the line into a passion so fiery she can't say no. Soon, his past rears its head and a vendetta calls his name in a mission gone horribly wrong. Will he survive to fight his way back to the woman who claimed his soul?

FOREWARD

If you HAVE NOT READ either the **Wicked Lovers** or **Devoted Lovers** series upon which the foundation of the Wicked & Devoted series is built, I've written these books so that you'll have no trouble jumping in and following along as I move forward. You will meet a host of new characters, and at the end of Wicked as Sin, if you're interested in getting to know them better, I've provided you a handy list of characters and their book titles. That's all you need to know in order to get started. I hope you enjoy your introduction to this new deep, delicious world!

If you HAVE READ the **Wicked Lovers** and/or **Devoted Lovers** series, let's talk about time. Real-world time and story-world time are not the same. The events of Wicked & Devoted kick off shortly BEFORE the events of *Falling in Deeper* (Wicked Lovers, book 11) and will carry through the same timeframes as *Holding on Tighter* (Wicked Lovers, book 12), then continue on through *Devoted to Pleasure* (Devoted Lovers, book 1), *Devoted to Wicked* (Devoted Lovers, book 1.5), and *Devoted to Love* (Devoted Lovers, book 2)—and beyond. This means, for instance, that while it's been years (in real-world time) since I created the stories of some of your favorite characters, only some months have passed in their world. But I promise you, there's a reason for this. Things are about to get mighty interesting...

I hope you enjoy your first foray into my Wicked & Devoted world.

Happy reading!
Shayla

PROLOGUE

Sunday, January 11
Sunset, Louisiana

Finally, he had her cornered. He intended to tear down every last damn obstacle between him and Brea Bell.

Right now.

For months, she'd succumbed to fears, buried her head in the sand, even lied. He'd tried to be understanding and patient. He'd made mistakes, but damn it, he'd put her first, given her space, been the good guy.

Fuck that. Now that he'd fought his way here, she would see the real him.

One-Mile Walker slammed the door of his Jeep and turned all his focus on the modest white cottage with its vintage blue door. As he marched up the long concrete driveway, his heart pounded. He had a nasty idea how Brea's father would respond when he explained why he'd come. The man would slam the door in his face; no maybe about that. After all, he was the bad boy from a broken home who had defiled Reverend Bell's pretty, perfect daughter with unholy glee.

But One-Mile refused to let Brea go again. He'd make her father listen…somehow. Since punching the guy in the face was out of the question, he'd have to quell his brute-force instinct to fight dirty and instead employ polish, tact, and charm—all the qualities he possessed zero of.

Fuck. This was going to be a shit show.

Still, One-Mile refused to give up. He'd known uphill battles his whole life. What was one more?

Through the front window, he spotted the soft doe eyes that had haunted him since last summer. Though Brea was talking to an elderly couple, the moment she saw him approach her porch, her amber eyes went wide with shock.

Determination gripped One-Mile and squeezed his chest. By damned, she was going to listen, too.

He wasn't leaving without making her his.

As he mounted the first step toward her door, his cell phone rang. He would have ignored it if it hadn't been for two critical facts: His job often entailed saving the world as people knew it, and this particular chime he only heard when one of the men he respected most in this fucked-up world needed him during the grimmest of emergencies.

Of all the lousy timing…

He yanked the device from his pocket. "Walker here. Colonel?"

"Yeah."

Colonel Caleb Edgington was a retired, highly decorated military officer and a tough son of a bitch. One thing he wasn't prone to was drama, so that single foreboding syllable told One-Mile that whatever had prompted this call was dire.

He didn't bother with small talk, even though it had been months since they'd spoken, and he wondered how the man was enjoying both his fifties and his new wife, but they'd catch up later. Now, they had no time to waste.

"What can I do for you?" Since he owed Caleb a million times over, whatever the man needed One-Mile would make happen.

Caleb's sons might be his bosses these days…but as far as One-Mile was concerned, the jury was still out on that trio. Speaking of which, why wasn't Caleb calling those badasses?

One-Mile could only think of one answer. It was hardly comforting.

"Or should I just ask who I need to kill?"

A feminine gasp sent his gaze jerking to Brea, who now stood in the doorway, her rosy bow of a mouth gaping open in a perfect little *O*. She'd heard that. *Goddamn it to hell.* Yeah, she knew perfectly well what he was. But he'd managed to shock her repeatedly over the last six months.

"I'm not sure yet." Caleb sounded cautious in his ear. "I'm going to text you an address. Can you meet me there in fifteen minutes?"

For months, he'd been anticipating this exact moment with Brea. "Any chance it can wait an hour?"

"No. Every moment is critical."

Since Caleb would never say such things lightly, One-Mile didn't see that he had an option. "On my way."

He ended the call and pocketed the phone as he climbed onto the porch and gave Brea his full attention. He had so little time with her, but he'd damn sure get his point across before he went.

She stepped outside and shut the door behind her, swallowing nervously as she cast a furtive glance over her shoulder, through the big picture window. Was she hoping her father didn't see them?

"Pierce." Her whisper sounded closer to a hiss. "What are you doing here?"

He hated when anyone else used his given name, but Brea could call him whatever the hell she wanted as long as she let him in her life.

He peered down at her, considering how to answer. He'd had grand plans to lay his cards out on the table and do whatever he had to —talk, coax, hustle, schmooze—until she and her father both came around to his way of thinking. Now he only had time to cut to the chase. "You know what I want, pretty girl. I'm here for you. And when I come back, I won't take no for an answer."

CHAPTER ONE

The previous year
Saturday, July 26

"Y ou okay?" Cutter Bryant, her best friend and pseudo older brother, squeezed her hand as they stepped onto the back patio of his boss's home.

Brea Bell took in the chaotic summer party—the smoking barbecue, the loud music, the clinking beers, and male laughter booming from his fellow operatives at EM Security Management, none of whom seemed to have brought a date. She was the only woman in the yard, and suddenly every man seemed to turn and focus on her. "A little overwhelmed."

"I'm not surprised. It's hot as hellfire tonight, and there's a lot of testosterone here." He glanced at the handful of men clustered in conversation across the lawn.

"You tried to tell me."

"For your own good. But you're a stubborn thing. Always have been." He gave her an encouraging smile. "Try to have some fun, huh?"

She nodded. "Thanks for inviting me. Daddy has been encouraging me to get out of the house and spread my wings a little."

But he would never let her spend an evening out with a man he didn't know well and wholeheartedly approve of. Since Cutter had known her from birth, he was one of the few who fit into that category.

"You need to find your future, Bre-bee. It's time."

Cutter was right. She couldn't simply be the preacher's dutiful daughter, helping Daddy care for the residents of tiny Sunset, Louisiana, for the rest of her life. She and Cutter had talked about that more than once. Brea agreed…but she didn't know where to start. Since she enjoyed helping the folks in town look and feel their best, she'd gone to cosmetology school rather than college. Nothing she loved more than contributing, relieving, serving, and assisting others. Their happiness fed her own.

But lately, she'd been fighting a restlessness brewing inside her. A wildness, like the devil was whispering temptation in her ear. Brea didn't dare answer, no matter how alluring the siren call.

"It is." She tucked a strand of her long caramel hair behind her ear and peered Cutter's way. "So your teammates came alone tonight. Does that mean they're, um…single?"

"All of them, except the bosses." He slanted her a sideways glance. "You're not looking to get married right away, are you? There's more to life than that."

Sometimes his overprotective nature meant he treated her not just like the younger sister he'd never had, but a girl.

"Of course I know. But I'm almost twenty-two and I've been on exactly two dates in my life. I think I'm entitled to want male companionship."

"Yeah. I just don't know if this is the best place to look. These men are hardened warriors—special operators, spies, snipers... They have to leave unexpectedly at a moment's notice. They've seen things, done things…"

"You, too. But you're a defender. A protector. And you're perfectly wonderful. Some woman will be lucky to have you someday."

But it wouldn't be her. Her connection with Cutter was—and always had been—purely platonic. Neither of them wanted their relationship any other way.

"I'm not in any hurry to get married. But, contrary to what you say, I suspect you are. So…" He sighed. "I'll give you some background before I introduce you around. Remember, I told you that Caleb Edgington formed this team a few years back, then turned it over to his sons? Hunter, his older"—he pointed to the hard-jawed man grilling burgers—"is a former SEAL. He's married to Kata, who's probably in the kitchen with his brother's wife. Logan, his younger, is also a former SEAL. He's the guy at the cooler watching Tara, the redhead, through the window with that dirty leer."

Brea was relieved to learn she wasn't the only woman here. "And the others?"

"Hunter and Logan's stepbrother, Joaquin Muñoz, is former NSA. He's the tall one with his back to the fence in the circle of men across the yard. His wife, Bailey, is a ballerina, but she's on tour right now. Josiah Grant, the buff guy next to him, is former CIA. The other two, Zy and Trees, are tight. They served together in some government program I'm not privy to know about." Cutter rolled his eyes. "Trees' real name is Forest Scott but everyone calls him Trees because—"

"He's incredibly tall." Brea blinked. "Wow."

"Exactly. He's a cyber security specialist and he's exceptionally good at it. And his buddy Zy—"

"Looks a lot like Zac Efron. The grown-up version, not the Disney kid."

Cutter laughed. "Which is why he's nicknamed Zyron. His real name is Chase Garrett, but around here he doesn't answer to that. Besides being our class clown, he's our demolitions guy. He loves blowing stuff up."

"That's a little scary, but…" Brea let out a breath. She'd come here to get out of her sheltered bubble and meet people. "You should probably introduce me to everyone on your team."

Cutter hesitated. "Yeah. I'm just going to warn you… We're missing one, Pierce Walker. I don't know if the bastard will show tonight. He's a loner, and you're not missing much. But if he turns up, avoid him, you hear me? He's no good."

"All right." Cutter was a good judge of character, so she'd take his word on that.

"That's my girl." He smiled her way, then they stepped off the back patio together.

As they crossed the lawn, Brea clung to his hand. She'd always been shy around new people, men especially. Thankfully, every one of his teammates smiled as they approached. Josiah, whose voice told her he wasn't from around here, seemed nice. Zyron and Trees both had Southern gentlemen's manners, though charm rolled off Zy's tongue while Trees seemed content to let his pal do the talking.

No denying each of them was fit, sharp, interesting, and attractive. But none sparked her interest. Honestly, that was all right. Like Cutter had said, there was more to life than getting married. Still, she couldn't lie. She'd looked forward to being some man's wife since she was a little girl. Her friends had all left Sunset to pursue their ambitions of becoming doctors or actresses or teachers. And that was lovely—for them. Even if it sounded old-fashioned, Brea wanted a husband, kids, home, and happiness.

That wasn't too much to ask, right?

After some small talk, Cutter led her to Hunter and his brother, Logan, respectively. The elder brother flipped burgers with intent focus. Though he was perfectly polite, it was obvious Hunter was a doer, not a talker. Logan, on the other hand, oozed charm. He smiled, winked, and laughed, making up for all the conversation she hadn't had with his brother. But under his façade she sensed something relentless, something dark. In fact, she felt that undercurrent in all the men here, even Cutter. They'd seen atrocities, stockpiled secrets, even committed sins in the name of national security.

Undoubtedly, she'd be better off with someone simpler. She could smile and nod the rest of the night, happy to make the acquaintance of Cutter's co-workers, then figure out how to meet a nice accountant or a handsome professor with whom she might share her future.

She loitered for an hour with Kata and Tara in the kitchen, helping to prepare macaroni salad and bake cookies. They were lovely and witty and funny. Gritty and interesting, too. Stories of Kata's son and Tara's twin girls had her giggling.

Together, they brought the food outside and set everything on a big buffet table as Hunter yelled to all at the gathering, "Chow time. Come and get it!"

Before she and Cutter could grab a plate, Logan snagged his arm. "Bryant, can you give me a hand throwing more cold ones in the cooler?"

"Sure." He turned to her. "Why don't you get your plate? I'll join you in a few."

And sit with all these strangers by herself? "Actually, I need to use the ladies' room first. Meet you at the buffet table?"

With a nod, Cutter turned to help his boss, his smile a white flash in the setting sun. Why couldn't he have been more than a friend in her heart? He was perfect in so many ways, and falling for him would have made her life so much easier…

As the others filled their plates and settled at a giant picnic table on the back patio, Brea hustled inside and found the powder room. As she finished washing her hands, the doorbell rang. A glance out the big kitchen window proved no one else had heard a thing over the loud music and even louder conversation. Rather than disturb Hunter, Logan, or their wives, she headed to the front door.

When she pulled it open, Brea found a mountain of a man standing on the other side. He towered over her, his shoulders taking up most of the portal. Beefy, inked arms crossed over a midnight-blue shirt, stretched tightly across his imposing chest. He had shorn dark hair, an even closer cropped beard, black eyes that saw inside her soul in an instant, and a scowl that told her she'd better not mess with him. He looked like the devil. He smelled like sex and sin.

Her heart lurched, and she utterly lost her ability to think. "Hi."

"Hey."

His eyes didn't leave her face, but she had the distinct impression he'd already taken in every inch of her from head to toe. Brea couldn't repress her shudder.

He glanced beyond her shoulder, out the big window in the family room, which overlooked the backyard. "I'm here for the EM party. This Hunter Edgington's place?"

"Yes." She stepped back to let him in since she couldn't seem to find more words.

He shut the door behind him and stared down at her. "You got a name?"

She inched back...though some forbidden urge prompted her to scoot closer. "B-Brea."

"Yeah?" He stepped into her personal space, following her until she backed into a wall and blinked up at him. "That's a pretty name."

"Thank you," she said automatically. "I like your..." *Everything.* Each part of him was put together so perfectly, he made her heart beat like a mad, fluttery thing and her stomach tighten.

"My what?" A corner of his lips lifted into something she could almost call a grin.

"Shirt," she improvised.

Oh, could she sound any more ridiculous?

"Yeah?" Amusement laced his voice.

"It's, um...a nice shade of blue."

He smiled, blindsiding her with the transformation of his face from desolate to dazzling.

"Good to know. I like your..." He scanned her up and down, his fathomless eyes traversing her slowly. "Dress. The lace is pretty, like you. Except..."

When he reached for her, one finger of his massive hand outstretched, her thoughts raced wildly. Would he touch her? Kiss her? Undress her? The way his eyes darkened told her all that—and more— had already crossed his mind.

Her heart thudded madly. "Except?"

He didn't answer with words, simply settled his fingers on her collarbone. The instant he touched her, their connection reverberated through her entire body, jolting and shuddering clear down to her toes. He glided one rough fingertip across her skin. Goose bumps erupted. Tingles spread. She reeled as he slid his digit under the thin strip of white lace draped over her shoulder and gave it a gentle tug.

Brea's eyes slid shut. She didn't know what he was doing to her or why, but if he wanted anything from her—anything at all—her answer was yes.

Then suddenly, his touch was gone. "Your strap was twisted."

He wasn't making a pass? No. But some forbidden part of her desperately wanted him to.

Embarrassed as all get-out, she sent him what she hoped was a blankly polite smile. "Thank you."

She expected him to release her then. Instead, he curled his fingers behind her shoulder and cupped it, drawing her closer. She could happily lose herself in his eyes. She ached to. Everything about him made her aware that he was a man...and that she'd never known the touch of one.

"You're a little thing."

"You're huge," she blurted, then blushed.

"You think?" He sent her a smug grin. "Or have you looked?"

Another rush of heat climbed to her cheeks. Did he mean what she thought? "Um, dinner just started, if you're hungry..."

"I am. But food can wait." His big, rough knuckles skimmed her cheek before he tucked a curl behind her ear. She barely managed to resist closing her eyes in pleasure. "Are you a friend of Kata's or Tara's?"

"Neither."

He paused. "Are you dating one of the other guys?"

"I..." She wasn't sure how to explain her relationship with Cutter.

"Brea!" She turned to find her best friend at the back door, his snarl warning the other man away. "Come here. Now, honey."

She jumped at the demand in his voice. He would never be so insistent...unless something was wrong. "O-okay." She faced the big, dark stranger again. "Excuse me."

For a second, he looked as if he might object. Something in her wanted him to, but he merely stepped back, his jaw set in a hard line.

Brea edged away. As soon as she reached Cutter's side, her breathing eased. Her nerves bled away. And when he curled a protective arm around her, she felt safe and sheltered.

But he didn't make her feel alive—not like the other man.

"Are you all right?"

Why was Cutter acting as if the newcomer might unleash terrible savagery on her in the foyer? "Of course."

He acknowledged her with an impatient nod. "Time to eat. Why don't you head on outside? I'll meet you at the buffet table."

And leave so he could berate the man for doing nothing but staring a little more than was truly polite and straightening her strap?

She shook her head. "I'd rather not go alone."

While Cutter weighed her words, Brea felt the stranger's stare all over her. She risked a glance his way. Sure enough, he hadn't peeled his eyes off her. He seemed especially fixated on Cutter's arm around her middle.

"Please. I'm famished." She added a pleading note Cutter had never been able to resist.

"In a minute. Before I go, I'm going to say something you won't like, Bre-bee. If you'd rather not hear, I suggest you either leave or don't listen."

She considered chastising him, but she knew Cutter too well. He intended to have words with this stranger. He wouldn't budge an inch until he did.

She let loose an impatient sigh. "Go on, then."

He turned to the other man with a killing glare. "Keep the fuck away from her, Walker."

Pierce Walker, the teammate Cutter had claimed was no good?

"Why?" the stranger challenged.

"She's mine."

Brea's eyes widened. *Cutter had not just made her sound like his girlfriend.*

Oh, but he had…

Pierce's eyes narrowed but he said nothing.

"Are we clear?" Cutter demanded.

"You want me to fuck the fuck off?"

"Yeah. I do."

"Too bad, Boy Scout." Pierce glared with contempt. "I don't take direction from you."

"I mean it. Stay the fuck away. Or else."

Before Brea could object that their language was horrible and that she didn't belong to anyone, Cutter swept her out the back door to the waiting feast. She glanced back. The dark stranger was still staring, the spine-tingling awareness she felt reflecting back in his hot black eyes.

She didn't know Pierce Walker, but one thing she didn't doubt? He intended to come after her.

* * *

"WHAT THE DEVIL was that caveman bit about earlier?" Brea turned to Cutter in his big truck with a piqued glare. "You let everyone think I'm your girlfriend."

He had the good grace to wince. "Mostly Walker. I was protecting you."

"He was merely talking to me."

"While he undressed you with his eyes. I told you, he's no good."

Brea didn't understand. Nor did she feel like being the agreeable good girl she'd been her whole life. "He was perfectly pleasant until you confronted him."

"Bre-bee, you don't know him. I hate to be crass with you, but the man is only after you for a piece of ass. Besides being a lousy teammate, he's a douchebag. And I'm using exceptionally nice language for your sake. He takes unnecessary chances on the job, he doesn't listen to anyone, and he refuses to compromise."

She slanted him a glance. "You're no social butterfly yourself, and you've always been as stubborn as the day is long."

"But I would *never* put myself—or others—in an unnecessarily risky situation because I was arrogant enough to presume I was right."

"And he did?"

"He does it all the time." Cutter gripped the wheel like the memories alone chapped his hide.

"Is he usually right?"

"That's not the point—"

"Isn't it? You've always said people should fight for what they believe in."

"And they should. But how am I supposed to trust him as a teammate—with my life—when he won't stick to the plan?" He sighed. "Brea, look…he's not the marrying kind."

They'd just met, and she wasn't expecting a waltz down the aisle… but they had shared something—a moment—and she wasn't ready to let go yet. "You know that for a fact?"

"Well, I doubt when I saw him at Crawfish and Corsets off Highway Ninety last weekend, coming out of the back room with one of the female bartenders while zipping up his jeans and wearing a smile, that they'd been swapping Bible stories."

Brea swallowed down absurd jealousy she had no right to feel. "Cutter Edward Bryant, maybe you shouldn't be casting stones. You haven't been chaste your whole life, either."

He squirmed in his seat. "But I have relationships. I usually date women for a while before we take that step. I don't just nail random females in the back of a bar at one in the morning."

"No?" She raised a brow. "What were you doing there, then?"

"The whole team had gathered to play pool. Zy beat the hell—I mean, the heck—out of almost everyone. Since Walker isn't a team player, he decided to use his 'stick' for other activities."

"Maybe he just hasn't met the right woman yet."

"Are you thinking that's you?"

Cutter's tone made her sound incredibly naive, and it pricked her temper. She crossed her arms over her chest stubbornly. "How do you know I'm not?"

He sighed, looking as if he mentally groped for his patience. "Brebee, I love you. No matter what our blood says, you're my sister and I will protect you with my dying breath. If you want me to die early or go to prison for murder, you go ahead and take up with that man. Do you know he's a killer?"

"What do you mean? You killed people in Afghanistan."

"Combatants who wanted to end me simply because I was American. I wish I hadn't been put in that position, and I didn't relish a single one of their deaths. I'll even admit I haven't been without sin or blame since I went to work for EM. The job can force you to make snap judgments about whether or not the enemy feet away from you will really pull the trigger so you should pull yours first. I never do it without due consideration. But Walker? His sole job responsibility is to kill."

That couldn't be right. "What do you mean?"

Cutter nodded. "He's a well-trained military assassin who wants everyone to call him One-Mile because that's his way of bragging about his longest kill shot."

The news hit her like a punch to the chest. Yes, Pierce Walker had reeked of danger, but Cutter made him sound like a cold-blooded murderer. "His actions are not for us to judge. That's between him and God."

"But you need to know the truth. When Walker is given a mark, he doesn't ask questions. He doesn't feel compunction or remorse. He doesn't care about the blood on his hands, and if he touched you with them"—Cutter gripped the wheel so tightly his knuckles went white—"if he defiled you, I would have to kill him."

"I've never known you to dislike someone so intensely."

"That should tell you something." He stopped at a light and turned to pin her with a stare. "Promise me you won't ever tell him we're not a couple. That would be like waving a red cape in a bull's face. Promise me that when he comes sniffing around—and he will—that you'll have nothing to do with him."

Cutter's demand came from a place of caring. As far as he was concerned, her father wasn't worldly enough to protect her from men like Pierce Walker, so he would do it for Daddy. Brea wasn't worldly, either. She knew that. The instant, blinding attraction she'd experienced with Cutter's teammate had been unlike anything she'd ever felt. No wonder it had made her want him to be the right man for her.

But her feelings hardly meant he was.

"Brea, please," he pressed. "Promise me."

"All right." Cutter was probably right, and she tried not to be disappointed. But she already suspected she'd never feel as alive again as she had those handful of minutes with Pierce Walker. "I promise."

CHAPTER TWO

One-Mile did what he had been trained to do whenever he locked his sights on a target. He watched, studied, and dissected. He learned a mark's habits, weaknesses, and quirks. He traveled their haunts and memorized their stomping grounds. Then he figured out how and when to strike.

Except this time, he wasn't here for a kill.

During the EM shindig at Hunter's house last night, One-Mile had watched pretty Brea Bell. He hadn't spoken to her again. Cutter, the uptight prick, would have felt compelled to cut him off at the balls and start something. A team getting-to-know-you wasn't the place for strife. But neither his stare nor his thoughts had once strayed from the beautiful brunette. In those few hours, he'd discerned three important things: She was every bit as warmhearted as he'd first imagined. She was attracted to him, too. And most interesting, she was probably as passionate about her sex life with Cutter as she was about taking her trash to the curb.

As he'd watched Bryant lead her out to his truck and drive away, he had debated the wisdom of pursuing Brea. Then he'd decided fuck it. She deserved the orgasms her boyfriend wasn't giving her.

One-Mile couldn't put his finger on the reasons he wanted Brea so fiercely. She wasn't his type. Usually, he gravitated to blondes who liked to show off their tits, but he'd never encountered her sweet sort of allure. He wanted to see where this inexplicable desire led—and not merely as a fuck you to Cutter. Bryant could pound sand—or his own cock—for all One-Mile cared.

Which explained why he sat in his Jeep now, parked on Napoleon Avenue just before noon the following day, watching parishioners meander out of the little white church across the street and hoping for a glimpse of Brea.

She was one of the last to file out. Immediately, she fell into conversation with two elderly women before a little boy tugged on her skirt. When she bent and wrapped her arms around him, her smile was genuine and contagious. Then she slipped the imp a piece of candy from her purse and ruffled his hair in a motherly gesture that made the boy grin.

Thank fuck Cutter was nowhere in sight.

One-Mile was tempted to cross the street and plant himself in her personal space just to see recognition transform Brea's face—and make sure he hadn't misinterpreted her excitement when their eyes met.

But he could be patient, so he leashed the urge. The right moment would come. First, he needed facts.

"How deep are your ties to Bryant, pretty girl?" he muttered.

He'd stayed up half the night trying to figure that out, using search engines far more in-depth than Google. Within a few minutes he'd tracked down her vitals. Brea Felicity Bell. Her twenty-second birthday was next Thursday. She'd grown up in Sunset. Her mother had died from complications of childbirth. She'd been raised alone by her father, a local Baptist minister. She'd gotten good grades and never been in trouble. Apparently, everyone loved her. She currently worked as a hairdresser at a family-owned salon—the only one in Sunset. She'd grown up next door to Bryant and his family, but Cutter had moved to an unpublished address some while back. Brea wasn't shacking up with him, thank fuck.

Those facts told One-Mile everything and nothing. What did she look like first thing in the morning? What would she taste like under his tongue? What would she smell like after he'd freshly fucked her? He was hungry to know. But she intrigued him far more than mere sex would satisfy—a first for him. What made her smile? What made her cry? What made her mad? What made her heart melt? He needed to figure Brea out, and he'd never manage that simply by staring. He had to talk to her without Cutter or that church crowd surrounding her.

For the next twenty minutes, she weathered the summer heat, shaking hands, exchanging hugs, and listening to the people of her father's congregation, all with a patient smile and kind eyes. Something about her goodness was so compelling, probably because he'd never seen anything like it. He damn sure wasn't drawn in by her sack of a dress, which covered everything between her neck and her shins in a pale pink fabric sprinkled with gray and lavender flowers. She wore the silky light brown hair he ached to wrap around his hands in a loose bun that emphasized her delicate features and her slight build. She'd finished it off with a pair of sensible wedge sandals and a sheer wrap, presumably to combat the blast of air conditioning inside the church.

There was absolutely nothing sexy about Brea's appearance, yet everything about her made him harder than hell.

One-Mile made his living listening to his gut, and it was telling him there was something between him and this woman. So he didn't give a damn if she had a boyfriend. To hell with being polite. And fuck walking away.

Finally, a man he presumed was her father approached. After they exchanged a few words, she nodded. He cupped her shoulder and brushed a kiss across her cheek before disappearing inside the church again.

Then Brea headed for her little white Toyota. One-Mile already knew the make, model, license plate, and VIN, so he wasn't surprised when she hopped into the vehicle and pulled out of the lot. She drove right past him without so much as a glance in his direction. No surprise she didn't take stock of her surroundings. Why should she? She probably didn't have a care in the world, much less any enemies.

She'd certainly never made her living by her gun, and he doubted anything ever happened in this sleepy town.

He was about to blow through Brea Bell's life and change it forever.

One-Mile turned his Jeep over and followed her down the road, then out of Sunset, south on I-49 toward Lafayette. On the outskirts of town, she pulled off. He followed at a discreet distance, though it wouldn't have mattered. She only looked in the rearview mirror when she changed lanes.

"Where are you going?" he mused aloud when she putt-putted down a bumpy two-lane road and pulled into an overwhelmingly brown strip mall that had seen better decades.

Was she stopping in for donuts? Or meeting someone, like Bryant, at the diner on the corner for lunch?

One-Mile pulled in and parked on the far side of the lot, near a barber shop, then watched as she bypassed all of those establishments in favor of the beauty supply on the end. She exited her car and locked it, then fished her phone out of her purse as she crossed the lot, not paying a lick of attention to her surroundings.

As long as he was around, she could have her head in the clouds. He'd keep her safe. But he'd be damned if he set foot in the foreign territory dominated by hair dye and nail polish. He'd rather clean a loaded gun.

As she disappeared inside, he rolled down his window, cut off his engine, then turned up Fall Out Boy. He tapped his thumb against his steering wheel to the beat of the music and stared at the glass door. As "Centuries" faded out and Radiohead's "Creep" filled his ears instead, he had to smile. Yeah, he felt a bit like a creep following Brea just to get a few minutes alone with her. All he needed now was Sting crooning "Every Breath You Take" to feel like a full-on stalker.

At somewhere near the ten-minute mark, instinct poked him between the shoulder blades. He rolled up his windows, then hopped from his Jeep. He'd no more navigated the lot and positioned himself against her car door, ankles crossed and arms folded over his chest, when she stepped out of the shop. Halfway across the lot, she looked up from the contents of her bag. Her gaze found his feet. He watched it climb his legs, his torso, his shoulders…and finally settle on his face.

As recognition dawned, Brea stopped where she stood. The bag fell from her fingers and onto the roasting asphalt. Surprise flared across her face. "Pierce."

He could imagine her whispering to him just like that when he shocked her in bed. The thought made him harder. "Brea."

"Did you...follow me here?" She scrambled to recover her purchases, looking anywhere but at him.

He debated on the best way to answer. But why lie? "Yeah. You knew I was coming for you. Can we talk?"

She looked around as if she was expecting someone. One of her girlfriends? Or a rescuer, maybe Bryant?

"I-I have to go."

"Five minutes."

She shook her head. "I can't stay. The heat... It's oppressive."

One-Mile couldn't argue. Since moving here, he'd quickly discovered that summer in Louisiana was like the crotch pit of hell. Today was particularly sweltering. But he also didn't think the sudden flush of her cheeks had much to do with the temperature. "Then let me take you to lunch. There's an air-conditioned diner right there."

"I can't."

"Is your father expecting you home?"

Brea frowned. "How would you know that?"

He ventured closer. "After last night, I learned more about you."

"You snooped?"

"Researched," he corrected.

"Why?"

"You want me to spell it out for you, pretty girl?"

"Please."

Her prim response did something perverse to his libido. He crooked his finger at her. "Come here, and I will."

She backed away with wide eyes. "I shouldn't be talking to you."

"Because?"

"Cutter made me promise I wouldn't."

One-Mile couldn't keep the cynical smirk off his face. So the good guy was afraid the bad boy would steal his woman? He ought to be.

But One-Mile refused to make Bryant's tactical mistake and put Brea in the middle.

"I'm just looking for conversation."

Her eyes softened with regret. "I'm sorry."

Because she was the kind of woman who always kept her word. As much as her pushback frustrated One-Mile, he admired her conviction. "How about a little help, then? I moved here a few months back, and I don't know much about this corner of the state. You've lived around here your whole life. Insider information would be helpful."

"You didn't 'research' me and follow me here so I could be your walking Yelp."

He grinned. Brea might be sweet but that didn't mean she wasn't sharp.

"No. But I won't ask you for anything more. And regardless of what Bryant might have said, I would never hurt you."

Her full, rosy lips pursed. His cock jerked. The things he'd love to do to her mouth…

"What do you really want, Mr. Walker? Say it."

Since she'd asked for the truth… "You. Naked. Under me. Crying out in pleasure."

She sucked in a shuddering breath. "Why me? Why not the bartender you…connected with last weekend?"

Cutter would only tell her about that forgettable twenty minutes if he'd noticed, as One-Mile himself had, that Brea was attracted to him.

"Tell me you don't feel the pull between us."

Brea cut her gaze away and sank her teeth into that plush bottom lip.

"You do. I know you do." He edged closer. "Look at me."

She didn't. "I really need to go. Please don't follow me again. And don't pursue me. This"—she gestured between them—"won't work."

"Why?"

"We're different."

"Opposites attract."

She shook her head. "Too different."

"Meaning?"

"Sex could never be casual for me."

One-Mile believed that. "I suspect that, with you, sex would be anything but casual to me."

Brea sucked in a shaky breath. "Stop."

"What, trying to show you the options Cutter told you to ignore?"

Finally, she whipped an annoyed glare his way. "He doesn't tell me what to think."

"Good. You're smart enough to make up your own mind." He cocked his head. "Let me ask you a question."

"I've said no in every polite way possible, and we're done with this conversation, do you hear me?"

He did, but she wasn't listening to him, either. "Are you afraid of losing your boyfriend? Or worried you'll figure out he isn't flipping your switch and I can?"

"I'm not dignifying that question with an answer. Goodbye, Mr. Walker."

When she tried to walk around him, he planted himself in front of her again. "Tell me the truth, and I'll let you go."

She flashed him a surprisingly fierce expression. "I don't owe you anything."

"You don't owe *me* anything. But you owe it to yourself to be honest."

Then, because he couldn't stay in her way without pissing her off, One-Mile stepped aside, leaving her a straight path to her car. He'd rather stay and talk, even with the stifling midday sun beating down and the beads of sweat rolling down his back. But he'd given Brea food for thought. Hopefully, she'd thoroughly chew on it until he found another opportunity to talk to her.

She flashed him a wary glance, then made a beeline for her compact. As soon as she reached the door and gave the handle a tug, her phone rang, its chime clanging like church bells. She ripped into her purse for the device as she settled into the passenger's seat. "Hi, Daddy."

Her father. The preacher. Her only parent. Besides Cutter Bryant, he might be a major stumbling block…

"What?" Brea breathed in shock. "Oh, my gosh. How long ago? Where are they taking him?"

One-Mile's radar went off. Something was wrong.

"University. Yes, I-I know where that is. I'll be there as soon as I can. Did the paramedics say anything else?"

Shit. Had someone called an ambulance for her father?

"Okay. Th-thank you for letting me know." Brea turned and squeezed her eyes shut. Tears leaked from their corners. "I'll be there as quickly as I can."

She ended the call, visibly shaking as she tried to shove her phone back in her purse and set it in the passenger's seat. The thin strap snagged on the lace trim at her shoulder. When she nudged, the leather stubbornly resisted. Finally, she ignored the bag altogether and tried—twice—to insert her key in the ignition. But her fingers shook. Her keys jingled. She huffed in frustration.

One-Mile hated seeing her rattled.

He knelt in the open car door. "Hey. What's going on? I can help."

She looked a split second from bawling. "My d-dad collapsed at the church shortly after I left. Th-they think it's his heart. I have to go."

Third time was the charm because she finally managed to stick the key into the ignition, but her purse strap was still stuck. She grabbed at it with impatient fingers and yanked. The strap finally flopped off her shoulder but clung to the crook of her elbow. The bag itself fell to the passenger floorboard, dragging her forearm with it. The more she struggled, the more she looked ready to scream.

Touching her now was risky, but he'd rather she tell him to fuck off forever than have an accident in the twenty minutes it would take her to reach the hospital.

"Brea." He wrapped his hand around her fingers, still clutching the keys, and gave them a squeeze. "You're in no shape to drive. Let me take you."

She opened her mouth, an automatic refusal seemingly perched there. Instead, she pressed her lips together again. "You're right."

Relieved that she'd acquiesced, he helped her from the car, reaching in after her to retrieve her purse. He took the keys from her grasp, locked the compact, and guided her to his Jeep.

Once he had her buckled in and they were heading down the road, he slipped into problem-solving mode. "Has your father had any problems with his heart in the past?"

"No." And she looked completely stunned by the fact he was dealing with it now. "He's had high blood pressure for a few years, but he's controlled it with medication. I've tried to keep him on a heart-healthy diet, but he loves fried chicken and beignets and..." She shook her head as tears started streaming down her face. "The doctor told him his weight has been creeping up for a while, and he's more sedentary than he should be. I've encouraged him to walk with me or try one of my spin classes. Something. But lately he's been so busy and preoccupied. I thought it would pass. I should have insisted."

"You can't blame yourself. He's a grown-ass man, and you've gone above and beyond."

"No." She closed her eyes as guilty fear closed up her expression. "I do the grocery shopping, and I've indulged him more than I should, telling myself that once the summer cookouts were over and pieces of peach pie weren't so easy to come by that I'd make sure he ate healthier. But what if it's too late?"

One-Mile both understood and hated how much she worried, but her ability to love with her whole heart was obvious. Her body pinged with anxious devotion. The way she willed herself to be at her father's side this instant confirmed it.

He'd never had anyone love him like that. And he wanted it.

One hand gripped the wheel. The other he curled around hers. He was surprised—and thrilled as hell—when she grabbed his in return and squeezed.

"Wait and see what the doctors say."

She turned to him with big doe eyes that melted him. "I'm afraid."

"I know. But I'm here, whatever you need."

More tears fell down her cheeks. "He's all I've got. My mother died shortly after I was born."

"I read that last night. I'm sorry." He didn't know how any woman died in this day and age as a result of childbirth, and he wished like hell Brea hadn't lost her mom when she'd come into the world. Growing up without a mom sucked; he should know.

"I'll be all alone if..."

She didn't finish that sentence. One-Mile was glad for a lot of reasons, mostly because she didn't need to borrow more worry by assuming Reverend Bell would kick the bucket. But how interesting that she hadn't included Bryant in her someone-she's-got category…

"You won't. How old is your father?"

"Not quite fifty. He's still so young…"

For this kind of serious heart shit? "Yeah. That will work in his favor. And he's got you."

She tried to accept his words with a nod. "Along with his congregation. And God. The power of prayer is strong. I've seen it work. I need to pray for him and ask his parishioners to do the same."

"Absolutely." If that made her feel better, she should.

Brea nodded, then bowed her head. Her soft lips moved in silence. One-Mile couldn't resist sliding his gaze over her profile, sweeping from her crown, down the slope of her nose, past the stubborn point of her chin, and over the sweet swells of her breasts with his stare.

He wasn't proud of how hard that made him, but Brea flipped every one of his switches. He couldn't give up the chance to visually drink her in.

Suddenly, her lashes fluttered and she opened her eyes. "I feel better."

"Good." Prayer had never done squat for him, but if it centered her, then he was in favor.

"I should make some phone calls."

"Sure. We've got another ten minutes before we get there."

Absently, she nodded, then ripped into her purse to grab her phone. She called back the woman who had informed her of her father's collapse in the church. Jennifer Collins, the kind widow, had apparently agreed to ring some of the other long-time church members and start a prayer chain before coming to the hospital to start a vigil with Brea. Then she reached out to the associate pastor and asked him to field whatever community issues came her father's way for the foreseeable future. Finally, she dialed someone who wasn't answering the phone.

"That man…" She huffed in frustration.

"Cutter?" One-Mile ventured.

"He only answers about half the time. I swear I don't know what he's doing the other half."

Probably saving the world. That's who Cutter was and that was their job. But as far as One-Mile knew, there were no pressing cases at the moment, so he had to wonder if maybe Cutter was doing someone else. Cheating didn't seem like the overgrown Boy Scout's thing, but if he wasn't being faithful to Brea, One-Mile would have even less compunction about stealing her from the bastard.

He didn't offer up that commentary, however, just watched her dial someone else.

"Hi, Mama Sweeney. You seen Cutter today? He wasn't in church."

There was a long pause, then One-Mile heard the other woman speak, though he couldn't decipher her words.

But Brea's face fell. "Oh. Well...um, if you see him anytime soon, can you ask him to call me? It's urgent. Daddy's had an episode with his heart. I'm on my way to the emergency room at University Hospital right now."

From what he could tell, the woman on the other end of the line conveyed an appropriate amount of shock and worry, before promising to have Cutter call her as soon as he turned up.

Brea ended the conversation, looking tight-lipped. One-Mile bit back a million questions. Fuck Brea being none of his business. Right now, she felt alone in the world, and he intended to take care of her, hoist as much of her responsibility as she'd allow onto his shoulders. But she seemed a million miles away.

"You okay?" he asked as he exited the highway.

"Fine."

But she wasn't. Her mood had taken another downturn after she'd talked to Mama Sweeney, whoever that was.

One-Mile squeezed her hand. "If you need to talk, pretty girl, I'm listening."

She turned to him with a wrenching smile that nearly broke his heart. "Thank you."

But she didn't share her thoughts or give him her troubles, just sat taut and mute until they reached the emergency room.

The instant he parked his Jeep near the door, she shoved off her seat belt, grabbed her purse, and dashed toward the hospital. One-Mile jumped from the vehicle and ran after her, locking the doors behind him with a click of his fob. By the time he caught up to her, she'd already spoken to an attendant, who went to fetch someone who could tell her about her father's condition.

She clutched her hands together, looking as if she waited for the verbal equivalent of a mortal body blow.

Normally, he didn't think too much about other people's problems. Everyone had shit to deal with, and he didn't expect anyone to listen to him whine about his. But it ripped him up to see sweet Brea hurting this much.

"Take a deep breath," he encouraged as he slipped his arm around her petite shoulders.

It was impossible not to notice that she fit perfectly against him, her delicate frame just the right height to hold close.

"What if Daddy is—"

"Don't borrow trouble. Let's wait for someone to give us the update. In the meantime, stay strong."

"I'm trying. But when I imagine life without him, I don't feel strong…" She buried her face in his chest and began to sob softly.

Brea had sought *him* for comfort? Granted, everyone else here was a complete stranger. But to draw solace from him, she had to trust him on some gut level she hadn't yet admitted to herself.

Tamping down his triumph, One-Mile wrapped both arms around her and held her tight against him. "I got you for as long as you need."

That didn't turn out to be long at all. The doctor, a forty-something no-nonsense woman, came bustling down the hall moments later. "Ms. Bell?"

Her head snapped up from his chest. "Yes."

"I'm Dr. Gale, one of the cardiovascular surgeons here at the hospital. I—"

"Is he all right? Is he going to make it?" Every muscle in Brea's body tightened.

A patient reassurance crossed the doctor's face. "Your father is stable and conscious now, but—"

"Can I see him?"

She shook her head. "I'm afraid not yet. We're running some tests…"

The doctor went on, explaining the preacher's condition. The only words Brea seemed to hear were bypass surgery, probably in the next few hours. Gaping, she pressed a hand to her chest as her face went sheet white and she wobbled on her feet. One-Mile steadied her.

The doctor addressed him. "Is she prone to fainting? Has she eaten today?"

He had no fucking idea. "I'll take care of her."

The woman nodded grimly. "It's likely going to be a long day. She'll need her strength. We should be finished with all the tests in about an hour."

That gave him enough time to see to Brea since she was too worried about her father to even think of herself.

When the surgeon disappeared down the hall again, he turned Brea to face him. "Talk to me. Did you eat breakfast?"

"Oatmeal about six this morning." She blinked up at him. "What if he doesn't make it?"

The terror on her face hurt him. "The fact he's conscious and talking is a good sign. She wouldn't perform the surgery if she believed he'd never pull through. I know you're afraid—"

"You don't understand." She wrenched from him.

"Then help me."

As quickly as the fight had filled her, it left. "I'm sorry. I shouldn't yell. You're very kindly letting me lean on you."

"I'm also the only one around to hear your fears and frustration. So let me have it. I'm a tough guy. I can handle whatever you need to dish out."

She shook her head. "I'll be fine."

"You're like a bottle of soda someone shook up. I can see you bubbling under the surface. Yank the lid off and spew." He tried to smile to lighten the mood. "I'll help you clean up the mess when you're done."

"I don't let loose like that. Ever."

"Maybe you should, pretty girl."

He couldn't push her anymore if she wasn't ready…but someday she'd pop the top on all that repressed tension. Then, watch out. Brea with her hair down and her gloves off would be a sight. One-Mile hoped he was there for that.

Hell, he hoped he provoked it.

For now, he led her to the cafeteria, got her a sandwich and a salad, then encouraged her to eat.

"Thank you for staying with me," she said as she pushed away the rest of her turkey on wheat. "You didn't have to."

"I did." He would be here for her as long as she wanted him. Probably longer. She just didn't know that yet.

"You barely know me."

He shrugged. "I want to know more."

But now wasn't the time. In fact, his moments alone with her were likely ticking away. Soon, the parishioners, Mama Sweeney, and probably Cutter the asswipe would show up. Brea would feel obligated to give them her attention and support. Then he'd be in her way. He had to maximize his time with her now.

"Later," he added. "Focus on your dad today."

"You know it will never work between us."

"Besides the sex thing, which I already answered, why not?" One-Mile was expecting a lot of blah-blah and bullshit about Cutter and their budding love or whatever the fuck she thought they shared.

"I don't know you."

"We can fix that. I'm game. How about you?"

She shook her head. "I know what you do for a living."

She didn't like it, but she also didn't understand that he was doing the world a goddamn favor by offing scum. "Good. Then we won't have to have that awkward conversation. What else?"

"You scare me."

He had to give Brea credit; that was honest.

One-Mile took a risk and held her hand. "I said I'd never hurt you. I meant it."

She squirmed in her seat. "Not that kind of scare."

So he made her heart race and her female parts tingle, huh? And she'd never felt that before? Cutter must be a literal wet noodle in the sack, but that wasn't his issue. Getting her to see a future without the Boy Scout was.

He dragged his thumb back and forth across her so-soft palm. "It's the good kind of scare."

She didn't look convinced. "Are you this adamant with every woman you pursue?"

It was a fair question. "No. But I've never met anyone like you."

"You really don't know me."

"I know my gut tells me that I shouldn't let you get away."

"Pierce..."

"One-Mile. Pierce was my father."

"You say that like it's a bad thing."

It wasn't good, but she loved her dad, so she'd probably never comprehend the bleeding asshole his had been. "Having someone else's name can be like wearing a too-tight jacket."

She seemed to weigh his words. "At least it's a nice name. And you could make it your own. But I can't, in good conscience, call you something that celebrates another person's death."

Of course not. She only saw the loss of life, not the fact that if he hadn't pulled the trigger for that fateful one-mile shot, a terrorist had been prepared to blow up a marketplace filled with women and children simply because American servicemen had been there. Still, now wasn't the time to push her more.

"If Pierce makes you more comfortable, fine." He'd rather her call him Pierce than not call him at all.

"Why don't you and Cutter like each other?"

"Are you asking me questions to take your mind off your worries?"

She sent him a faint smile. "I might be."

Reading people could sometimes be the difference between life and death. "Try not to worry too much."

"I don't think I can stop it."

One-Mile palmed her crown, feeling the softness of her hair as he pulled her closer. "Think positive. You done here, pretty girl?"

She looked at her half-eaten sandwich and nodded. "We should get back to the ER."

He'd rather linger where it was unlikely anyone—especially Cutter

—would find them, but Brea would feel better if she were closer to her father. "Let's go."

Sure, she could find her own way through the hospital, but he couldn't resist settling his palm on the small of her back and guiding her to the crowded room that smelled like antiseptic, puke, and fear. When they arrived, a tall man who looked like an older version of Cutter and a tiny woman who shared his eyes headed straight for Brea.

She bolted for the woman. "Mama Sweeney!"

"Oh, baby girl…" The older woman hugged her fiercely. "We're here for you and your daddy. Try not to fret."

"That means the world to me." Brea turned to the other man. "Thanks for coming, too, Cage."

One-Mile hung back, gritting his teeth as the other man folded her into his big arms.

"Of course," Cage assured. "I don't have to be back in Dallas and on duty until midnight. I'm sure my little brother will turn up long before then."

"Most likely." Brea's stilted smile didn't quite mask her worry.

"I left him a voicemail on our way over. But you know Cutter isn't the sort to disappear all night without a word. Of my two boys, he's the good one," Sweeney teased as she elbowed her older son.

Cage rolled his eyes. "You only think that because he's better at fooling you."

Brea's boyfriend had been out all night? And his family wasn't even trying to reassure her that Cutter hadn't danced the mattress tango with another woman?

Maybe they thought he was working. One-Mile knew better.

"Hush," Sweeney scolded Cage before she settled Brea into the nearest chair. "Honey, sit down before you fall down and tell us the latest from the doctor."

Brea did, looking alarmingly pale by the time she glanced his way. "Did I forget anything?"

"No."

Cage zipped a cautious stare his way. "We haven't met."

"Sorry." Brea jumped to her feet. "Cage, this is one of Cutter's peers, Pierce Walker."

"I prefer One-Mile." He stuck out his hand to Cutter's older brother.

As they shook hands, nothing on Cage's face said he'd heard the name before. "Good to meet you. Which branch did you serve?"

"Marines. Sniper."

Understanding dawned as Cage nodded. "Hence the nickname. Hell of a kill shot, man."

He'd rather not talk about it with Brea listening. "What do you do?"

"I'm a cop in Dallas."

It fit. Cage had that sharp, gritty edge he never saw on a salesman or an accountant. "Glad you could come before you have to get back for your shift."

"Always. She's like my sister." Cage stared him down. "You a friend of Cutter's?"

He and Bryant would become pals on the twelfth of never as hell was freezing over. "We just work together."

Cage's face closed up. Obviously, he'd read between the lines.

Brea tugged on Cage's sleeve. "You don't have any idea where Cutter is?"

"I don't. He dropped you home after the party, and we went out for a beer. I left the bar when they shouted last call. He stayed to, um…talk to some folks."

Folks who were female, no doubt. That lying motherfucker was covering his brother's ass. Was Brea too trusting to believe her boyfriend was cheating? One-Mile wanted to strangle Cutter. If Brea ever gave him a chance, he wouldn't dishonor her like that.

"I hope he's not hung over. I got concerned when he didn't show up for church this morning. I'd planned to go by his apartment after my errand, but then Jennifer Collins called…"

Cage slid into the seat beside her and gave her hand a squeeze. "He'll turn up."

Yeah, hopefully not smelling like skank. Oh, he'd love Cutter to do something stupid enough to prompt Brea to sever their relationship, but she didn't need the stress of finding out her boyfriend was a two-timing douche today.

She squeezed Cage's hand in return. "I know."

"Brea," a familiar deep voice called from the sliding double doors.

Speak of the devil…

As Cutter strode toward them, heads turned. Cage and Mama Sweeney looked relieved to see him.

Brea stood. "You made it."

"As soon as I got Mama's message." When Cutter reached her, he enfolded her in his arms, lifting her off the floor and against his body while she buried her face in his neck with a sob. "I saw you'd called. Why didn't you leave a message?"

"You might have been busy, and I didn't want to be a bother."

Was she kidding? She should expect her man to drop anything—everything—when she needed him. He sure as hell would if Brea belonged to him. Had Cutter given her a reason to think he'd put her last?

"Bre-bee, you're never a bother." He set her on her feet and cupped her face. "I'm always here for you. I always will be."

She gave him a shaky nod, rife with thanks.

That was it? She wasn't going to ask the bastard where he'd been all night and why he hadn't answered the phone until three o'clock in the afternoon?

No one else seemed to think it was odd, either. Sweeney hugged her son. Cage gave his brother a shoulder bump. Then they updated him about her dad's condition.

"I'll be praying for him," Cutter assured with a nod, then marched One-Mile's way, cutting a scathing look in his direction. "Why are you here?"

"She was in no shape to drive herself."

"You were with her when she got the call?" Cutter demanded, brow raised.

One-Mile didn't see the point of stating the obvious.

"Would y'all mind giving us a minute?" Cutter asked his family. "Maybe get me a cup of coffee. I could use one."

"Whatever you want, little brother. Let's go, Brea." Cage took her arm.

Brea twisted from his reach. "I'd rather stay."

Cutter scowled. "You don't need to hear this, Bre-bee."

"I'm not leaving. The doctor might return with an update."

"Let her stay, son," Sweeney implored.

"All right. But One-Mile and I are going to have a man-to-man talk." Cutter jerked his head toward the door. "What I have in mind is probably best said outside."

Did the fidiot think he was going to beat him up in the parking lot? It would be hilarious if he wasn't so annoying.

As Sweeney and Cage exited for the cafeteria, Brea propped her hands on her hips. "You will not speak a cross word to Pierce, do you hear me? He got me here in one piece. He fed me and took care of me and—"

"Ask yourself why he'd do all that," Cutter fired back. "It wasn't out of the goodness of his heart, Bre-Bee. I guarantee he's focused on the desperation behind his zipper."

One-Mile hated being run out by the prick, but the last thing Brea needed right now was to be in the middle of their bickering. "I'll just go, pretty girl. I wish your father the best."

"But—

"It's fine," he cut into her objection, then pinned Cutter with a glare. "Bryant, maybe you should try getting your filthy mind out of the gutter."

As One-Mile headed for the exit, the asshole followed. "I have a few things to say before you go."

The moment they were out of Brea's earshot, he whirled on Cutter. "I'm not obligated to listen to your annoying-ass lecture, especially when it looks like you spent the night cheating on your girlfriend. So fuck off."

Bryant pointed a finger in his face. "Brea is off-limits to you, asshole."

"That's for her to decide. She's a grown woman."

"Who's too naive to know who you really are, so—hey!" the Boy Scout yelled. "Don't you walk away from me."

As he headed to his Jeep, One-Mile gave Cutter a one-fingered salute before he revved out of his parking spot and lurched toward the freeway, Brea Bell still on his mind.

Friday, August 8

BREA HUSTLED up the walkway of the surprisingly well-kept mid-century modern home in Lafayette, questioning her sanity for the tenth time in as many minutes. Loud rock music throbbed behind the front door as she clutched the plastic food container in one hand. With the other she rang the bell, her fingers shaking—along with the rest of her body.

What the devil was she doing here? Courting danger. Pierce Walker was more man than she could handle. She was likely to get herself in over her head.

But Brea owed him her thanks. And, okay…she was dying to see him again.

What could five minutes alone with the man hurt?

Suddenly, the volume on the music dropped under a dull roar and heavy footfalls got louder as they headed her way. Then the door whipped open, and Pierce stood on the other side of the threshold, scowling.

He was covered in nothing but ink, body hair, and bulging muscle from the waist up. Well-washed jeans hung low on his hips. He dangled the neck of a half-empty beer in one hand. His bare feet were built like the rest of him—big and overwhelmingly masculine.

Brea sucked in a silent, shaking breath. "Hi."

"Brea." His scowl disappeared. "This is a surprise."

How was it possible that his eyes had been on her a handful of seconds and she somehow felt naked?

"Sorry to drop by. I-I just wanted to thank you." She held out the container to him.

He took the dish from her hands. "For what?"

As Pierce propped himself against the doorframe and stared, she nearly lost herself in his fathomless black eyes. She forced herself to blink, but her wayward gaze wandered down his body. A Marine crest tattoo covered his right pectoral. More dark ink enveloped both shoulders, emphasizing every ridge and swell of his sizable physique. Well-washed denim cupped the substantial bulge between his legs.

And she utterly forgot everything she'd planned to say.

"Brea?"

His deep voice jolted her. She jerked her gaze from places it didn't belong and cleared her throat. "Um…helping me get to the hospital the day Daddy collapsed. And for bringing my car to me afterward. It was very kind of you."

"No problem. How's he doing now?"

"Recovering. His surgery went well. Since you thoughtfully left me your contact information in my console, I meant to come sooner to tell you how much I appreciated your help, but I've been taking care of him. I finally got a few minutes, so I-I brought you these cookies. Since I didn't know what you liked, I baked a few different kinds…" She dropped her gaze to collect her thoughts and stop rambling, but her stare glued itself to him again, this time fixating on his ridiculously delineated twelve-pack abs. "But you don't look like you eat many."

He laughed. Pierce Walker was menacing when he scowled, but when he smiled he was stunning. Something wild and reckless quivered in her belly, urging her to put her hands on him, press herself against him, beg him to somehow stop this breathless, fluttery yearning she'd only ever felt with him.

"Because I don't have anyone baking me cookies." He peeled the lid off the top and peered down. "These look good."

"I baked the chocolate chip without nuts. I didn't know if you were allergic."

"I'm not."

"I also included checkerboard, cinnamon sugar, and gluten-free almond wafer."

"Thank you." He curled his fingers around her shoulder. They burned like a brand as he scooted her breathlessly close to his naked torso and locked the door behind them. "Why don't you come in and let me get you something to drink?"

"I shouldn't stay. I would never want to interrupt your…" Goodness, what *had* he been doing? It was a Friday night. Maybe he was getting ready to go out. Or heaven forbid, planning to stay in…with female company.

"Game of pool. You're not interrupting. Stay. Like a lot of things, it's a lot more fun when you're not playing alone." He winked.

His seemingly suggestive words sparked a reaction low in her belly. "I-I've never played."

He raised a dark brow. "Ever?"

"Daddy isn't much for games. My friends aren't, either."

"What about Cutter?"

She shrugged. "He's never shown any interest."

He sent her a stare that looked somewhere between stunned and dubious. "You sure? I've seen him play."

That didn't surprise Brea. Cutter had a whole life she barely knew about. "I'm sure he does, but not with me."

"I find that hard to believe."

Were they still talking about billiards? "Anyway, I won't keep you…"

"Don't go. One game." He wrapped his arm around her middle and ushered her deeper into his house. "What do you say?"

She risked a glance up at him. "You're sure I'm not in your way?"

"No. I'm thrilled as hell to have you here, pretty girl."

That low, deep declaration of his did something to her insides. Heat crawled up her cheeks. She ran her tongue across her suddenly dry lips. "O-one game, then."

"Let me get you a drink. Water? Tea? Beer?"

Brea shook her head. "Nothing. I also wanted to thank you for the thoughtful birthday gift you left me at the salon yesterday. I'm sorry I wasn't there, but I got it this morning. The wine was a lovely gesture."

He finished off his beer, then cocked his head at her. "You don't drink, do you?"

"Not much, but I'm looking forward to trying this." One of her fellow hairdressers who was a wine enthusiast had assured her it was a more than decent bottle.

Pierce led her deeper into his house. One wall was floor-to-ceiling windows. Movement outside hinted at trees in the yard, swaying in the dark. The adjacent wall was covered in white subway tile with dark grout. Over that he'd hung ten identically sized bright graphical pieces of art—skulls, poker cards, crossbones, masks, and the like—in two perfectly straight rows. Black modern furniture went with the vibe. A big vase of yellow daisies sat on top of a round, glass-top table, adding the lone homey touch. The living room was flanked by floating stairs with an angular steel railing that probably led to his bedroom. Beyond that lay a big pool table with a red felt top. His kitchen, with cabinets stained a warm, mid-tone brown, hugged the far wall.

The place seemed so him—vivid, sexy, contemporary, unexpected.

"This is really nice."

He smiled. "Thanks. I bought it a few months back. Gutted and rebuilt it."

That impressed her even more. "You did an amazing job."

Pierce grabbed a cookie from the plastic container and tossed it in his mouth. In fascination, she watched his sharp jaw work and his Adam's apple bob. Even the way he chewed dripped masculinity. It did something wicked to her when he closed his eyes.

"Hmm… Your cookies are delicious, pretty girl. I knew they would be."

The low dip in his voice nearly made her melt. "I like to bake them."

"I'm going to love eating them." He licked his full lips. "I'll do it all night if you let me."

He definitely wasn't talking about anything she whipped up in her kitchen.

She blushed. "Let me know when you run out. I'll be happy to make more." She turned for the door. "But I really should go."

He blocked her path. "You promised me one game, remember?"

"I don't know how."

"I'll teach you." He set the cookies and his empty beer aside, then sauntered closer. "Stay."

She probably shouldn't…but Brea couldn't resist. "All right."

Pierce gathered up the colorful balls on the table and racked them in a triangle, arranging each in numerical order. When he'd finished, he lifted the rack away, settled the plain white ball in front of the triangle's point, then grabbed a cue. "Do you know the object of the game?"

"To put your balls in your pockets?" When he laughed heartily, Brea realized her blunder. Her face seemed to heat to a thousand degrees. "I meant to shoot the balls you've chosen into their assigned—"

"I know what you meant. And you're mostly right." He grabbed the blue cube on the rim of the pool table and chalked the tip of the cue. "I'll explain along the way. Take this."

She wrapped her fingers around the stick he proffered in her direction. "Now what?"

"Bend over the table, behind the cue ball…"

Brea did, more than vaguely aware of her shorts creeping up her thighs, dangerously close to the under curve of her derrière, then glanced over her shoulder. "Like this?"

He tore his gaze away from her backside, then frowned. "Damn, you really are a little thing. You might have to stand on the tips of your toes to get your arms on the table for a good shot."

She did, feeling the muscles in her legs tighten and her butt lift in the air.

"Yeah." Pierce's voice sounded rough. "Like that."

Brea glanced back. She didn't want to notice that the bulge behind his jeans had grown…but she'd be lying if she said she didn't. The notion that a man like him found her attractive made her feel a little feverish and giddy.

The man is only after you for a piece of ass, Cutter had warned.

She straightened and turned—only to find him suddenly plastered against her body. She gasped, automatically setting her hands on his chest to put space between them. But he was like solid stone under her touch.

Pierce's hands dropped to her hips. "Would you rather do something besides play pool?"

Yes, please. "No. This is fine."

His fingers tightened on her. The heat of his touch penetrated the khaki twill of her shorts. Suddenly, she found it hard to breathe.

"Then turn and bend over the table again." He waited until she complied, and Brea was achingly aware of his body heat bracketing the backs of her thighs, of the sexual stirrings his closeness roused. "You're right-handed?"

"Um, yes."

"With that hand, hold the cue about five inches from the bottom. Now place it near your hip. Don't hold it so tight. You want to be relaxed but controlled. Good. Align your body with the cue ball. This will help your aim. Exactly. With your left hand, make a *V* with your thumb and index finger, like this." He demonstrated. "You'll balance the tip of the cue in that crevice."

Brea watched, acutely aware of the veins bulging in his forearms, the size of his hands, the length of his fingers, the hair dusting his knuckles.

Then he took hold of her hips again. "Spread your legs, pretty girl."

Her stomach tightened. "Why?"

"Your feet are too close together. You'll find it hard to stabilize when you take your shot. Go on. Yeah, just like that. Now lay the rest of the fingers of your left hand on the table and make a bridge for the *V* to rest on. You got it."

"Now what?" she asked.

Brea only half listened to his answer. She was excruciatingly aware of his body heat blistering her, of his hips packed against her backside as he leaned over and utterly surrounded her with his big body.

"That means you need to bend over a bit more."

"Oh," she breathed as she rushed to comply.

"Good. Now hold the cue steady and eye the ball. Like that." He sounded hoarse as his fingers gripped her tighter. Then he pressed his entire chest over her back and breathed against her neck. A shiver wracked her. "Hold still. Yeah. Now take your shot."

How the devil was she supposed to concentrate when he was all over her? When his musky scent swam in her head and she kept closing her eyes to drink him in? It was hard to concentrate on balancing the cue when her body kept urging her to press back into him with a moan.

But Brea did her best.

The tip of her stick barely poked the cue ball. The white orb rolled lazily across the table, made a polite clap with the first of the balls in the triangle, barely jostling them before rolling away.

"Not a bad first effort. Next time, put a little more force into it." He eased away, seemingly reluctant to put space between them.

"It was horrible." She straightened, and her hungry stare climbed him again. "Show me what I should have done?"

He hesitated, then set his pool cue aside. "You didn't come to play pool. Cutter made you promise not to talk to me, so why are you here?"

"To thank you."

"You could have left cookies for me at the office. But you came to my house. On a Friday night. With your hair curled and your makeup done, wearing pretty white lace." Pierce fingered the scooped neck of her top before he wrapped his hand around her neck and tilted her face up to meet his stare. "Look me in the eye and tell me why you're here."

"I don't know."

"Yes, you do. You're afraid to admit it."

Goodness, Pierce could see right through her.

She swallowed. "Terrified."

His fingers on the back of her neck tightened. "I'm more than happy to give you what you want, but you have to look me in the eye and say it out loud."

Brea dug her nails into his forearms, her heart pounding. "I don't understand."

"I won't settle for less than your enthusiastic consent when I take you to bed."

She gaped. "Don't you mean if?"

Abruptly, he released her. "If you really think it's still a question, you're bullshitting yourself. And we don't have a whole lot more to say."

"Wait. This is happening too fast." Brea looked up at him, not even sure what she was silently begging for.

But he knew. "I'm cutting to the chase, pretty girl. Let me tell you what isn't going to happen. I'm not going to seduce you. I'm not going to push or pressure or force you. You're coming to me because you want it. From me. And no one else."

"C-can't we get to know each other?"

Brea was grasping at straws. Pierce wasn't the sort of man who formed cute, benign friendships with girls. He had sex with women. Which meant he had no use for her.

As she'd feared, she was in way over her head.

"I'm sorry. That was a stupid question. I'll go." She looked away, humiliation blazing her cheeks as she charged for his front door.

Now if she could just manage to make it outside before her composure disintegrated…

Pierce grabbed her elbow and pulled her back. "It wasn't stupid. I want to know more about you than your body. But I know exactly where this attraction is heading. Whether you want to admit it or not, we'll wind up in bed. I'm just saying that I want your full consent when we get there. If you can't give me that when the time comes, say goodbye now."

Brea dragged in a deep breath. As far as he knew, she belonged to another man. Of course he would want her consent before anything happened between them. And she respected that he wanted a completely willing sexual partner.

That wasn't her.

She shook her head and backed away. "I shouldn't have come."

Brea whirled around and darted for the door again. She'd embarrassed herself enough.

Behind her, she heard Pierce give chase, his footsteps heavy as he spun her to face him. Brea expected him to pull her close, but she gasped when he shoved her back. Her spine made contact with the foyer wall. His hands spread on either side of her head. He pressed every inch of his body against her. Then he dipped his head as if he intended to kiss her here and now.

Brea's belly flipped with excitement. She gripped his bare shoulders, thrilled by his satiny skin over hard, steely muscle. Anticipation rolled through her as she tilted her head up to him and closed her eyes in surrender.

She wanted Pierce Walker's kiss so badly…

It never came.

Seconds later, Brea blinked, her lashes fluttering up until she focused on him. He studied her with a dissecting stare even as he pressed the hard length of his manhood against her belly. "I know you want me."

She looked away. "Let me go."

Pierce merely thrust his fingers in her hair and tugged until she had no choice but to look at him. "I want you, too, pretty girl. So fucking bad I can almost taste you. That's why I waited for you outside your church a week ago last Sunday. That's why I followed you to Lafayette. That's why it's taking every bit of my restraint now not to kiss you."

"Why don't you?" She really wished he would.

"Because you have to be willing to admit what you want between us. Until that day..." He eased away with a shake of his head, then opened the door. "Unless it's an emergency, don't come back. If you do, Brea, you better be ready to confess that you want me—and me alone—to strip you down, get deep inside you, and give you every bit of pleasure I'm dying to."

Every cell in her body flashed hot. She gaped at him. Some wayward, wanton part of her ached to give in. She was a grown woman. She wasn't saving herself for marriage, just until sex meant something. If she spent the next hour with him, who would know? Or care? And why should it matter to anyone but them?

Before she could make up her mind, Pierce nudged her onto the porch. He cradled her face in his hands and lifted her face to him. Hope leaped. *Please God, let him have changed his mind.* But he merely pressed his lips to her forehead before shutting and locking the door between them with a final click.

CHAPTER THREE

Thursday, August 14

"I t's okay, Bre-bee. Don't be upset."

Through the open door of his boss's office, One-Mile heard Cutter's crooning tone. He risked a glance at Logan Edgington. How quickly could he wrap up this pointless chat with his boss and eavesdrop on the douche who didn't deserve his girlfriend? Because One-Mile hadn't stopped thinking about Brea Bell in the last six days. He didn't care if he had to fight dirty. He wasn't giving up on her.

"Uh-oh. I don't like your expression…" Logan grumbled.

One-Mile didn't give a shit.

"Tell me what you're thinking," his boss pressed.

"Gotta pee," he lied.

"Wait—"

One-Mile didn't. He dashed out the door to plaster himself against the wall, around the corner from where Bryant was having his low-voiced telephone conversation with Brea. Thank fuck that, despite a life spent around firearms, he still had superb hearing.

"You know your dad," Cutter murmured. "He's a perfectionist and he cares about the people of his congregation. Since he's recovering from surgery and can't handle his responsibilities without help, it makes him cranky. Besides, the doctors told you he might be irritable until they stabilized his meds."

"I know. I don't blame Daddy, just saying he's being difficult," Brea said on speakerphone. "I've been telling him for the past few years that he needs to rely on Tom more. He's the associate pastor, after all. And I think the stress of trying to do everything himself is one of the reasons Daddy had a heart attack. But when I pointed all that out, along with the fact that Tom wouldn't appreciate me taking over his duties, Daddy nearly blew a gasket."

Cutter sighed, sounding slightly impatient. "He's just not himself right now. It's not fair of him to put you in such an awkward position or force you to juggle your own job and his, but he's not being difficult on purpose. If it helps, I'll make a few phone calls, see if I can get the church van fixed before you need to pick everyone up for Sunday services. Will that free you up to run over to the Rutherfords' house this evening and pray with them? Shame about their son's overdose."

"Just awful. Aidan was only sixteen." Compassion filled her voice, along with real tears. "If you could find someone to fix the van, that would definitely give me more time to spend with those poor people. But I'm not stepping on Tom's toes. He's coming with me."

"I think he should. Stephanie Rutherford must be devastated."

Brea sniffled. "She loved Aidan so much. I want to give her and her husband all the comfort and fellowship I can."

Despite how frazzled and stretched thin Brea was, she was still worried about everyone else. She had such a big, beautiful heart. One-Mile ached for a chunk of it.

"Where's the van now?" Cutter asked.

"At the church, 'round back. Keys are in the glovebox. If you find a mechanic, can you leave me the bill in Daddy's office? I'll pick it up tonight after I drop Tom off."

"Sure thing. Just take a deep breath, Bre-bee. This will pass."

"Thanks. I know you're right. Hey, my three-thirty client just walked in. It's a cut and color, so I won't be able to answer for a bit if you have an update."

"Got it."

Cutter hung up. The SOB ended the call without a single romantic word. Hell, without even saying goodbye. No wonder Brea wasn't excited about their sex life. Hard to be thrilled about a cheating, dismissive asshat…

When he heard Cutter sigh and start across the tile floor, One-Mile peeled away from the wall and turned to head down the hall—only to find Logan right behind him.

His eavesdropping boss hustled them into his office and speared him with a vivid blue stare. "So it really is like that, huh? Damn it. Shut the door."

One-Mile hesitated, then complied. "Like what?"

"Dude, everyone saw how you looked at Brea during the party. You get that she's Cutter's, right?"

One-Mile shrugged. "He's wrong for her. And if he can't treat her well enough to hold on to her, that's his problem."

"You've got some giant balls. How serious are you about her?"

His feelings didn't much matter until he could figure out how invested she was in Cutter.

When Brea had delivered the cookies to his house last week, she hadn't withheld her consent because she wasn't feeling him. One-Mile knew that. Hell, her amber eyes had darkened with desire every time he even came close. His guess? She'd hesitated because of the Boy Scout. Did she think she was in love with Cutter?

"Serious enough to fight for her."

Logan sighed. "I was afraid you were going to say that. Your shit can't affect the team."

"I won't bring it to work if Bryant doesn't. But there's already no love lost between us."

"Yeah, you really pissed him off during that first mission in Mexico."

"He wasn't listening, and I didn't have the patience to stand around while he dithered and flapped his jaws. The fact that I was right and he hasn't gotten over it isn't my problem."

Logan sat back at his desk, arms crossed over his chest. "Jesus, you remind me of my brother."

Which was probably why he and Hunter butted heads. "Yeah?"

"He married Kata the night he met her, did you know that? He took one look at her, and he knew."

No shit? A few weeks ago, One-Mile wouldn't have understood. Today, he got it. "They happy?"

"Fucking as in love as I've ever seen. I knew with my wife right away, too. But we met in high school, and things got fucked up. I lost her for a few years. When we met up again, she was engaged to another guy."

Until now, Logan had never shared anything personal, but One-Mile wasn't too thick to grasp that the man was delivering some message.

"How long did that last after you found her again?"

"Not long." Logan tapped his thumb on his desk, clearly pondering his next words. "Especially after the asshole watched me go down on Tara…and I made sure he knew she enjoyed the hell out of it."

One-Mile grinned. "Damn, you shit-stirrer."

Logan shrugged. "We all gotta be good at something…"

"So…you get where I'm coming from with Brea?"

"That you don't give a shit about her relationship with Cutter? Yeah, but think hard. Is it really worth starting a shit storm if she's just a fuck? Or a way for you to provoke Cutter?"

"She's not." Even the intimation irritated One-Mile. "And I wouldn't put the time or effort into scheming something to piss off the Boy Scout when a simple fuck you would do."

"Fair enough." Logan stood. "That's not why I called you in here. I need the rest of your reports on the latest Mexico trip. We all hate paperwork, but we have to keep our documentation squeaky clean so Uncle Sam doesn't shut us down."

"It's done. I'll email the shit now."

"Good. Then get your ass out of my office and send Cutter in so I can have a nice, long chat with him about being prompt and thorough with his."

What was Edgington saying? "How long?"

"Probably long enough for you to go to Brea's rescue."

He'd never seen any of his bosses as potential bros. He worked for them. They gave orders, and he completed the dirtiest of the dirty missions on their behalf. End of story. But Logan was proving that he was all right. "Thanks, man."

As he turned and reached for the door, his boss called after him, "You're welcome. But if you make work ugly, I'll make your life hell."

That didn't scare One-Mile. He twisted around long enough to salute Logan, then hauled ass out of the office and headed to Sunset.

Mid-August was still hotter than fuck, and he wished he had some idea what was wrong with Brea's van, but he had a few hours to figure it out. Since he and machinery usually got along just fine, he hoped it wouldn't be too tough.

When he arrived at the church, a fiftyish woman who identified herself as Mrs. Collins poked her head out...but didn't shake his hand. No surprise. He probably looked big and violent to her sheltered suburban eyes. He didn't give her his name, just said he'd come to fix the van for Brea. The woman nodded and disappeared inside.

About thirty minutes later, he figured out the vehicle was over-heating and the likely culprit was a faulty water pump. He managed to run one down and get it installed way before the sun set. Then he knocked and let himself in the church's back door.

"Yes?" Mrs. Collins eyed him and his tattoos like he was the devil and if she let him too close, his sin might rub off on her.

But she was probably someone Brea knew and respected, so One-Mile made nice. "The van is fixed. Do you have a piece of paper so I can leave Brea a note?"

He'd rather text her, but she'd never given him her number. Sure, he had it. Finding her digits hadn't been hard. But he wanted her to *choose* to tell him.

"This way."

Mrs. Collins led him down a blessedly air-conditioned hallway that ended in a small office with white walls bare of everything except a cross. In the middle of the room sat a painfully neat desk. A plaque squatted front and center that read Reverend Jasper P. Bell.

She retrieved a sheet of paper from the nearby printer and a pen from the top drawer. "There you go."

Mrs. Collins hovered awkwardly, watching him like she worried he might steal something. He tried not to roll his eyes. The truth was, he'd saved pretty much every penny Uncle Sam had ever paid him. Between that, his lucrative post-Marine contracts, and the money his granddad had left him, he'd managed to sock away a couple million dollars. He had zero interest in swiping the preacher's stapler.

"Thanks. How's the reverend doing since his surgery?"

Mrs. Collins looked surprised. "Brea told you about that?"

"Yeah." But he hadn't heard anything new in almost a week.

"Oh. Well, Reverend Bell is recovering nicely, thank you. Do you, um…know Brea?" Clearly, that possibility surprised her.

"We've met."

The woman relaxed. "Isn't she a doll? She's done an amazing job taking care of her father and keeping the church activities running while he's out."

That didn't surprise One-Mile. "Do you work here?"

"I just volunteer. I teach third-grade math at the elementary school down the street. But since Jasper's surgery, I've tried to step in and help more."

Probably because she wanted to be more than Jasper's parishioner. One-Mile could tell by the way her eyes lit up when she talked about the man.

Whatever. He'd rather hear about the preacher's pretty daughter. But—wild guess—probing Mrs. Collins about Brea's sex life with Cutter would get him booted from here.

Instead, he leaned over the desk, jotted a quick note explaining how he'd fixed the vehicle. Then he invited her to come by his place to pick up the plastic container she'd delivered her cookies in and stay for a round of pool…or whatever she wanted. "I'm sure she appreciates you. Got an envelope?"

He didn't need Mrs. Collins snooping.

"One minute." She disappeared around the corner and returned with a crisp white envelope.

He tucked the paper inside, sealed it, jotted Brea's name on the front, and left it on the desk. Then he nodded at Mrs. Collins and headed home, wondering when—or if—he'd see Brea.

Given her schedule, One-Mile didn't really expect any company soon.

But a couple of hours later, he was kicking back with a beer, eyeing the pool table where he'd taught her how to play so he could shamelessly rub up against her, when someone started pounding on his front door. He doubted Brea was the one demanding entry with a fist... which meant she probably hadn't been the one who read his note.

But he had a good idea who had.

Shit.

After racking his pool cue, he headed across the house and yanked the door open. Sure enough, Cutter Bryant stood on the other side, foaming mad, like a chihuahua with rabies.

"Damn it, I thought I'd taken the trash to the curb, but here you are..."

Cutter bared his teeth and shoved him back. At the unexpected push, One-Mile stumbled until he found his footing. Bryant marched in and slammed the door, then hurled his wadded-up note at his chest. One-Mile caught it reflexively.

"Listen to me, asshole. I'm only going to say this once more. Keep the fuck away from Brea. Stop talking to her, stop pursuing her, and stop writing trash like that to manipulate her into coming here so you can hook up with her."

Who the fuck did Cutter think he was, opening her mail, then barging into *his* house to start shit? Normally, he would beat the hell out of the asswipe...but that wouldn't win him any gold stars with Brea.

"Or what, you'll bore me to death?" He feigned a yawn. "I've already heard this speech, and I hate reruns. So get the fuck out."

Cutter didn't move. "You act big and bad, like you don't give a shit about anything. But I see through you. You're a gaping, know-it-all sphincter. And an insecure bully. Deep down, I think you feel powerless. Did your mommy not love you enough as a kid, Walker?"

Bryant couldn't know a damn thing about his mother, but it was still a low fucking blow, and it took all of One-Mile's restraint not to unleash his fury on the cockroach.

"Are you too much of a pussy to throw a punch? Is that why you're trying to hurt my feewings?" he snarked.

"Fuck you. Stay away from Brea. I mean it."

"You act like I'm going to hurt her. I fixed the van to *help* her. So get off my ass and get the hell out of my house."

Cutter didn't budge. "I'm serious. If you keep after Brea, you'll ruin her."

Dramatic much? "For what? I just want to get to know her."

The Boy Scout scoffed. "You want to take her to bed."

Of course he did. One-Mile refused to lie. But he wanted more than Brea's body. Still, he didn't owe Bryant any sort of answer. He'd only be giving the bastard more ammo.

"You think you have me all figured out. I'm the player who wants to sex up your girlfriend and break her heart. But you don't know a thing about me, asshole." He gave Cutter a shove backward. "And you're no fucking good for her yourself. You were too busy banging some girl you met in a bar the night before to be there for Brea when her dad collapsed. So I stepped in, you cheating douchebag. Get over it."

"I've explained that day to Brea. We're square, so where I was is none of your business."

Bullshit. Cutter was taking advantage of her goodness and spewing lies to cover his ass while he stepped out on her. Why should she settle for that, especially when One-Mile was more than happy to appreciate her—and only her?

"You're a selfish fucking prick for hanging on to her when you won't be faithful. What about her happiness? Her future? Or have you even thought past your dick?"

Cutter's jaw hardened as he spotted Brea's clean plastic container on the table in his foyer and snatched it up. "I don't have to justify myself to you. She's my concern, and I'll take care of her—always. But Brea is off-limits to you." He pointed a finger in One-Mile's face. "And if you step one more toe over the line, I swear I'll fucking kill you."

"Try it. We'll see who winds up dead."

———— ·=·· ————

Saturday, *August 16*

"Brea!" her father called across the house from his recliner.

"Coming, Daddy." She hustled into the living room with his cup of coffee, a piece of dry, multigrain toast, and his morning medicine, then set everything on the table beside him. "Eat up and take your pills."

She was surprised to see that he'd showered and shaved already, but not at all shocked by his sour expression. "Capsules of nonsense from a snake-oil salesman."

"No, medicine prescribed by one of the best heart surgeons in the state," Brea corrected. "Please take it. We don't want to put your heart at risk again."

She couldn't. The news that he had collapsed and that she'd nearly lost him had devastated her. Though Pierce following her shopping that day had rattled Brea, she thanked God he'd been there. She had been in no shape to drive herself to the hospital.

Daddy grumbled but sighed with resignation. "Fine. When you're done with your last client, I need you to run by the church and pick up my mail. If you get there by five, Tom will be meeting with the new youth group. Sit in on that session so you can tell me how he's doing. Then if you can head out to the Richards' farm... Apparently, Josette is having female surgery on Monday, and she's asked for someone from the church to pray with them."

"Tom should do it. That's his job, Daddy." And he'd let her know on the way home from the Rutherfords' place the other night that he'd appreciate her taking a step back.

Her father scowled. "He gives a decent sermon, but he hasn't learned how to compassionately connect with the community. You have. You know and love all these people. And you've got that gift of making everyone feel special."

Brea appreciated that but... "I have to work all day. If I sit through the youth meeting, then go to the Richards' farm for an hour or two, when will I eat? Plus, I'd planned to grocery shop and do some laundry tonight."

Well, she should...but she found herself resisting the urge to seek out Pierce instead. She'd heard nothing from him since he'd tried to teach her to play pool. Admittedly, she was a little disappointed. It was foolish, but she'd hoped he might ask her on a date.

Is he really the dinner-and-a-movie type?

She needed to clear him from her head. Seeking Pierce out, even to thank him with cookies, had been impulsive, reckless, and desperate— three things she'd never been with a man. But he filled her with such exciting, unexpected feelings. Forgetting him was impossible.

"You can do that after church tomorrow," her father insisted. "I know it's an imposition, but we have a duty to this town. I can't see to these people myself, and I raised you to think of others first. I need you, baby."

And there it was, the button he pushed ruthlessly anytime she resisted doing something he asked. It only worked because he was right. She would feel terrible if she put her needs above those around her. "I'll take care of everything."

He smiled. "That's my girl. So Cutter is taking you to breakfast before your first appointment this morning?"

"He is." And she felt a giddy, guilty excitement at being able to get out of the house and relax for an hour.

"You ought to marry that boy. His daddy was a drunk, and Sweeney was better off without Rod, but Cage and Cutter both turned out to be good boys. Cutter would take care of you, Brea."

He would, and they would both be miserable. "We're friends, Daddy. That's all."

"So you keep saying." He sighed. "Then I'll pray you find a right-eous, God-fearing man who makes you happy."

Brea sighed. Her father didn't mean to sound either old-fashioned or judgmental, but she wasn't going to change him. "Thank you."

A knock put an end to their conversation. Brea hustled to the door and let Mrs. Collins in just as Daddy took his first bite of toast and downed one of his pills. "Good morning."

After some small talk, Jennifer sat on the ottoman at her father's feet and smiled when her father grumbled about LSU's first football game of the season still being another two weeks away. Thankfully, Cutter let himself in a moment later. Brea kissed her father's cheek and promised to check in before thanking Mrs. Collins for spending the day with him.

Forty minutes later, she found herself picking at her plate, dreading the two shampoo-and-sets on her schedule…and wondering again if Pierce had decided he wasn't interested in her after all.

"You've barely touched your waffle, Bre-bee."

Brea glanced up at Cutter and forced a smile. "That's not true. It's just a lot of food. Want the rest?"

"You know I don't eat that crap."

"But how do you choke down six eggs and a half a chicken for breakfast?"

"I'm a growing boy." He patted his flat stomach, which she knew was all abs. "And I need protein to keep up my strength."

"You're plenty strong," she said with a roll of her eyes. "Thanks again for getting me out of the house this morning."

"You're welcome. I figured you needed a break, and Jennifer Collins is all too happy to play nursemaid to your dad."

She swatted his arm. "You make it sound like they're engaging in hanky-panky."

Cutter shrugged. "It wouldn't surprise me. They both lost their spouses years ago, and I think they're sweet on each other."

"That hardly means they're having sex," Brea insisted in a low hiss. "Daddy had heart surgery less than three weeks ago, and they're not married."

"But if they were lovers, you'd forgive him, wouldn't you? He might be a preacher, but he's also a man."

What was Cutter getting at? "That's for God to judge, not me. But Daddy isn't the sort to commit carnal sins."

Her best friend leaned forward, elbows on the table. "You're twenty-two years old, and your mama died shortly after you were born. Do you really think he's gone more than two decades without sex because he's a man of God?"

Brea squirmed. "I try not to think of it at all."

"Yeah, I try not to think about who's been 'comforting' Mama since my dad ran off decades ago. But I'm telling you now, don't be shocked if your father is involved with someone. My money is on Mrs. Collins."

"That's absurd. She's just a very kind lady."

He scoffed and shook his head. "Bre-Bee, when you're confronted with things you don't know how to handle, you have a habit of burying your head in the sand. That won't always work."

"I don't like conflict," she defended. "How does it not upset you?"

"Sometimes it's a necessary evil."

Like his job, which she didn't like much, either. "I guess I should go. Gabrielle Brown is bringing her mama in this morning. They're both insisting on having a perm. Gabi swears those are coming back in style."

"She's got hair down to her ass."

"Backside," she corrected. "And you're right. So it's going to be a long day."

"Then let's get you to work."

Cutter stood, tossed a few bills on the table, then escorted her out of the restaurant. They were surrounded by familiar faces who stared, probably either wondering why the two of them weren't married or when they would be. Wouldn't they all be surprised to know that she'd never had a romantic thought about him...but she'd had more than a few lustful fantasies about the tattooed military assassin he worked with?

She waved to some of the townsfolk across the room, then stopped to admire Mrs. Jenkins's granddaughter, who had just turned four yesterday. Cutter urged her along, his hand on the small of her back, until they finally reached the sidewalk.

"I thought we'd never get out of there." He wriggled like he wore a too-tight sweater.

She laughed. "You like people as long as you're protecting them. Heaven forbid you have to talk to them."

He grinned. "You know me so well."

"All my life." She bumped shoulders with him. "That's why you're my best friend. What are you doing today?"

"Mama is working. Cage got off duty a few hours ago, so he's on his way back to town." He shrugged. "I might head back to Lafayette and run a few errands. You know, get ready to raise hell tonight."

"As much as you hide it from me, I know you're capable of that."

Cutter opened his mouth to say something. The revving of a motor-cycle cut him off. Brea turned—and stopped in her tracks when she spotted a big man in a black helmet, leather jacket, well-worn jeans, and combat boots cruising toward them.

Instantly, tingles sizzled across every inch of her skin, awakening her aching nipples. They shocked her even more by pooling between her legs.

Brea couldn't see behind the man's glossy black visor, but he handled his bike with easy confidence. He stared in a way that told her she was his sole focus. She was magnetically drawn to him, as if her soul compelled her to follow his. Only one man had ever affected her that way, and every time she saw him, the feeling grew stronger.

Pierce Walker.

Was he in Sunset looking for her?

With his stare still glued to her, he revved his engine again and turned off Napoleon Avenue, heading left on Landry. She craned her head to watch until he disappeared behind the buildings and she couldn't hear his engine anymore.

"That son of a bitch," Cutter grumbled.

"Shush. He's only riding down the street."

Cutter gently guided her down the sidewalk, but she could feel rage pinging from him. "Walker is sniffing around you, Bre-Bee. He smells blood."

"What the devil does that mean?"

"You think he's a harmless kitten, that under all his BS he's got a good heart. That man is a hungry lion ready to eat, and you're the little rabbit he intends to sate his hunger with."

His intimation sent heat rolling through her. "You don't know that."

Cutter scoffed. "Yeah, I do. He's not even trying to hide it. You're just too nice to understand. He was pleasant at the EM party. He took you to the hospital when you needed help. He ate the cookies you baked him—"

"How did you know about those?"

"I didn't fix the church van. He did. But I intercepted the note he left you, 'inviting' you back to his place to pick up your container since he'd spent the evening 'eating your cookies.' I hope he meant your snickerdoodles and not your pussy."

"Cutter Edward Bryant!" He'd never spoken to her like that.

Still, a vision of Pierce, big and inked and naked, with his dark head between her bare thighs as she writhed in ecstasy, shot a bolt of fire through her bloodstream.

"I'm serious," Cutter growled. "He'd like to."

She knew. He hadn't kept that a secret. "Well, he never touched me, especially...there."

"And now he won't. I warned him away again. This time, I made sure he knows I mean it."

Brea stopped their stroll by putting her foot down. "Did you ask me what *I* wanted?"

"It's not him. You have better taste than that."

Admitting that she didn't would only start an argument. And why bother? Other than eyeing her on the street just now and supposedly fixing the church van, Pierce hadn't given her any real indication he was interested in more than sex. Besides, how could she introduce him to Daddy? Unless Pierce was willing to put a ring on her finger, that was impossible. But the notion seemed highly unlikely. He might give her a night of sin but never his last name. Time to stop indulging in this stupid fantasy that the bad boy wanted her for anything more than a fling.

Time to forget him.

Brea looked down the sidewalk. The door to the beauty shop opened. Rayleigh, the owner, stuck her head out and shot her an Insta-gram-ready brow.

"I've got to go. I'm sure Gabrielle and her mother are waiting for me. I'll see you later."

"Call me if you need someone to run you out to the Richards' place later."

Brea was tired just thinking about the twelve-plus-hour day in front of her. "Thanks."

Cutter leaned in and kissed her cheek. "I'm only trying to protect you."

She sighed. "I know."

After giving him the only smile she could manage, she headed inside the salon. Four hours, two perms, a shampoo-and-set, and a no-show later, she propped her feet on a vacant chair in the break room and waited for her next haircut. She was playing a crossword app on her phone when it rang. It was Cutter.

Brea almost didn't answer. He probably wanted to remind her of all the reasons Pierce wasn't right for her, and she wasn't in the mood.

But as her finger hovered over the decline button, something told her to answer. "Hi. What're you doing?"

He paused. His silence was somehow rife with tension. "Brea, I want you to listen to me carefully."

"What's wrong?"

Had he gone by to check on Daddy and found him collapsed again?

"I'm in a situation. I've always managed to make it out safely in the past...but I don't think this one will end that way. I'm sorry. I called to say goodbye."

CHAPTER FOUR

Brea's heart stopped. Her world came to a standstill. "What are you saying?"

But she knew. Cutter lived steeped in danger, and her worst fear, that something had finally proven stronger than him, had come true.

"Cage is on his way. Stay put. He'll explain. But—"

"No!"

"Don't make this harder," he barked, his voice gravelly with resolution and something she'd never heard in his voice—fear. "I've called the rest of my family and said my goodbyes. I love you, little sister. Take care—"

"Stop. There must be something you can do. This can't be happening. I don't..." *Know what I'll do without you.*

The words pressed on her chest, cutting off her breath and forcing out tears.

"I negotiated the release of a group of hostages. Saving fifteen lives at the price of one is a good deal. My end will be quick, and you'll go on. Live well." He let out a shuddering breath. "For me."

"Cutter, no. You can't just—"

But the line went dead. The reality that she'd probably never again talk to the brother of her heart slammed into her chest.

She believed in a benevolent God. Sure, bad things happened in this world…but why Cutter? Why now? Brea didn't understand anything about this—except that she had to do something to stop it. Surely, His will couldn't be so cruel as to let someone as wonderful as Cutter die for doing a good deed.

As she leapt to her feet, Rayleigh poked her head in the door. "Cage is here for you, honey. I think something is wrong."

"Cancel the rest of my appointments," she barked as she grabbed her purse and burst out of the break room.

"What's going on?" the woman called after her.

Brea didn't answer, just ran toward Cage, who waited near the entry, face somber. He wrapped his arms around her and squeezed her tight, as if he needed to give comfort as much as to receive it. She freely embraced him, but didn't want any consolation. She just wanted Cutter home safely.

"Tell me everything. Where is your brother? How did this happen?"

Cage glanced around. Brea followed suit and realized everyone in the salon was staring. There was nothing this small town loved more than gossip, the juicier the better.

She had lovingly nurtured this community all her life. She'd loved everyone openly and without reservation. Now they gawked like rapt bystanders, watching as if she and Cage were acting out a sensational TV spectacle.

She was being dramatic. Of course they wouldn't know what to say. She barely did. Still, their curious stares and pitying expressions irritated her.

"Let's talk in the car," Cage grumbled. "I need to get back to Mama."

She nodded feverishly, then sent Rayleigh an imploring glance. "I've got to go."

The woman's face softened. "I'll cancel everything for you."

Brea ran out the door, Cage hot on her heels. Thankfully, he'd found a spot at the curb and helped her into his truck.

As soon as he got behind the wheel, he faced her. "After you two had breakfast, Cutter stopped at the grocery store on his way home. A man was inside, threatening to kill his estranged wife. Some bystanders tried to help, but he pulled a gun. Most people ran to safety, but he shot the butcher simply to prove he meant business, then trapped fifteen people inside the store with him: four men, eight women—including his soon-to-be ex-wife—and three children. When Cutter pulled up, the police hadn't arrived yet and all hell was breaking loose. He intervened."

Of course. Not only did Cutter see it as his solemn duty to protect others, he'd negotiated hostage situations in the past. "So he arranged their release?"

"Everyone except the estranged wife. The gunman wasn't willing to let her go…at first."

But Cutter had worn the man down until he gave in and agreed to release the woman?

Brea turned to Cage with a gasp. "Cutter exchanged his life for hers, didn't he? That's why he was calling."

Cage nodded grimly as he started the truck. "He made the deal less than an hour ago. The gunman allowed him to say his final goodbyes to his family and relay his demands to the police."

"What does he want?" Not that it really mattered, but she had to know how much time Cutter had left.

"A black Camaro with a full tank of gas, ten thousand in unmarked bills, and two fifths of Jack Daniels."

The man didn't sound like he had his priorities straight. "Nothing else?"

As they stopped for the light at the corner near the salon, Cage pulled at the back of his neck. "No. The gunman knows he's already lost. That makes him reckless, stupid, and dangerous."

And Brea knew Cutter. Even if he died, he would be satisfied he'd won if all the hostages went free. "How long do the police have to deliver his demands?"

"Three hours. And thirty minutes of that have already passed."

Unless something happened, Cutter would be dead before the sun went down.

Dread gonged in her chest. "What are the police doing? Tell me they have some plan to catch this man before—"

"Cutter asked everyone not to intervene." Cage didn't sound happy. "Since he and the entire EM Security team are reserve officers, the police are honoring his wishes."

"What?" She'd ask if Cage was serious or Cutter was insane, but she knew the answer.

"I'm pissed, too. Fuck!" He took out his frustrations by beating the steering wheel with his big fist. "I'm sorry but…"

Brea waved away his apology. She'd never spoken that word in her life, but she'd sort of like to right now. "So the police are just going to let this happen?"

"They'll try to catch the guy when he leaves the store, but…pretty much."

"What about you? You could—"

"Step in? Don't you think I wish I could? Even if my brother hadn't asked me to stand down, I'm a cop in Dallas. I don't have any jurisdiction in Lafayette. If I went in there and killed that guy, I'd probably go to prison for murder." He shook his head in frustration. "My hands are tied."

She understood the laws and why they existed, but she couldn't accept giving up now. Thank goodness Cage had given her an idea. "Well, mine aren't. Take me to my car."

He shook his head. "Cutter told me to bring you to Mama to make sure you're safe and—"

"Let me go." When Cage hesitated, she pressed on. "If there's even the slimmest chance I can save your brother, don't you want me to try?"

"What do you have in mind?"

If she told him, he'd only waste time trying to talk her out of it. But Cutter wasn't the only one who could be sacrificial. "Please don't ask. I'd rather not lie to you."

"You can't go anywhere near that grocery story, you hear? You can't put yourself in danger."

She shook her head. "I won't. I promise."

The light turned green. Cage paused, then cursed as he slung an illegal U-turn in the middle of the street. He pulled into the parking lot behind the salon with a sigh. "If my brother makes it through this, he's going to kill me. And I don't care. If you can do anything…"

When he braked beside her compact, she laid a hand on his. "It's a slim possibility, but I'll do everything I can."

With that promise, she jumped out and slid into her little car, screeching out of the parking lot before Cage could maneuver his big truck around to follow her.

It should have taken her at least twenty minutes to reach Lafayette. She made it in twelve. Leaping out of the car and dashing up the walkway to the mid-century modern, she frantically rang the doorbell.

"Please be home." If not, she'd have to figure out a plan B, but that would take time she didn't have. "*Please* be home."

Suddenly, the door jerked open. Shirtless and scowling, Pierce Walker stood in the entryway, scrutinizing her with fierce black eyes. "What are you doing here?"

"I need your help. Please."

He hesitated, and she wondered if he would turn her away. Then finally, he stepped back and invited her in with a bob of his head. "Tell me what you need."

She rushed inside. "Cutter's in danger. He negotiated the release of some hostages from a gunman holding them at a nearby grocery store, but he wouldn't let his estranged wife go. So Cutter offered his life in exchange for hers. He's planning to kill Cutter in about two hours." Tears stung her eyes as she surged forward to grab his steely arms. "I know I'm asking for a lot. I know this isn't your fight. I know you don't like him. But I love him so much. Please… Please, save him. I'll do *anything*."

ONE-MILE STOOD over Brea's petite form, searching her big, pleading eyes. She was begging him—of all people—to save her boyfriend's life.

How fucked up is this?

"What makes you think I can do anything?"

"Aren't you a Lafayette PD reserve officer?"

He nodded. "But that means I have even less power to make things happen in this situation than a beat cop. I'm sure it's being handled—"

"Cutter told them all to stand down. Besides, I doubt any of their officers possess your…skill set."

Now he understood. *Oh, hell.*

One-Mile slammed the door behind Brea and crowded close. Her scent wafted across his senses and slammed into his brain. The soft sway of her breasts burned his chest with the rise and fall of every breath. His lust surged. Jesus, he ached to touch her, to fucking kiss her until she forgot Cutter Bryant had ever existed.

Fat chance.

"And you'll do anything if I save him, is that right?"

"Yes."

"So the pretty little preacher's daughter is offering to fuck me as payment to commit murder?"

She flinched but her stare didn't waver. "Yes."

Well, that answered his most burning question. She was so committed to Cutter that she would give a middle finger to her good-girl morals and do the nasty with a man who scared her in order to save the bastard's life.

Son of a bitch.

He'd deal with that later. But he only wanted Brea if she was wet and hot for him, not because she was martyring herself for another man. Even so, he hated to see her in distress. And she'd never forgive him if he didn't intervene. Caring at all probably made him a schmuck since she didn't give two shits about him. But he wouldn't shut off his internal compass for her or anyone, and it told him to move heaven and hell to keep Brea in his life. Besides, it wasn't as if he had any qualms about ending a scumbag who'd held innocents hostage. Plus, his bosses would either fire him or slit his throat—his money was on the latter—if he could have saved Cutter and hadn't.

Reality tasted really fucking bitter.

He managed not to slam his fist into the nearest wall. "I need a few minutes."

Without a word, he marched to the other side of the house, tore into his home office, then opened the gun safe bolted into the floor.

Brea tiptoed up behind him. Of course he knew. Not only could he hear her, his goddamn body was attuned to her. Every time she came within ten feet of him, his skin fried with lust. His dick got so fucking hard.

"Is that a yes?"

He yanked his MK-13 from where he'd nestled it, retrieved the scope and a tripod, then fished out a box of .300 Magnum rounds. From deeper in the closet, he retrieved a gun case and arranged everything inside, then shut the lid with a final click. "Why not? You want someone dead, pretty girl, I'm your man."

"You're angry." Brea's face said that troubled her.

He grabbed a long-sleeved camo T-shirt from the hanging rod above, thrust it over his head, and lied like a motherfucker. "Nope. Just putting on my game face."

Why tell her he was jealous? It served no purpose except to make him feel pitiful as fuck.

"I'm sorry." She laid a hand against his chest and looked up at him, her expression imploring him to understand. "I know I have no right to ask, but only you can help."

The shitty thing was, she was right. Sure, the Lafayette Police Department had a SWAT unit. Some of their officers had spent some time in the military. A couple had even served in war zones. But if someone was going to nail this guy from a few hundred yards away without alerting the perp while keeping the loss of civilian and LPD life to nil, he was the guy.

It just pissed him off that Brea was only eager to crawl into bed with him in order to save Bryant.

"That's why I'm on it. Stay here."

"Cage and Mama Sweeney are waiting for me back at—"

"No." He pinned her with a glare. "If you want this done, stay here."

She wrapped her arms around herself, but she nodded. "All right."

Fuck, he wasn't trying to scare her, but he also didn't need anyone except him and the cops to know what he had planned—if they even agreed to let him try.

"I'll be back." One-Mile turned for the door.

Brea grabbed his arm, folding one hand in his. "Please be careful."

Was she saying that because she actually cared or simply because she didn't want his blood on her conscience?

"The gunman will never know I'm there until I put a bullet in his brain."

She flinched but grabbed him tighter. "Will you keep me posted? I'll text you my number."

She really had no idea who she was dealing with. If she was never going to want him, maybe it was time to scare the hell out of her so she'd give him a wide berth. Because if he didn't get distance between them, he didn't know how much longer he could stop himself from tasting the sweet pink bow of her lips. And once he got his mouth on her…

Fuck.

One-Mile leaned into her personal space and braced himself against the doorjamb above her head, glaring down. "I already know it. I know everything about you because I made it my business. I'll call when there's something to say."

She swallowed and glanced up at him nervously. "Thank you."

He raised a brow. "You can thank me later."

By staying the hell away.

He left his bedroom and the house, dragging his phone out of his pocket as he launched himself into his Jeep. Time to compartmentalize all this destructive touchy-feely shit and get down to business. Which of his three bosses would listen without losing his head and pave the way for him to get busy?

One-Mile finally settled on Hunter, dialing the former SEAL's number as he turned down the main drag out of his neighborhood. Logan seemed to think he spoke the same language as his older brother. So far, he and the elder Edgington sibling had circled each other. Now he had to hope the younger Edgington hadn't been blowing smoke up his ass.

"What do you want, Walker? It's a Saturday. I'm spending it with my wife and son."

"Unfortunately, unhinged gunmen with an ax to grind don't work Monday through Friday. And your golden boy, Bryant, didn't waste any time playing the hero and offering himself up as the sacrificial lamb."

"What the…" Hunter sounded blazingly pissed as he swallowed a curse. "Kata, take the baby." After some rustling, heavy footsteps clapped across the hardwood floors. "That goddamn son of a bitch. How long do we have?"

"Less than two hours before time's up on the gunman's demands."

"And the shit hits the fan. Why the hell did the police clue you and not me?"

"They never said dick to me. Brea asked me to intervene."

"Fuck." A hundred questions hovered in his expletive, but to Hunter's credit, he didn't ask those now. He just cut to the chase. "You think there's a kill shot to get?"

"I'm on my way to find out. Can you make a few calls, take care of some red tape for me?"

Hunter hesitated. "I could try, but I know who will succeed."

One-Mile knew exactly who he meant. "Your dad."

"Bingo. Everyone respects the hell out of the colonel."

Since One-Mile was in that camp, too, he totally understood Hunter's reasoning. "Good thought. I'm heading to the scene. Let me know."

"I'll have my dad get in touch with you after he's reached out and touched the right people. Thank God he knows everyone in this damn town."

And was at the top of the good ol' boys' food chain.

"Thanks."

"I appreciate you intervening, especially when Brea's request puts you in an awkward-as-fuck position."

Did everyone fucking know he had a hard-on for her? "Your point?"

"Logan and I knew Cage in high school. I know you don't like Cutter much, but…rough childhood. His mom and his brother are good people."

And Cutter was also everyone's favorite at EM. "I got it. I'll take care of it."

Then he hung up. What more was there to say? He'd been tasked with saving the hero before he slunk back to the dark corners of humanity because no one liked to admit that people like him were a necessary evil.

When he reached the scene, the police had cordoned off all entrances to the strip mall that housed the grocery store. Caleb Edgington had apparently worked fast, because the beat cops keeping the parking lot secure let him through right away.

He didn't have to wander through the pandemonium to find the person in charge. A short, forty-something balding guy approached him, eyed him up and down, then stuck out his hand. "You must be Walker. I'm Major John Gaines, the precinct commander."

One-Mile shook his hand. "Tell me what you know."

"Sure. First, we're glad you came. Our SWAT unit is very qualified but…"

None with his credentials. "I'm sure they are."

"You're a little bit of a celebrity among the ranks. A one-mile kill shot is… Well, I don't need to tell you how rare that is."

Fewer than fifteen people in the world had ever actually managed one, but he wasn't here to discuss that. "Any further contact from Bryant or the gunman? Does he have a name?"

Gaines finally got the picture that he wasn't up for a trip down memory lane. "No additional communication. The gunman is Richard Schading. He and his wife, Emily, have been married four years. She's a checker here. Apparently, their relationship has been rocky, and she filed for divorce after he got fired from his last job. She's pregnant, and Richard is convinced another guy knocked her up. I think he went into the store with a murder-suicide plan. Mr. Bryant talked him out of it."

"Is the wife free now?" If he could talk to her, she could give him the scoop, especially her husband's habits and what he might be planning next.

"Not yet, just the others. Schading swears that once we meet his demands, he'll let her go."

So he was intending to use Bryant as a human shield in his getaway. And once they cleared the area, Brea's boyfriend would be a defenseless duck who'd get a quick bullet to the brain. It was also possible the gunman would kill both Cutter and the wife, then turn the gun on himself. Offenders like this were emotional, which made them as unpredictable as they were crazy.

"Where and how are you supposed to make good on his demands?"

"There's a back door. He wants us to leave the Camaro with a full tank of gas running there, money and the booze in the back seat before five."

One-Mile glanced at his phone. He had time, not a ton...but it would have to be enough. "I need to scope the area back there." He gave a visual sweep around the parking lot. "I'm assuming you have the building surrounded?"

"Yes, and we've advised him of that. We've also evacuated the rest of the businesses in this strip mall."

That was a plus. "Once I'm in position, you need to clear everyone out from behind the building."

"And leave you alone?" Gaines's scowl said that wasn't happening. "I don't think—"

"If Schading sees your men surrounding him with weapons drawn, we don't know how he'll respond. If he doesn't feel hemmed in and threatened, he'll be more predictable. And I'll stand a better chance of getting off a clean shot."

"What if you miss?"

"I don't. But if you think you've got this under control, I can leave."

Gaines gritted his teeth as they exchanged numbers. "When you're in place, give me the word. I'll tell everyone back there to clear out."

"Perfect."

The other man scowled. "You're every bit the arrogant asshole I heard you were."

As the precinct commander turned away, he heard a familiar laugh behind him. "Look at you, making friends wherever you go."

One-Mile couldn't not smile back as he turned to find Caleb Edgington. He stuck out his hand. "Good to see you, sir."

"You, too," the tall man with silvery temples said. "Don't mind Gaines. He has short-man's disease."

"I know his type."

"I'll soothe his little feelings," the colonel promised. "What are you thinking here?"

"I need to scout out back."

"Want me to walk it with you?"

"Yeah." He welcomed the colonel's seasoned opinion.

"Happy to." Caleb kept pace beside him as they used the nail salon beside the grocery store as a thruway to the back of the strip mall. "How have you been getting along with my sons since my retirement?"

One-Mile hesitated. "You want the truth?"

"I don't want bullshit."

Fair enough. "They're all right. But I hired on expecting to work for you."

"I know. I'm sorry that didn't happen."

"I get it. Things change. People move on."

"But you depended on me—all of you—and I let you down. That's bugged the hell out of me." He hesitated. "Did you know Bryant felt the same?"

"No."

"The evening after I delivered the news in our team meeting, he called to ream me a new asshole."

Finally, something he respected Bryant for. "I wanted to."

"I figured you would, so I kept you busy with another job." Caleb winked.

"Sly dog."

"I've learned a few tricks over the years, but give my sons a fair shake. They're all-around badasses and good men."

"Yes, but they're not you, sir."

"I appreciate that, but they'll win you over in time. I'm sure of it. They're just not used to handling someone who scares them."

None of them seemed to be shaking in his boots. "Come again?"

"Not literally, but you're a different breed than their SEAL teammates."

Those guys were like brothers. Hell, closer than family in some cases. Snipers like him tended to be loners. "You're saying they don't know how to relate."

"Logan is trying. Hunter and Joaquin are watching how you shake out. Bryant is easy for them to understand. He's damn good at what he does, and he has a noble streak a mile wide…"

While One-Mile himself was morally gray. "Got it."

"You don't. They know you're important. Special. They just don't know how to take you. And it's not like any of them are well known for their interpersonal skills."

One-Mile smiled. "So you're asking me to be patient?"

"I'd appreciate it. They only took over the business a few months ago. A lot of this is new for them, but especially someone like you."

One-Mile wasn't dumb; the colonel was buttering him up, but he understood the basic message. He wasn't a team player since that wasn't his role, and that made relating to him difficult. He also had a chip on his shoulder because Bryant had Brea, and he wanted her way more than he should. The colonel's sons were running a security firm, not overseeing a daytime drama. Hence, Logan's warning to keep his angst out of the office.

"I'm reserving judgment, doing my job, and keeping my nose clean. Speaking of which…" He scanned the alley behind the grocery store.

It looked typical. A lot of concrete, a couple of dumpsters, painted brick topped by a flat industrial roof. A retaining wall blocked off access to the street behind the strip mall. A residential development lay directly beyond that, leaving the gunman's easy path of escape an adjacent highway that led straight out of town. It also limited the places One-Mile could set up a shot in the immediate vicinity.

But across from the cookie-cutter neighborhood, he saw possibilities.

"Give me a minute."

At the colonel's nod, he jumped and grabbed the top of the eight-foot retaining wall, then hoisted himself up for a look-see over the whole vicinity. To his left, he saw a bank, but he didn't like the pitch of its roof or close proximity to the grocery store. If Schading was observant enough, he'd be spotted up there. Behind that stood a doctor's office, but that roofline was also too sloped to provide the proper stability for his setup. He could see rooflines beyond that but didn't know this part of town well enough to know what businesses they housed.

One-Mile whipped out his phone, found a satellite map, and answered his own question in the next thirty seconds.

He jumped down to join the colonel in the alley once more. "There's a two-story storage facility across the street about four buildings back. I'd like to set up there."

The colonel gawked over the wall at the building he'd indicated. "I won't ask you if you're crazy. I know the answer."

One-Mile shrugged. "Not the first time I've been accused of that."

"You know that's over a thousand feet away."

He nodded. "I've hit double that."

The colonel sighed, then slapped him on the back. "Which is why I hired you. I respect that you're not arrogant, just factual."

"I do my best, sir. Sure there's no chance you'll take over the business again?"

"The boys have already renamed it Edgington-Muñoz, so no. I'm out." He shrugged. "Carlotta and I have decided to travel instead. We're taking a cruise."

"I can't picture you at the buffet before shuffleboard."

The older man closed his eyes. "It sounds horrible, doesn't it? But still better than this high-stress, life-and-death shit." He clapped One-Mile on the back. "I'll talk to Gaines and get you on that roof. How long do you need to set up?"

"As much time as you can buy me. The good news is, I'll be shooting to the northeast, so Schading will have the sun in his eyes, not me. I need a weather report. Not the hotter-than-fuck part; I know that. But I could use a thorough wind forecast. I need to know if I can expect the current conditions to hold."

"Get your gear, and I'll have a chat with the powers that be. I'll meet you back at your Jeep in a few."

One-Mile headed back to his vehicle, struck by the stillness of what must be a typically busy parking lot. Beyond that, motorists rubbernecked, trying to see what all the fuss in the strip mall was about. Their lives went on as soon as the light turned green. Someone's was going to end today, and he would be the one pulling the trigger.

He just hoped Schading was the only person on the scene who met his end.

As much as One-Mile disliked Bryant, his squeaky-clean heroics, and his hold on Brea Bell, he didn't wish death on the guy. He'd tried to do the right thing, and One-Mile respected that. Besides, his passing would destroy the pretty preacher's daughter. And if she thought he was killing for any reason other than to please her, she was fooling herself.

It didn't take long for the colonel to approach, Gaines in tow.

The precinct commander eyed him. "You sure about that location?"

The guy who had never been a sniper was going to question his strategy? "It's the best balance between getting the right angle and being difficult for the gunman to spot."

"Our SWAT guys think we'd do better to put someone on the roof of the grocery store, so that when Schading walks out with the wife and Bryant, the car will be in front of him. He'll get distracted by his getaway and leave you a really easy shot from behind."

One-Mile shook his head. "Or he sees the obvious plan coming a mile away and looks on the roof, spots me, then kills someone to prove a goddamn point."

"That's the risk we take."

He shook his head. "Maybe that's the risk *you* take when you don't have someone who can hit this shot. But since I can and I'm probably the person he kills to make that point, I vote we do it my way."

"Let him do his job, John," the colonel encouraged in knowledge-able tones. "He's the best. I hired him myself."

Gaines cursed. "I need to make a few phone calls. We'll have to clear out as many civilians as we can."

One-Mile shrugged. "If that makes you feel better... I'm not going to miss and hit any of them, but if you're worried Schading will fire back, I promise he'll be dead before he even realizes he's taken a bullet."

"We'll see," the commander grumbled, then walked away.

"He's got to cover his ass. If anything goes wrong, the department could have the shit sued out of them, and the optics would be horrible around the community."

"Valid points." One-Mile wasn't used to worrying about shit like that, just about getting the damn job done.

"He'll come through."

Sure enough, fifteen minutes later, Gaines ambled back with a scowl. "You got your way. The police chief isn't thrilled, but he's on board. The bank is closing now. The doctor was having a staff meeting that he's wrapping up, and the light industrial offices behind that are already closed. The storage facility only has one employee on shift. He's scheduled to leave at five, so he's going to slide out early. You'll have a clear shot."

He could set up and get to work now. Best news he'd heard all day.

After that, shit happened quickly, which suited One-Mile just fine. To the police's credit, they cleared all traffic from the vicinity with minimal disruption. If Schading had any accomplices outside the store —and they'd seen no indication of that—it would simply appear as if all of these businesses had gone dark for the rest of the weekend. They'd also managed to block off the alley to the east and the street access, as if the city intended to bring in a road crew to fill some potholes.

Thirty minutes later, he'd set up his tripod, positioned his weapon, and gotten his scope in place. Then he did what snipers had to learn to do if they wanted to be any fucking good: he waited. He refined the shot, felt the wind and heaviness of the air, factored that into his mental calculations, then texted Caleb to let them know he was ready, along with a host of other instructions to make sure no one spooked Schading or blocked his shot.

Fifteen minutes later, a black Camaro rolled into the alley. The gunman hadn't left specific instructions about where and how he wanted the car positioned, other than to have it stocked with a full tank, money, and Tennessee whiskey. So One-Mile had been very detailed, and it looked as if the message had been communicated correctly when a uniformed officer left the running vehicle in the middle of the alley with the driver's side facing the retaining wall. Only the driver's door would be unlocked, which would force the gunman to walk around the car to escape. If he wanted to take Cutter as a hostage, Schading would either have to shove Bryant in first before he could take his seat or unlock the passenger door, escort Bryant to it, and force him in before finding his own seat. Either way, he'd be out in the open and vulnerable as fuck for far longer than One-Mile would need to get off a successful shot.

Not long after the officer left the Camaro idling, the grocery store's back door opened. Cutter was first to emerge, hands high in the air, blood dripping from his left temple. Schading was right behind him, gun in his grip as he jabbed Bryant in the back, prodding him forward. With his free hand, he gripped his wife by the hair and dragged her out behind him.

The woman trembled and cried, mascara running down her face. She was a little thing, with a hint of a baby bump. Schading yanked on Bryant's shirt, then turned back to shout at his wife. The terrified woman cowered and tried to make herself as small as possible. One-Mile felt really fucking sorry for her. Bryant must have had the same reaction, because he started talking, clearly trying to take the gunman's anger down twenty notches. The bad news was, while Brea's boy toy stood there and played the hero, he was shielding Schading from the shot One-Mile had painstakingly lined up.

Finally, the gunman shoved his wife to the ground. And because he was such a Prince Charming, he kicked her a couple of times. Cutter was clearly itching to use this distraction to launch more heroics. Not that he didn't understand Bryant's urge to punch this abusive asshole in the face, but the Boy Scout could help most by getting the fuck out of the way.

Schading's temper seemed to ratchet up as he waved the gun in his estranged wife's face. She shrank back and curled her arms around her belly protectively.

One-Mile would lose zero sleep over ending this douche.

He wrapped his finger around the trigger, triple-checked his sights, and held his breath…

Before he could pull the trigger, Bryant opened his mouth and started flapping his jaws again. Schading whirled, turning his crazy-eyed glare on Cutter, and charged toward him like an enraged bull. Then he shoved the gun against Bryant's bleeding temple and shouted something that looked expletive-filled.

Fuck, this was heating up too furiously and too fast. If he didn't act now, Schading might lose his shit, decide to take his wife hostage after all, and blow the head off his expendable tagalong, Cutter.

With a rapid mental ticktock in his head counting down the seconds, One-Mile realigned his shot, curled his finger a little tighter around the trigger...and squeezed.

CHAPTER FIVE

The crack of his shot resounded in his ears as the rifle kicked back, but he stayed with the scope and watched the bullet plant itself dead center in the middle of Schading's forehead. The would-be gunman crumpled to the concrete. Blood splattered onto the screaming woman behind him and pooled around his body.

Cutter whipped his gaze around, searching for the source of the shot. The Boy Scout couldn't see him, but he seemingly realized the ordeal was over and blew out a deep sigh of relief before turning his attention on the newly minted widow. More blood rolled down his temple as he bent and helped the shaking woman to her feet.

Cops rushed in from everywhere. A pair of EMTs followed with a gurney. Gaines marched in, the colonel by his side, followed by another guy who looked too bleak to be anything other than the coroner. Someone drove the still-idling car away.

One-Mile stood and stretched. The phone in his pocket buzzed with a message from Caleb Edgington that read Good job, Walker. He didn't reply. He hadn't done anything heroic or amazing, just taken out the trash.

What exactly did he tell Brea now? She'd be both relieved and horrified. Sure, she'd asked him for this…but it wouldn't take long for the reality to hit her that she'd begged him to kill a man. Then she'd probably tie herself in guilty knots. Would she even speak to him after that?

His thumbs hovered over the keyboard, but he didn't have a choice. With a grumble, he tapped in her number and typed out a message.

`I'm done. Stay put.`

Brea only wanted to know one thing.

`Is Cutter all right?`

As soon as the words appeared on One-Mile's screen, he cursed. Of course she wanted to know. She'd pleaded with him to save the son of a bitch's life because she loved him so much. Naturally, his fate was the first she'd ask about. He'd been an idiot to hope differently.

`Fine, just a scratch or two.`

`Thank you.`

For the update or for killing someone who had threatened her lover?

Shaking his head, One-Mile pocketed his phone. Time to blow this fucking shit show.

With short, sharp movements, he packed up his weapon and the rest of his equipment, then hopped in his Jeep and returned to the strip mall. When he arrived on the scene, Gaines sent him a businesslike nod. The colonel gave him a thumbs-up. The cops around him stared either in worship or terror.

Cutter jerked away from an attentive EMT applying pressure to his bleeding temple and scowled. "That was *your* kill shot?"

Why lie? "Yep."

"Why the hell did you get involved? I had the situation under control. I'd been talking to Richard for hours. I was just getting him to the point of admitting his impulsive plan wouldn't work and surrendering."

"Well, it didn't look that way when he pressed his barrel against your skull."

He rolled his eyes. "He hadn't yet pulled the trigger. I was less than three minutes from getting him to surrender."

"Or being dead, because he didn't look ready to raise a white flag to me. So stop bitching. It's done. He's dead. If you'd rather, next time I won't save your life. Hell, I wouldn't have this time except Brea begged me."

"What?" Cutter looked like his head was about to spin off into another dimension.

"She asked me to make sure you came home in one piece. I did. Now I'm leaving."

The colonel approached and clapped him on the back. "I'll take care of the red tape from here. We'll call you if we need anything, but Gaines and I both saw the whole thing. There shouldn't be too many questions."

One-Mile nodded. "Thanks."

Cutter was still sputtering. "Where is she?"

"My place." He just smiled. Yeah, it was a petty jab, but one that seemed to bug the hell out of Bryant.

"I'm coming with you to take her home."

"That's not a good idea." The colonel stepped in when the nearby EMT shook her head stubbornly. "Word is, you probably have a concussion. I think you should get checked out."

"I've had worse."

Caleb's affable expression fell away. "You're going to the hospital. My sons will insist. So am I. You won't be cleared to work until you do."

"Fine," Cutter muttered, then turned his back on the older man and glared One-Mile's way. "Why did Brea come to *you* for help?"

"You'll have to take that up with her." And One-Mile was done talking.

With a wave at the colonel, he turned and headed for his Jeep. Time to get back to the pretty preacher's daughter. Now that he'd done as she'd pleaded, was she expecting he'd demand her to pay up?

⸺ ·⊰·⊱· ⸺

BREA PACED the open length of Pierce's house from the kitchen to the front door and back again. As soon as she'd received his text that the gunman had been vanquished and Cutter had survived, she'd broken down and cried. Then she gathered herself and called Cutter's family to tell them he was alive. After his initial rush of relief, Cage began asking pointed questions about how she'd gotten that information and what exactly she had done to intervene. Brea forced a smile in her voice, then she did something she hadn't done since she was a child.

She lied.

"Nothing much."

Pierce had kept his end of their bargain. Now she had to be brave enough to repay him—with her body.

As she passed the kitchen table again, she grabbed the glass of water she'd poured herself hours ago and swallowed it down. She didn't drink alcohol much, but in that moment, she wished she'd sought out something stronger to fill her glass.

Still, intoxication wouldn't change the truth. She had promised Pierce Walker sex.

So tonight, she would give herself to him without regret. Tomorrow, she would repent for her sins. Afterward, their paths would never cross again.

The buzz of the automatic garage door snagged her attention, followed by the purr of an engine, signaling Pierce's return. Suddenly, Brea felt like a bunny trapped in a wolf's lair. Her hands went clammy. Her breath rattled in and out of her lungs. Her heart pounded like a wild thing.

She should have been terrified of crawling between the sheets with a man she barely knew. Sickened that he'd agreed to accept sex in exchange for a human life. Ashamed that she'd bartered away her virginity instead of saving it for a man she loved.

But when she thought of Pierce touching her, stripping her down, and covering her body with his, the flesh between her legs twisted with a shameful ache. She might lie to Cage about tonight to save face or to Cutter to spare him guilt, but she wouldn't lie to herself. She wanted Pierce Walker. Everything about him as a man that should repel her instead tempted the woman inside her.

Brea eased her empty glass onto the table and took a deep breath before she forced herself to approach the garage door. She folded her hands to steady herself, hoping Pierce wouldn't see her tremble.

The engine cut off. A car door slammed. Then he stepped inside the house—all six and a half feet of him—his big shoulders filling the doorway.

His black eyes fell on her immediately. "You're still here."

She nodded. "You told me to be."

Something passed across his face. Approval? Desire? Whatever it was, she felt the answering ping inside her.

"You okay?" he asked.

He had been the one to run headlong into danger. And unlike Cutter, Pierce hadn't ridden to the rescue out of the goodness of his heart. He'd done it because he wanted her—desperately enough to risk his safety, intensely enough to take another's life just to have her.

That made no sense to Brea. In a roomful of women, she was never the prettiest. Or the smartest. Forget the most gregarious, so she was never the most popular. She definitely wasn't the funniest or the sexiest or the most interesting. Why had Pierce agreed to something so perilous and horrific to have *her?*

"Other than some frazzled nerves, I'm fine." Another lie to mask her confusion, her desire. "What about you?"

He shrugged, his big body moving with stealthy grace. "Fine. If you didn't know, the EMTs took Cutter to the hospital for some tests, but he'll be all right."

"I heard. I called Cage shortly after I received your text. He said his brother rang before the medical team took him away. He and Sweeney are on their way over there. Cutter is going back for an MRI on his head before they stitch him up."

Pierce hesitated, then set his keys on the foyer table. He tucked his gun case on the floor underneath. "They're waiting for you, right? Go on."

He was letting her leave? Just like that? Without expecting anything in return? "But...I owe you. I'm prepared to give you what I promised."

He looked her up and down, then raised a brow at her. "No, you're not. And I don't want a martyr. Get out."

When Pierce brushed past her and headed for the kitchen, Brea whirled, frowning as she watched him pluck a tumbler from the cabinet. Her frown deepened when he filled it with whiskey and knocked it back in one swallow, ignoring her.

He'd not only given her a reprieve but seemingly released her from their deal altogether. She should be thrilled. She should be breathing a sigh of relief and running for the door. Instead, she felt shocked and disappointed. Angry, even.

What the devil was wrong with her?

It didn't matter. Cutter was at the hospital. Cage and Mama Sweeney were waiting. She should be beside them. They might need her moral support and prayers.

Still, she couldn't just leave without saying something. "I don't understand. You did something extraordinary for me today that I—"

"It's the same damn thing I did for Uncle Sam on the daily for eight years."

The math on that astounded her. He'd seriously killed that many enemy combatants? "But you were paid for your work. I owe you."

"Fuck that. I'm not your charity case, and I won't have you feeling guilty because you 'endured' my filthy hands all over you. Besides, I don't want the Boy Scout's leftovers. So get the hell out."

He poured another tumbler of whiskey and swallowed it back. Brea just stared. What was up with him? He pretended his kills didn't matter, as if he'd prefer to be alone and screw the rest of the world. But under all his bluster, she felt his hurt and loneliness. He was lost, wounded. And he had no one.

Except maybe her.

Brea softened. "Despite what you think, I committed tonight to you and I'm prepared to see this through. But if you don't want to have sex with me, then—"

"Oh, don't kid yourself." He slammed his glass on the table and stalked toward her on almost silent footfalls, spearing her where she stood. "Can you honestly say that you believe, for even a single second, that I'm not desperate to fuck you?"

Given everything he'd admitted the evening she'd brought him cookies? Given the way he was looking at her right now? "No."

"No," he confirmed. "I wanted you the second you opened the door at Edgington's house, skirt swishing and good-girl smile in place.

I wanted you even after I knew you were Bryant's. Even when you refused to admit you want me, too. Hell, I even wanted you when you told me how much you love Cutter and offered me your body to save his life. I've imagined you, masturbated to thoughts of you, dreamed of you. So don't think, for one instant, that I've changed my mind."

His words stunned her. Brea's heart raced. "Why are you telling me this?"

"Because I'm being straight-up honest and I want the same from you. *That's* how you can repay me."

His demand terrified her…but she couldn't refuse. "A-all right."

"Good. Now we might get somewhere." Brea barely had time to grasp that he'd seen through her before he grabbed her arms and pulled her against his hard body. "I'm touching you. How does that make you feel?"

Heat radiated from him like a furnace, singeing all her exposed skin. She gasped. "Hot."

"And?" His nostrils flared. His eyes turned impossibly blacker.

When she tried to draw in a steadying breath, his scent filled her head instead. He smelled like musk. Like man. Like the most tempting sin. Her knees wobbled. Her eyes went wide. Her heart quaked.

And her whole body came alive.

What was it about Pierce Walker?

"That, right there." He pointed at her. "You want me, too, despite your better judgment. I see it all over your face. But you're still reluctant to admit it. You promised to stop lying."

Shame filled Brea. Her dishonesty was a selfish sin she wreaked on him to protect her pride. Pierce hadn't demanded that she give him her body, but she owed him her truth.

"You're right. I've thought of you, too," she whispered. "Even when Cutter told me to avoid you, even when I knew my father would never approve. And even when you scared me. I told myself none of what I'm feeling is logical or practical. But nothing has stopped my attraction to you."

"You're finally admitting you want me?"

Answering gave him the sort of power over her she could never take back…but her honor and his rough voice compelled her. "Yes. You make me ache in ways I shouldn't. In places I shouldn't. And I can't seem to stop."

Pierce grabbed her chin and lifted it. "What do you want from me?"

Did she dare answer him?

Brea bit her lip. "You already know."

"Spell it out." His fingers tightened. "I know what your eyes are telling me, pretty girl. But I want to hear you say it. Full consent."

This again? But why would he want that now...unless he intended to touch her?

"Pierce..." She tilted her head back, let her eyes slide shut again. "We shouldn't."

"Give me the words, pretty girl. I'm not asking for anything else."

What choice did she have? Sincerity was such a small price to pay him for saving her best friend's life.

Knowing she'd probably never be this close to Pierce again, Brea rose on her tiptoes and swayed against him, stealing a forbidden caress of her cheek against his hair-roughened one. "I want you to kiss me."

"I want that, too," Pierce groaned as he cupped her face, forcing her to meet his stare. "But I'm weak when it comes to resisting you. Don't say that again unless you actually mean it."

Something hot and twisted jolted through her body. "Or what?"

"Brea, I'm trying to do the right thing. When you look at me with those pleading eyes... And, fuck, your plump, pink mouth is so close, all I can think of are the indecent things I'm dying to do to it."

Probably the same things she'd secretly wanted him to do.

Her ache tightened. "What is this connection between us? I don't understand."

"Fuck if I know. I've never felt anything like it."

She hadn't imagined a yearning this strong was possible. It was bigger than her, and every time she tried to ignore it, the desire only grew.

Must be why folks call it temptation...

Brea searched his face, fighting her own impulse to touch him. And the fire in his black stare told her he knew it.

If she dared to repeat her desire, he'd be all over her. She wasn't sure she would have the will to resist him when he pushed her for everything she'd never given a man, then demanded more. But if she chose the coward's way out, she'd be lying, letting them both down, and leaving herself to forever wonder *what if.*

Which was really the bigger sin?

The truth was, Cutter didn't need her right now. His wounds weren't mortal. Even if he had a concussion, he would wake up tomorrow to live another day, secure in the knowledge that he was surrounded by community, family, and friends who loved him.

Who did Pierce have?

Tonight, he had her.

"I want you to kiss me," she whispered. "Now."

He tensed. "You're sure?"

"Yes."

"Even though it's wrong?"

According to Cutter, it was. Her father and God would concur, too. Pierce would probably break her heart in the end. Right now, none of that mattered more than giving him her honesty.

"Yes."

"Even though this could get out of control?"

"Yes."

"Brea. Baby…" Desire darkened his expression. "Don't say I didn't warn you."

Pierce's breaths came fast and harsh as he thrust his big hand in her hair, fisted the strands, and lowered his head.

She'd been kissed a few times, mostly by polite boys who hadn't taken things too far because they'd been afraid to incur the wrath of Reverend Bell or Cutter Bryant. Once, she'd made out on a bus ride home with a football player after a game in Baton Rouge. He'd kissed her with a lot of gusto and very little finesse before he'd tried to feel his way under her shirt. When she'd shoved away his wandering hands, he'd called her a prude and told his teammates she was a waste of time. Afterward, she'd felt angry, ashamed, and determined not to suck face with a boy again.

But the instant Pierce covered her mouth with his, she realized she'd never truly been kissed.

He pried her lips apart, surged inside, and touched her somewhere deeper than she'd ever felt. Sparks flared and zinged. Her skin stretched tight. Heat burst into a bonfire in her belly, awakening more of this dizzying need.

Brea threw her arms around Pierce, pressing her throbbing nipples against his chest in search of relief. He was hot and impossibly hard. Rubbing against him only increased her torment.

Their shirts were in the way. She needed his bare skin against hers. Ached for it. Craved it.

With an impatient fist, she tugged his camo T-shirt up his torso. The velvety skin and rigid muscle across his abdomen and ribs tempted her. She dug her fingers into his back, pulling him closer, feeling him deeper. It still wasn't enough.

At her touch, he groaned, twined their tongues together again, and reached behind his head. He interrupted their kiss just long enough to yank his shirt off and toss it to the floor.

She got a glimpse of his bare torso—big and hair-roughened, littered with tattoos and the scars of war, panting with desire—before he covered her mouth again and took her lips.

He seized her soul.

With shaking fingers, she braced herself on his steely shoulders and crashed into him, returning every jagged breath and stroke of his tongue as she curled her leg around his. As if he shared her desperation, he grabbed her thigh in his big hand and dragged it over his hip before backing her against the kitchen table and nudging her needy feminine flesh with his erection.

Pleasure spiked. Pierce swallowed her cries.

Under him, she wriggled, her blazing need burning through her misgivings and modesty. It demanded she get even closer, feel more of him—now.

Brea grabbed his steely biceps and writhed shamelessly. He ground his erection against the spot that made her wild for him. Pierce tore his mouth from their kiss, tossed his head back, and groaned out a curse.

Then he met her gaze. Instantly she knew if he'd been wearing gloves before, they were off now.

Good. She wanted to taste him, to feel him, to give herself to him.

She wanted to be his, even if it was for a night. Even if it was a sin. Even if she burned in hell for this desire. It couldn't be any worse than twisting in agony without him.

His hands took a rough plunge down her body, skirting dangerously close to the sides of her breasts before he filled his palms with her backside and lifted her off her feet. Her flip-flops fell to the floor as he set her on his kitchen table, spread her legs, and made himself at home in between. "Want your shirt off?"

"Yes."

Pierce gripped the hem of her floral tank and yanked it over her head. His stare fell on the skin he'd exposed. Beneath the lace-trimmed cups of her white bra, her nipples tightened and stabbed the modest cups. She shivered.

His rapacious black gaze skated down her bare belly, to the denim shorts clinging to her hips, to her bare feet with their painted pink toes. Then he settled his big palms around her hips and dragged her flush against him again. The sensations jolted her system. The longing between her legs torqued up, becoming pure torment.

"Pierce..."

"Jesus, pretty girl. You're perfect." He swept one hand across her abdomen, searing wherever he touched, before he dug his steely length right against her ache again. "Oh, fuck, yeah... You with me?"

Brea didn't hesitate. "Yes."

"You want more?"

"Yes."

"I want to suck those pretty nipples. What do you say to that?"

His demand sounded immoral. Wicked. Sublime. "Please."

"Tell me to take off your bra, pretty girl."

Her head was spinning. Her heart was chugging. She felt ready to burst into flames. "Take off my bra. Hurry."

Pinning her in place with his hungry gaze, Pierce lifted one hand to the strap bisecting her back and unfastened all three hooks in the blink of an eye.

Brea swallowed. This was happening. This was real. Pierce Walker was about to lay eyes on her naked breasts.

He let go. Her bra fell away.

His black eyes fastened on her, firmly affixing to her nipples. They drew up even tighter under his scrutiny, the tips so engorged they throbbed. "Fucking gorgeous."

His words made Brea blush. But she wanted more than his praise; she wanted relief from this endless ache.

She wound her arms around his neck and arched, flattening herself against his muscled torso. The jolt of his skin directly on hers was electric. She gasped at the new, foreign sensations.

"You feel so damn good," he groaned.

"You feel better."

But the skin-to-skin contact wasn't enough to satisfy her. She wriggled again, needing something more.

Pierce eased away, gaze fastened on her breasts again, as his fingers crept up her torso. "Tell me to touch them."

"Please." She prayed that would end her torment. "Touch them now."

She hadn't even finished speaking before he had her breasts in his scorching palms. He cradled them, testing their weight, squeezing. Then he swept the sensitive crests with his thumbs.

Tingles spread throughout her body. She hissed in pleasure and arched closer to Pierce, shoving herself deeper into his grip—and under his spell—silently begging for more.

"Like that?"

"Yes," she gasped.

"Want more?"

"Please." His touch made her need more insistent.

She feared only one thing would end it.

With a devilish smile, he flicked his thumbs across her nipples, bending the peaks—and her—to his will. Heat flared from the tops of her breasts to the tips of her toes, then zipped between her legs, twisting into a greedy, destructive inferno.

"I want your nipples on my tongue. Tell me to suck them."

His suggestion made her flare even hotter. And if he took her breasts in his mouth, he'd only destroy her that much faster.

Brea couldn't bring herself to care anymore.

"Yes." She clawed at him. "Please."

He skimmed his knuckles along the side of one of her mounds, back and forth, moving ever closer to her aching peak. "Please what?"

She knew why he kept prompting her with these questions, but she wished he'd stop. She didn't want to think, didn't want to consider every step down this road paved with lust and sin. But he was determined that she not only allow him to join her but *invite* him down the path of ruination with her.

"Please suck my nipples, then take off my shorts and lead me upstairs. Do whatever will make this ache go away. I need it. I need you. I consent."

SHOCK PINGED THROUGH ONE-MILE. He'd fantasized. He'd hoped. But he hadn't truly believed Brea Bell would agree to let him spend the night inside her. "You're sure?"

"You can end this agony, right?"

"You bet I can, pretty girl." But given the chemistry between them, he had a sneaking suspicion the ache would only come back stronger, over and over again.

In fact, he was betting on it.

"Then yes," she groaned as she tried to wriggle off the table. "Hurry."

He would because he was dying to be inside her, but no fucking way would he let her go until they were both thoroughly satisfied. And maybe not even then.

One-Mile crowded her back onto the flat surface, then scooped her pert little ass in his hands again, crushing her against every hot inch of his body. Then he laid her out and swooped in for another unrestrained kiss. Just like the first time he tasted her, the instant her honey-sweet flavor hit his tongue, she ramped up his hunger.

He dove deep into her mouth, driven by the need to take all she gave. Brea melted, arms around his neck, drawing him closer as she writhed artlessly beneath him. He rocked against her, grinding where he ached to penetrate her.

His desire for her became a searing, infinite need. One-Mile ate at her mouth, hell-bent on imprinting himself on Brea Bell forever. He tried to slow his roll, not overwhelm her. Hell, he tried to let her breathe.

Not happening. Her every touch and little whimper only jacked him up more.

He jerked back, chest heaving as he sucked in air. Beneath him, Brea looked stunned and blinking, her rosy, swollen lips gaping in surprise. *He* had put that look on her face, and it made One-Mile harder than he'd ever been. He gripped her thighs and tried like hell to think. Because if he didn't find some goddamn self-control, he'd strip her where she lay and fuck her until she screamed.

"Do you need to tell anyone you'll be unavailable for a while?" The last fucking thing he wanted was to be interrupted, especially by annoying-as-fuck Bryant.

"No," she breathed. "My dad is playing cards tonight with friends. I doubt the hospital will release Cutter before morning. But I'll turn it off just in case."

The hitch and shiver in her voice torqued up his arousal.

"Do that."

"You have to let me up."

Reluctantly, he did, never taking his rapt gaze off of her as she pulled the device from her purse. She checked it…then silenced it.

Finally, she was his…at least for the night.

And the fact that she would rather spend it getting orgasms from him instead of holding her convalescing boyfriend's hand said that, while parts of her heart might still be with Cutter, the rest of her wanted only him.

One-Mile could work with that. He had every intention of blowing Brea's doors off in bed. Given her good-girl mentality, he'd bet Cutter had been her first—and only—lover. He hated that she'd given her innocence to the prick, but he would happily provide her a point of comparison. And since Brea was the sort of woman whose body followed her heart, if he did this right, she would soon be waving *adios* to the bastard for good.

When she swayed toward him again, he dragged her against his body and lifted her. "Wrap your arms and legs around me."

She didn't hesitate to sling her thighs around his hips and grip his shoulders, then squirm to get closer. He groaned. Goddamn it, despite how tiny she was, they were going to fit together perfectly when they fucked.

He grappled for the patience to at least get her clothes off before he ruthlessly impaled her.

With his hands full of her ass, he charged for the stairs. When she skimmed her lips across his bare shoulder and started kissing her way up his neck, his gait turned to a run.

"You're playing with fire," he warned.

"I already know you're going to burn me."

Her whisper shuddered down his spine. No doubt she'd leave him some blisters of her own. If she didn't realize that, she was either delusional or totally unaware of her own appeal.

Climbing the stairs took for-fucking-ever. When he finally reached the landing, he was out of breath—not from exertion but from his weeping cock rubbing the molten heat between her legs. When she sank her teeth into his shoulder, then lapped at the spot with her little tongue, he was damn near ready to crawl out of his skin.

"Brea…"

"Hmm… You have this hint of salt. I want to know if the rest of you tastes like that."

At the image of her mouth all over him, One-Mile picked up his pace toward his bedroom, melting with lust. It was taking so fucking long to get down the hallway. If he didn't get there quickly, he'd shove her against the nearest wall and get inside her just to give them both some goddamn relief.

"You can put your mouth anywhere you want on me, pretty girl. Just wait until we get to the fucking bed."

She lifted her wide gaze his way, wearing a hint of a smile. "You sound impatient."

"You think?"

When he grumbled, her smile widened. "So I get to you?"

"After one look, I wanted you. But after one kiss, I knew I'd do anything to have you."

The smile slid off her face. "Why?"

"We're about to find out." He bent and laid her flat across his rumpled sheets. "Let's take our chemistry for a spin."

One-Mile didn't give her a second to rethink or regroup. He covered her body with his and dove into her mouth, praying the balm of her kiss could soothe the rough edges of his agony. Beneath him, she parted her legs as if him sliding between them was the most natural thing in the world. It fucking felt that way when he notched his cock against her pussy again, which he hoped like hell was wet enough to take him. She cried out under him, her nails already digging into his skin like a kneading kitten's.

Brea tore her lips from his with a gasp. "Pierce…"

"You asked me to suck your nipples."

"Yes."

Craving a taste of her, One-Mile cradled one of her breasts in his palm and dragged his tongue over its tight crest.

Yeah, he'd held bigger tits, but none as sweet as hers. This was a pair he could be happy with for the rest of his life—symmetrical, bouncy and round, slightly heavier at the bottom, but still delicate, like her. Her rosy-brown nipples tempted the fuck out of him. They were small and taut, and he wanted to suck the sugary little buttons until she melted for him.

After his first lick, both her peaks swelled to stab the air—pretty, pouting, begging. He turned his mouth to the other and pinched the first, gratified when she arched toward him, as if she was surrendering these luscious little tips to him entirely.

Greedily, he wrapped his lips around the closest one, sucking it deep. He reveled in the toss of her head as she dug her nails into his back again.

"Oh… My…" she panted. "Yes."

One-Mile wasn't up for conversation, but he loved hearing her stream-of-pleasure babble. So he drew her deeper into his mouth, swirled his tongue around the captive crest, then released her slowly, teeth nipping gently along the way.

"Please…" She curled her fingers into his short hair and pulled him closer. "More."

He didn't argue, just switched breasts. This nipple looked as earnest and engorged as the first. With his thumb and fingers, he plucked at the peak he'd just popped from his mouth. Then he engulfed the other, pulling it ruthlessly between his lips, tonguing it, then gently biting, pecking, gripping.

He kept at her, first one breast, followed by the other, until he reduced Brea to incoherent animal sounds and she twisted in agony beneath him.

"How's that ache now?" he murmured as he dragged his lips up her neck to nip at her lobe.

"Do something. I need..." She bit her lip and stared with helpless eyes. "I need you."

One-Mile was only too happy to oblige. Sure, he'd love to take a leisurely tour of her body, get his hands wherever she had curves, and let his mouth linger anywhere she might taste good. That would have to wait until round two. Right now, he didn't think either of them could stand another second of him not being inside her.

Jesus, his cock ached. Brea was like a fever; he was fucking sweating with need for her. He had to take her. Possess her. Own her.

As he shucked his constraining pants and kicked them aside, Brea propped herself up on her elbows and stared, her eyes wide, her mouth hanging open. How should he interpret that fucking expression? She gaped as if she'd never seen a man's cock, but she must have. She'd been with Cutter for years, and he was no monk.

"Pretty girl?" He knelt on the bed and leaned over her.

She jerked her stare to his face, blinked, then dragged him down for a drugging kiss. "I'm here. Yes. Hurry."

No fucking way he would deny her anything.

As he crushed her swollen lips beneath his, One-Mile tore into the button at the waist of her shorts. Next, he yanked down her zipper. He tugged the denim and her underwear away all at once, jerking them down her thighs. Later, he'd take a gander at whatever pretty, lacy shit she'd worn that would undoubtedly tempt the hell out of him. Right now... He dropped his stare to the one place on her body that would no doubt seduce him most.

Oh, sweet pussy.

Soft and pink, hiding shyly behind a tuft of dark hair. And so fucking wet.

His mouth watered, and he dropped between her legs, bending them, then tossing them over his shoulders as quickly as he could. "I'm so fucking hungry."

"Pierce...oh—"

She stopped talking the instant he filled his mouth with her succulent flesh. The tart-sweet flavor of her teased his tongue as he explored her folds and valleys. She was lush and ripe—like a fucking fantasy. He ate at her ravenously, wondering if he'd ever get enough.

Under him, she cried out, head thrashing from side to side. Her thighs suddenly tightened around his head. Her fingers thrust into his hair as she began scratching at his scalp. Her little moans became high-pitched pleas that reverberated in his ears and messed with his restraint.

Fuck, he loved heaping pleasure on her.

One-Mile pushed her thighs wider, dragged his tongue up her center again, and let out a gruff groan as she gushed into his mouth. The clit he took between his lips was engorged and hard as hell. God, he'd love to mouth-fuck her half the night, but she wasn't going to last. And neither was his nagging cock. If he didn't get inside Brea soon, the fucker would drill a hole in his mattress to find relief.

Under his insistent tongue, her hips wriggled. Her harsh breaths filled the room. Her cries grew louder. He could fucking smell her—under his nose, on his lips, all over his sheets. It made him hungrier. Fair or not, he demanded more from her.

Reluctantly, he released her thighs to clamp his fingers around her hips so he could use his grip to press her onto his tongue. Every fucking time he lapped her up, she gave him more sweet cream. She was making him crazy. Goddamn hysterically insane. He was always in control, always aware of everyone and everything around him, threats assessed, escape routes mapped. Right now, his fucking house could burn down but he wouldn't give a shit about that or the danger until she fucking came on his tongue.

When her clit swelled even more and began to quiver as it turned to steel, One-Mile knew he had her.

Yeah. Oh, fuck, yeah. Give. It. To. Me.

As if she read his mind, Brea did, exploding with her next gasping breath as she stiffened and tossed her head back with an ear-piercing scream that made her entire body quiver and jolt.

Into his mouth, she pulsed and flowed. He plunged his tongue into her so he could feel the hard clamp of her body throbbing with the ecstasy he gave her.

He licked her through the pinnacle, making sure she rode every euphoric moment that twisted on and on until her body went limp, leaving Brea to gulp in recovering breaths of air. Smiling, One-Mile licked his lips as he climbed up her body.

Slowly, her lashes fluttered open. She blinked up at him, her eyes so golden they looked molten. Her stare was like a battering ram to his solar plexus. With just a look, she staggered him, knocked the breath from him.

Bullshit. She destroyed him.

"You good?" he managed to get out.

Her lips curled into a little smile. "Ahhhmazing. Can you make me feel like that again?"

He was already on fire, but her words poured gasoline over the blaze. Fuck waiting another second. "Right now, pretty girl. Right the fuck now."

His entire body buzzed with need as he took his cock in hand and fit it against her snug opening. He stared, forcing her wide eyes to meet his as he began to rock and thrust inside her, slowly shoving his tip past her swollen flesh.

Jesus, she was so fucking tight.

One-Mile eased out, rooted to her opening again, then pushed harder. She gasped in a catch of breath that had him freezing in place. She sounded as if she was in pain. He would have sworn he felt something inside her give way—almost as if it...broke.

What the fuck?

Before he could ask, the force of his next mindless thrust sent him delving deep. He tumbled inside her unimpeded, until he was blessedly submerged balls deep.

Dear God...

Her scalding heat surrounded him in a feeling unlike anything he'd ever experienced. An involuntary shudder wracked his body. Holy fuck. This woman was going to burn him the fuck alive. Right now, all he could think was how badly he ached for the flames.

He'd process these last few moments—how he felt and what it meant—then they'd talk. But later. Much fucking later.

Now was for making Brea scream his name.

"Oh, damn, pretty girl…"

When he looked down, he was surprised to find her eyes screwed shut tight.

"It hurts," she whimpered.

Fuck, the last thing he'd ever want to do was cause her pain. He had to find the control to be gentler—somehow. She'd had a massive orgasm, and while she was swollen he'd battered into her like a damn blunt-force object. He owed it to her to make her feel good.

But his goal was to give her so much fucking pleasure that she'd never want to spend another minute naked with Cutter Bryant.

"I'm sorry," he crooned. "I'll slow down. No more pain."

Slowly, she relaxed around him. "Really?"

"None. I promise." To prove it, he stroked softly into her, down, down, until his crest nudged her cervix.

Oh, holy hell…

"That's better," she sighed breathlessly.

"Yeah?" He kissed her overheated cheeks, swiped his thumb across the perspiration at her temple.

She nodded. "That feels…good."

Fuck, did it ever. He thrust a bit faster, still watching her face for any sign of discomfort. Thankfully, nothing but soft excitement filled her face. And when her lashes lifted from her cheeks, opening his view to the windows of her soul once more? Yeah, his cock nagged and ached for relief, but the vise in his chest squeezed even harder. Her expression played hell with his self-control.

Those fiery golden eyes of hers said that, at least for now, she totally belonged to him.

His fingers on her hips tightened. He tried so fucking hard to hold back and stay in control of his rhythm, but his body was done waiting.

His thrusts picked up pace. "A little or a lot?"

"A little." She writhed under him, moving with him as he slid in and out of her like melted butter. Then she tightened with a cry. Her gaze bounced up to his in shock a second before she liquified under him with a moan. "Oh. No, a lot."

So he'd found her sweet spot. *Fuck, yes.* "More?"

She clarified her incoherent sob with a wholehearted bob of her head.

One-Mile took that as a hell yes.

He tucked his hands under her ass and lifted her closer, tilting and opening her wider to penetrate her deeper. The shift didn't just give him access to the most untouched corners of her body but put him in direct contact with her still-sensitive clit.

As soon as he did, she gasped and shuddered, her stare going wide with both shock and a hundred silent questions.

He just smiled as he settled into a quick tempo. She'd figure it out —pretty quickly if her reaction was any indication.

There was something so unbearably intimate about staring into her eyes as he fucked her. Every emotion, every thought, every shred of bliss? He saw them all. One-Mile swore he wasn't reading just her body but her mind. And she was telling him that she couldn't hold out much longer.

"Pierce!" She clamped down on him.

He filled her faster and ground down on her clit just to help things along, because goddamn it, he'd held back for her as long as he could. Everything inside him was poised and screaming at him to let go of his restraint and fucking explode.

Hell of a time to remember that he'd monumentally screwed up and—for the first time ever—forgotten a condom.

He didn't care. Whatever happened next? Yeah. Bring it. He didn't need anything more than this moment, right now, to know that Brea Bell belonged to him. Whatever she had with Bryant was history.

He'd make sure of that.

If there were consequences from tonight…the timing might not be optimal, but the end result suited him just fine.

Beneath him, Brea suddenly went wild, rocking with him, nails in his back, lips on his neck, her cries in his ear. Then he felt her cunt clenching, her breath stopping, the air stilling, and the need building in his heavy balls bursting.

Teeth bared, he growled as his restraint broke. He shoved his way inside her with a dozen rapid-fire thrusts that had his headboard beating the wall—and Brea clenching on him as she let loose a shrill shriek of ecstasy and shuddered wildly under him.

Jesus. Holy hell. Fuck, fuck, fuck... But no self-talk could stop the overwhelming wall of rapture. It flattened him, undid him, turned him around, twisted him, then spit him back out. After long, mind-blowing moments, he finally found the other side of ecstasy, gasped for air, and tried to process what the fuck had happened. He felt different. He felt changed.

He felt like hers.

Under him, she heaved a sigh, lips parted, eyes closed. The tension in her body eased, except the occasional pulse of her pretty pussy around his softening cock.

She blinked up at him, clearly stunned. "Oh...my goodness."

That was her version of *holy fuck*, and it made him laugh. He slicked back the damp hair clinging to her forehead and cheeks. "Yeah, you could say that."

"I had no idea..."

Cutter must be a real deadbeat in the sack. No wonder she was here instead of with him. Keeping her might be even easier than he'd imagined. With chemistry like theirs, it would be years—hell, maybe a lifetime—before they got enough of each other.

"How do you feel, pretty girl?"

The smile that curled up her pouty mouth was almost self-conscious. It matched her still-flaming cheeks. "Happy. Like I'm floating. Best feeling ever."

One-Mile laughed, stupidly thrilled. Whether she knew it or not, she'd just admitted that was the best sex of her life. The fact that she loved being with him and wanted more only made him feel on top of the world. This was Christmas in August—but better. Unless he missed his guess, it wouldn't take much to make sure he could unwrap her every single day.

"It is." He laid a soft kiss on her lips. "It was amazing."

"Yeah…"

Her voice still had that dreamy quality when he reluctantly withdrew. She winced, biting her lip and clearly holding in a cry. Shit. Had he somehow hurt her?

"What's wrong?"

But the words had no more left his mouth when he sat back on his knees and looked down.

Blood.

One-Mile already knew from having his mouth all over Brea that she wasn't in the middle of her period.

The moment he'd pushed his way into her slammed back through his brain. The tightness. The feeling of something giving way. Her admission that it had hurt.

The obvious occurred to him, but…how was that possible? From his research, it seemed she'd been Cutter's girlfriend for years—at least based on her barely used social media accounts. The asshole had taken her to her prom. He'd held her hand and posed for a dozen pictures during her high school graduation. He'd been her first haircut when she'd finished beauty school.

If she had been anyone else, One-Mile would have dismissed even the small chance that she'd been innocent when he'd carried her up to his bedroom less than an hour ago. But this was Brea. She was a preacher's daughter. She was a good girl to the core.

Oh, shit. Maybe Cutter hadn't been cheating on her the night before her father's heart attack as much as getting some relief because he really was a Boy Scout who had agreed to wait for Brea until marriage.

At least that might have been his plan until One-Mile had barged in and ruined her.

Oh, holy fuck.

"Brea…" He forced her to meet his stare. "You promised me the truth tonight, so be fucking honest. Were you a virgin?"

CHAPTER SIX

Brea gaped. She crossed protective arms over her breasts. Self-preservation warred with her innate desire to be honest. But the way Pierce kept staring tied her tongue. Thinking seemed impossible. She wished she could crawl inside her skin and hide.

He'd figured out she was a virgin. Was he mad? Shocked? Dismayed? Did he feel guilty? Responsible? Disgusted?

Those possibilities had her eyes stinging with mortifying tears. Why couldn't she stop feeling so horribly vulnerable?

Brea bolted up from the bed and scanned the room for her clothes. "I already answered your questions."

"I have more."

She shook her head. "I'm sorry. I have to go."

Pierce stood, utterly naked and unconcerned, and prowled toward her with narrowed eyes. "So…what? Now that we've fucked, you're done being honest?"

She flinched at his question. "Please. That's enough."

"If you're measuring honesty, it's never going to be 'enough.'"

Finally, she found her panties and snatched them up, doing her best not to stare at his big, naked body. "I meant that I don't appreciate your language and I don't owe you my personal information."

"As the guy who unwittingly took your virginity, I disagree. By the way, isn't lying a sin?"

"Yes." Technically, so was having sex outside of wedlock. She would have a lot to repent for after tonight. "But I was merely asking you to drop the subject and respect my privacy."

He scoffed. "Since I've had my dick deep inside you, I think we're past privacy."

Brea managed to step into her underwear, but it didn't make her feel less naked under his black stare. "I'm leaving."

Her dratted bra was nowhere to be found. Where the devil had he tossed it?

A blip of a memory flashed through her brain of Pierce stripping it off of her downstairs...just before she'd begged him to touch her breasts. What had she been thinking?

Nothing—beyond him easing the unrelenting ache inside her.

"Stay." He gripped her arm. "We need to talk."

Pierce spoke like he wanted to have a serious conversation...but his stare caressed her nipples, still tight and tingling from his attention. His penis began rising again.

An answering desire stirred between her legs.

She ignored it, plucking up her shorts and slapping them over her breasts. "No, we don't."

If she stayed, she feared they wouldn't spend much time talking.

"Since you were a virgin, even if you'd rather not admit that, I'm assuming you're not on birth control."

She froze. She'd had no reason to be on birth control. And he hadn't used a condom.

Brea's mouth fell open on a silent gasp. She staggered back. How had she been so careless?

Pierce's grip was the only thing that kept her from falling. "That's what I thought. Where are you in your cycle?"

She couldn't think beyond her dismay. "Pierce, please... I have to go."

"Not until we figure out how likely you are to get pregnant." His grip tightened. "Refusing to talk won't solve anything."

You have a habit of burying your head in the sand. That won't always work... Cutter's warning drifted through her head. He was right, but she wasn't ready to face the stark reality of her choice and its potentially monumental consequences.

"Please stop talking. And let go." She yanked her arm from his grip.

He released her so abruptly she stumbled back—only to get another eyeful of him in his head-to-toe naked glory.

Heat flared through her.

Brea had never imagined being blasphemous enough to think that God had a sadistic streak. But why else would He make the only man she'd ever found irresistible be the one her friends, family, and community would never approve of?

Biting her lip to hold in a cry, she turned away and dashed down the stairs.

Pierce followed, his heavy footfalls sounding determined not to let her get far. "You didn't ask, but I'm clean. I've never had sex with anyone else without a condom."

Of course she hadn't thought he'd been pure, but when she imagined him being as intimate with another woman as he'd been with her, jealousy twisted a knife in Brea's chest. Her stomach turned in a sick grind. Her eyes stung again.

She had to get out of here.

Brea dashed down the stairs and darted to the kitchen, plucking up her bra and shirt as she crossed the room to her purse. Pierce was right behind her, his breath hot on the back of her neck.

"Stop running, damn it, and talk to me. We'll work through it."

She whirled on him, the tears she'd been trying to hold back spilling like hot acid down her burning cheeks. "I've given you everything I offered you in exchange for Cutter's life. Now we're even. I need to go."

His eyes narrowed. "You're kidding yourself if you think the only reason you let me take you to bed was to save your boyfriend's life. I made no secret of the fact I wanted you. But you fucking wanted me, too. Woman up and own it."

He was right, just like she knew she should be honest with him about her relationship with Cutter. But when he looked at her, Brea felt

more exposed than she had when he'd stripped her naked and penetrated her.

"There's nothing left to talk about."

"Bullshit. You're afraid. I get it. But this fucking wedge of distance
you're driving between us right now isn't helping." He stalked
toward her.

Brea juggled her clothes and her purse in her hands, backing up for
every step he prowled closer. "Stop."

"Not when you're upset." He wrenched the items from her grasp
and tossed everything on the kitchen table. Then he lifted her off her
feet and carried her to the sofa, plopping down on the nearest cushion.
He settled her over his lap, facing him so she straddled his hips. His
big hands swept up her back, urging her head onto his shoulder. "Talk
or cry or whatever you need. I'm here."

The sincerity in his voice told Brea he really would be there for
her...but he was too close for her to breathe, much less rub two
thoughts together. A terrible awareness consumed her—of his big arms
around her, his warm breath in her ear, his hard, naked chest flattening
her sensitive nipples, and his heart chugging in time with hers.

As if he felt their connection, too, his penis hardened even more,
surging between them, nudging where her ache swirled and
thickened.

"Pierce..." Brea meant to pull away.

Instead, she found herself writhing against him.

"I'm trying to be a good guy, pretty girl, but if you keep that up,
I'm going to fuck you again," he groaned. "In thirty seconds—or less."

Fresh need tightened between her legs. Brea's head told her that
would be terrible. But her body loved the notion, heating and softening all at once, arching to get even closer.

Pierce cursed, then lifted her breasts in his massive palms and
sucked one nipple into his mouth. She gasped...and her protest faded
into a wail of pleasure.

Why was she resisting him? The damage was already done. She
was no longer a virgin. They had already had unprotected sex. Would
another few minutes of sin really matter?

Of course she was rationalizing, but when Pierce tongued her sensitive peaks, then sucked one deep into his mouth, she dug her nails into his shoulders and gave in. "Oh…"

As he moved to thumb her stiff crests again, he slid his tongue up her neck. "It's so right between us. Say something if you don't want more, but otherwise… All it takes to feel good is a little shift and"—he yanked the crotch of her panties out of his way slowly, giving her time to refuse him as he fisted his erection and adjusted her directly over his swollen head—"fuck…"

He gripped her hips and gave her a gentle push down. Gravity did the rest of his dirty work. Together, they destroyed her resistance. When she finally enveloped every inch of his hardness, she sank against him with a long, agonized gasp.

Having Pierce inside her, filling her so completely, shocked her even more than the first time.

"That's it," he growled in her ear. "You're not too sore?"

Brea felt a slight sting everywhere her flesh stretched to accommodate him, but this time it only hurt in a good way. "Not enough to stop."

He urged her up the length of his shaft, then urged her back down. "You like the bite?"

Beneath her, he lifted his hips, his erection scraping her swollen sex as he shoved inside her, prodding some nerve-rich spot deep.

"Yes," Brea hissed, her head falling back with a moan of surrender as her blood raced and her heart careened.

"Grab on to my shoulders. I'm going to fuck you until you can't think about anything but us."

She was already there.

A voice of caution in the back of her head tried to scream at her to stop, to consider whose daughter she was and what she was doing. But Pierce's raspy breaths and rough hands distracted her from anything resembling reason. His male musk swam in her head. He overwhelmed her. He intoxicated her.

He owned her.

As he shafted her up and down his length, her ache tightened, her pleasure multiplied, and her objections fell silent. All that remained were his long fingers encircling her, his big body driving under her, and his thick cock filling her. Brea found herself rocking with him, swaying and grinding, gasping and keening toward the pinnacle of pleasure he was already so close to giving her.

"You look fucking beautiful." He pinched her nipples, his grip tightening even after she sucked in a shocked breath of pained bliss. "Open your eyes. I want to watch you come."

Brea lifted her lashes slowly. Immediately, his black stare fused itself to her. The intensity of his arousal seared her. His cheeks flamed with it. His jaw clenched with it. His entire body tightened with it. The sight of him—along with the feelings surging between them—mesmerized her. Everything about him more than accelerated her desire. A connection she'd never felt with another human being overwhelmed her. It wasn't purely sexual, but it was as if, with some click, her soul attached itself to his.

It was shocking. It felt irrevocable.

Her hunger climbed. She ached to be even closer, craved her mouth on him. She needed him in every way a woman could touch a man.

With a cry, she fastened her lips over his. Pierce might have been physically underneath her, but he took charge, tangling his fingers in her hair, locking their mouths together, binding them in ways she'd never imagined. Brea couldn't help but melt as she ground down on him, stroke after frantic stroke.

Finally, he tore his lips from hers with a gasp, then grabbed her hips tighter, thrusting himself hard and deep and sure, as if she was his and he had every right to claim her in any way he liked. "Give it to me. Orgasm number three. I want it now."

She keened as she plunged down, taking him deeper than ever. The tension gathering in her belly and between her thighs coalesced, knotting up so tightly she panted, dug her nails into his bare shoulders, and unraveled with a scream.

"Yes. Oh, fuck…" His fingers bit into her as he rammed up one last time, teeth clenched, tendons in his neck flexing as ecstasy overtook him. "Brea!"

Together, they fell into the abyss, clinging, clutching, holding on for dear life. Pleasure threatened to drag her into an addicting, sublime darkness as she panted, her head lost in a dizzy sway she no longer had the will to fight.

This climax was shockingly stronger than the first two. And when she finally opened her eyes again, she found Pierce's inky stare locked on her. The feeling of falling into him unnerved her. The longer she studied him as they tried to catch their breath, the deeper she fell. Something about being with this man in this moment... She felt as if she'd somehow tied herself to him for all time.

Like he was her destiny.

Ridiculous. God had a plan for her. And as much as she was loath to leave Pierce's arms because this would probably be their last few moments alone, He wouldn't curse her to lose her heart to a man her family and community would shun, right?

Pierce pulled her in, kissing his way up her cleavage, her collarbone, her shoulder. "Stay tonight."

She shouldn't. She couldn't.

But she was so very tempted.

The truth was, her father would go to bed early because, even if he wasn't giving the service tomorrow, he would want to be well rested for his first Sunday back in the church since his surgery. Cutter wasn't leaving the hospital tonight. It was already past visiting hours, and he wouldn't expect to see her until he was officially discharged in the morning. So the two people most likely to care where she spent the night would have no idea she wasn't at home, tucked chastely in her bed.

This might be her only chance to stay with Pierce, indulge her need for him...and purge him from her system for good.

Still, she had one question. "Why?"

"Want me to keep being honest with you?"

"Please."

Pierce looked at her as if he never wanted to let her go. "I've never felt about a woman the way I do about you."

Brea's breath caught. A wave of pleasure washed over her. Another rush of it flushed her cheeks. "I'd have to be up really early."

"Any time I get with you is better than none."

His words softened her heart. She felt the same. It probably wasn't smart but… "I'll stay."

A smile stretched across his face, transforming him, before he nuzzled his face in her neck. "I'll make sure you don't regret it, pretty girl."

Normally, she'd suspect he meant something sexual. And she didn't think for one second that he'd keep his hands off her the rest of the night. In fact, she hoped he didn't since the thought of him inside of her again made her whole body flash hot, as if she wasn't already spent. As if he hadn't utterly satisfied her minutes ago. But something about the way he watched her or touched her—Brea couldn't exactly put her finger on it—convinced her he wasn't simply wanting to hook up again.

If she were honest, she wasn't staying strictly for the sex, either. She more than liked him, despite all the reasons she shouldn't. But everyone in her life behaved as if she was a girl; Pierce alone treated her like a woman. Didn't she deserve one night with a man who made her feel good?

Maybe Pierce wasn't her sin but her reward—albeit temporary—for always being everyone's dutiful friend and helpmate. And maybe she was fooling herself. Even so, Brea resolved to pack as much pleasure as she possibly could into this one night and leave tomorrow with no regrets.

She smiled. "Are you going to feed me before you take advantage of me again?"

"I could." He nuzzled her. "Or I could just chain you to my bed and fuck you all night."

That should not turn her on so much, but it sounded both forbidden and wonderful. "How about both? I can fry eggs in less than five minutes."

Pierce cradled her face, and the way he looked at her again—as if she meant the world to him—had her stomach flipping over and upside down with a giddiness that spread through her body. If she wasn't careful, she would fall for him.

He pressed a passionate kiss to her bruised lips, something slow, urgent, and thorough. Something that told her what the rest of her night was likely to be like. Something that excited her almost more than she could contain.

When he finally lifted his head, he brushed his thumb across her tingling lip. "As long as I get to watch you cook naked, hell yes."

Sunday, August 17

PREDAWN DARKNESS SURROUNDED Brea as she slowed her car and killed her headlights. She wished she could turn off her guilt half so easily after creeping from Pierce's bed and tiptoeing out of his house. What would he think when he woke to find her gone?

Nothing polite. He wouldn't care that people had expectations of her—that her father required her in the front row at church or that Cutter needed a nursemaid after his release from the hospital. He wanted her all to himself. And if she could have been selfish for a bit longer, she would have stayed.

But that wasn't her reality. She had responsibilities and, unlike Pierce, she enjoyed people relying on her.

It was just frustratingly inconvenient today.

Shoving aside that reality, Brea brought her car to a complete stop in front of her house and let out an exhausted sigh. Since she didn't see any lights on inside, thank goodness, she figured Daddy must still be asleep. Hopefully, she could sneak in a shower and a power nap before they left for church.

Flushed and boneless, her whole body sensitive and beyond sated, she turned off the engine and eased from the seat. She winced against the soreness between her thighs, but the tingly, uncomfortable ache reminded her of Pierce. Of the best night of her life.

He'd kept her up half the night before he'd curled her against his big furnace of a body for a couple of hours of rest...only to awaken her again with his teeth in her shoulder and his heavy erection working its way back into her snug, swollen sex with a low male groan.

The memory nearly had Brea staggering against another bomb of desire detonating inside her. The urge to throw caution to the wind—to climb back into her car and return to Pierce—assailed her. She'd give almost anything to jump into his arms again and stay for good.

That was a lovely fantasy. Maybe if she wasn't a dutiful small-town preacher's daughter and he wasn't an outsider who killed for a living, they could find some way to be together. But all the what-ifs and wishes in the world weren't going to change reality.

They were doomed.

She had given Pierce her virginity more to satisfy her own desires than to save Cutter, and she would have to both atone to God for her sin and live with her actions. But right now...she didn't regret a thing.

Brea eased her car door shut, slung her purse over her shoulder, then, shoes in hand, crept toward her house.

"I never thought I'd see you doing the walk of shame."

That all-too-familiar voice made her heart drop.

She whirled. "Cutter..."

Brow raised, he sauntered in her direction, eyeing her up and down as if he had no idea who she was anymore. Shame rolled through her, but she beat it back. Who was he to judge? He wasn't her father or God. She might not have needed to give herself to Pierce Walker to save him, but she'd offered. Her heart had been in the right place... even if the rest of her had been far less altruistic.

"Listen. I can—"

"Explain?" he cut in sharply.

At the rebuke in his voice, she pressed her lips together mutely. He'd already grasped the situation. Nothing she could say, short of lying, would convince him of anything less than the truth. And she saw no point in compounding her sin with a falsehood.

"Help you home. I didn't think you'd already be released from the hospital, and I'm sure you shouldn't be out of bed. Why are you?"

He drew closer and clutched her arm. Even though the shadows hid the disapproval in his expression, Brea could feel it. "Been too 'busy' to look at your phone?"

She'd turned it off last night, and Pierce had kept her far too busy to even think about turning it back on. "Sorry."

"I called. Repeatedly. Until three this morning. Then I sent Cage out to find you. But you weren't home. You weren't at the church. You weren't at the hospital, either. Then I remembered that bastard Walker telling me—after he served as the shooter's judge, jury, and executioner—that you were at his house. That you were *waiting* for him there. And sure enough, that's where my brother found your car about an hour ago. And since there's no way you and Walker were having a deep, existential conversation in the middle of the night, I checked myself out against doctor's orders and had Cage drop me off at my truck so I could come after you." Cutter clutched both of her shoulders and dragged her under the nearby streetlamp in time to see a guilty flush crawl up her face. "Dear God. What the fuck did Walker do to you?"

She winced, both at his shout and his choice of slurs. "Please lower your voice and calm down."

"Calm down? I worried he took advantage of your naiveté. That he seduced you but..." Cutter's grip tightened, along with his mouth, which flattened into a grim line that promised retribution. "He left his mark all over you. You reek of him. Your cheeks are whisker burned. Your lips are bruised and swollen. He fucking *ravaged* you." The tightness in his voice told Brea that notion pained him. "Son of a bitch. He said you begged him to intervene on my behalf."

Had he really thought she wouldn't? "I-I was terrified for you."

"Not as afraid as I've been for you. I knew damn well what he wanted the moment he laid eyes on you." A scathing, cynical stare twisted his face. "He demanded you give it to him, didn't he?"

She shook her head and tried to think of some way to explain that wouldn't make him even angrier. "That's not what happened."

He clenched his jaw, turning deadly still. "Shit. Then it's worse than I thought. Because now that I see what he's done to you, the only other way I'll believe you spent a night in his bed was if he forced you. By all that's holy, I swear I'm going to kill him."

"Don't. You can't. He—"

"Don't try to sugarcoat what that motherfucker did to you."

Cutter only used that language around her when he was beyond furious. He underscored that fact by curling up his fist, rolling a growl up from his chest, and punching her driver's-side window.

Brea jumped and started—then blinked in horror when he reared back to do it again, as if he wasn't satisfied that the glass hadn't shattered the first time.

"Stop." She grabbed his elbow and hauled back with all her might.

He whipped a furious stare on her, then snarled out another curse as he shook out his hand. "You shouldn't have gone to Walker on my behalf. You promised me you'd stay away."

"You needed me, and I—"

"He's dangerous. I hope you fucking get that now."

"Cutter, please. Listen…"

"No. I know you. I know you sacrificed yourself for me. And I know what you're doing right now. Don't you dare try to make me feel less guilty."

"I'm not. I'm telling you that—"

"It wasn't too bad?" he scoffed. "A conversation with the asshole is torture. I can't imagine how you endured a whole night with him fucking on top of you." He clenched his hands into fists again with a guttural grunt. "I would have gotten myself out of the situation. And if I couldn't have, it wasn't worth whatever he put you through. I don't even want to think about how much he bent you to his will—and hurt you—without wanting to kill him."

The longer she let Cutter linger on this subject, the angrier he would become. And he wasn't calm enough yet to hear that Pierce hadn't forced her to do anything. He might not be for a while.

"It's over. Right now, I'm worried about you. You should never have left against doctor's orders. You have a nasty concussion. Don't break your hand, too. You need rest. I'm so thankful you're alive. Please don't worry me more."

"I'm fine. I'm taking you to the hospital to get a rape kit."

She blanched. "No."

"You're going to let him get away with defiling you?" His incredulous stare curdled her stomach.

"He's not getting away with anything. I'm focused on you right now. I'm worried about *you*. Nothing else matters."

Cutter raked a hand through his hair, angry knuckles reddening. "You can't expect me to let this go, Bre-bee. I understand why you might not want to tell everyone in Sunset or even your father. I don't agree because this isn't your shame. But I understand."

"You don't understand at all. Let it go."

"Are you fucking crazy?"

"Keep it down, bro," Cage hissed as he made his way down the driveway to join them on the sidewalk. "You're going to wake up the whole neighborhood if you don't."

Cutter whirled on his brother. "I'm supposed to be calm when Walker fucking raped her?"

"Don't say that. You don't understand," Brea insisted.

"Oh, I understand perfectly." Her best friend looked murderous.

She turned to Cage with an imploring gaze.

The older Bryant brother nodded. "Bro, you're not supposed to be out of bed. And you're definitely not supposed to be driving." He plucked the truck keys from Cutter's grip. "Today isn't the day to fight this battle."

Cutter looked gutted. "You're taking her side?"

"I'm taking yours," Cage insisted. "That pain pill should be kicking in about now… The one that warns against operating heavy machinery or an automobile."

Cutter clutched his head. "We can't let Walker get away with this. He needs to die."

Brea groped for her patience. "He did nothing wrong."

But one look at Cutter's face told her that he'd never believe her. He saw her as a little girl. He would never believe she had chosen to have sex with a man who wasn't her husband, especially someone he held such a low opinion of. If burying her head in the sand was sometimes her downfall, Cutter's was being stubbornly blind. He didn't want the truth, so it didn't exist.

"He did everything wrong," Cutter growled. "And you let him take whatever he wanted from you to save my miserable ass. I will never forgive myself."

Before she could say another word, he pivoted toward his mother's house and marched for the front door, leaving her alone with Cage. His expression was more measured, equal parts righteous anger and curiosity. "Want to talk about it?"

Brea shook her head. She loved Cage like family, but she'd never been as close to him as she was to Cutter. The last thing she wanted to do was share her personal life with more people or bring anyone else into this strife. "I don't, except to say that your brother is wrong."

"Walker didn't rape you?"

"No. Not at all."

"That fits. You might be pious and soft-spoken, but if he'd hurt you, then you would have said so."

"Thank you for being rational."

"Cutter will be, too. Eventually. I hope." He winced. "Right now, he's just angry."

"Your brother is so stubborn. We both know he may never change his mind."

"Without a significant slap upside the head? Maybe not," Cage conceded. "Anything I can do to help until then?"

"Get him back to the doctor. He shouldn't return to work until he's been medically cleared."

"I'll do my best. I need to be back on the road to Dallas. My shift was supposed to start about…now."

Brea closed her eyes as more guilt enveloped her. No, she hadn't called Cage and demanded that he spend half the night looking for her. Cutter had done that. But if she'd looked at her phone sooner or checked in or reached out… "I'm sorry."

He shrugged. "I could use the extra day off. I'm going to escort Mama to church this morning. Then I'll be heading down the road. You should probably take a shower before your father wakes up. I know you don't wear makeup often, but you might want to put on some today."

She blushed again. "Are the marks that obvious?"

He grimaced and pulled at the back of his neck. "Afraid so. I don't have a particular beef with Walker. I don't even know him. But I know you. So I know the guilt is probably eating you up inside. And if you exchanged your body for my brother's safety, I regret whatever you had to endure, but I'll forever be grateful that Cutter is alive today."

Then Cage was gone.

Brea swallowed, standing stock-still until she heard the soft thump of their front door closing.

God, she didn't even know what to feel anymore. Guilty, yes. Sorry? Some of that, too. Exhaustion, worry, uncertainty. Somewhere in there, shock that the world felt so different in some ways but exactly the same in others. Still, under it all, giddiness prevailed. Pierce Walker had more than touched her. He had stolen a piece of her heart. And rather than wring her hands and wonder how on earth she'd ever get it back, all she could do was wonder if—no, how—she could spend the night in his arms again.

CHAPTER SEVEN

Tuesday, August 19

One-Mile started Tuesday in a foul mood. Over forty-eight hours had passed since he'd last pressed his lips to Brea's—while buried deep in the sweetest, snuggest cunt he'd ever felt. Then he'd awakened alone. After cursing a blue streak, he'd tried repeatedly to reach her.

Calls and texts on Sunday morning went unanswered. Fine. He'd figured she was sleeping or, better yet, breaking up with that asshole Bryant. But a few hours later, he'd rolled up to the little white house of worship her father preached at and, from his Jeep across the street, he'd seen her talking to a group of middle-aged moms. Cutter had been fucking glued to her side, his arm wrapped around her waist as if he owned her.

Brea hadn't objected, simply curled up against him as if she was where she wanted to be.

The sight had been a punch in the gut.

After that, his mood had rolled downhill.

By Monday morning, he'd been itching for a fight. Since he'd promised Logan he wouldn't bring their shit into the office, One-Mile had been more than prepared to beat the shit out of the asshole in the parking lot. But the Boy Scout had been a no-show. Normally, he would have relished a day without the insufferable bastard. Not today.

Later, he'd learned the bosses had insisted Bryant get medically cleared before he darkened their door again. Whatever. All One-Mile had cared about was the fact that Brea still hadn't responded to him.

This morning she finally had—texting him four brief words.

`I need some space.`

That told him where he stood. Brea had enjoyed her night of fun with the bad boy and was now kicking him to the curb. He should just say *fuck it* and do his damnedest to forget her. But he already knew he'd fail.

Besides, two and two wasn't adding up. Brea hadn't merely fucked him to save her boyfriend. If she had, she would never have given him her virginity or let him take her repeatedly Saturday night. She would never have kissed him with such innocent gusto. She would never have moaned so uninhibitedly every time her pleasure climbed. She would never have screamed so loudly when her climaxes hit. She would never have clung to him while she slept like a baby. She'd wanted *him.* Her needing space now? That was either Bryant breathing suspicion down her neck or her good-girl guilt barking. Maybe both.

He was going to call bullshit—and call her bluff.

Once he'd tracked her down, he'd coax, cajole, or seduce her into listening to his pitch to leave her boyfriend—who had never treated her like a woman. Then she could move in with him. Sure, it was fast. Yes, he was probably crazy. One-Mile expected obstacles. But he wasn't wrong about them. Brea Bell was his. The more he thought about it, the more his gut told him that was true.

Cutter was nothing more than a speed bump.

One-Mile slammed the door of his truck and locked it before shoving his way into EM Security Management's offices. Just inside the lobby, their pretty blond receptionist, Tessa Lawrence, sat at the front desk, doing her best to ignore Zyron. But the big lug had perched his ass on the edge of her desk to flirt shamelessly, despite the fact their bosses had a strict policy against fraternization and the woman didn't seem inclined to say yes. Even now, Tessa looked pale and nervous as she focused on her computer screen, typing away as if Zy didn't exist. But he didn't take the hint, instead asking her out—yet again—in low, suggestive tones while flashing his Hollywood smile.

Dumb ass. Her baby was only a few months old, and her ex-boyfriend's desertion only a few weeks older than that. The last thing a woman like Tessa was looking for was some asshole to nail her.

As he passed them, Zy scowled—the nonverbal equivalent of *get the fuck away from my woman.* One-Mile held up a hand. His fellow operative was welcome to fall flat on his face all day with the cute receptionist. He wasn't interested in any woman except Brea.

When he reached the dark corner of the building that housed his desk, One-Mile slumped into his chair and booted up his computer, eyeing the avalanche of unread messages dropping into his inbox. Updates on hotspots around the world. Information that might affect current and upcoming cases. Forensic reports on incidents they'd wrapped. Miscellaneous shit about new toys the bosses had acquired. Paperwork reminders. And on and on…

His mood went from dark to black as hell.

Why hadn't Brea told Bryant to fuck off? Did she love the stupid Boy Scout, in spite of the fact he didn't light her fire? Or had things changed? Now that she was no longer a virgin, had she and Cutter decided to screw waiting for marriage and fucked?

The thought made One-Mile homicidal.

He launched himself to his feet and headed for the coffeepot, wondering if Bryant would show up today. As he rounded the corner, he picked up a clean mug from the shelf and looked up.

Speak of the SOB…

"I want to talk to you."

Cutter barely glanced away from the java he poured. "Fuck off."

Maybe the asshole didn't understand. "It's about Brea."

Bryant slammed the pot back onto the brewer. "You're never touching her again, so whatever happened over the weekend? Forget it and move on. She's going to."

Was the Boy Scout bullshitting him? "You and me. Outside."

"Not happening. I've already been warned against drama in the office. Since I can't kick the ass of my esteemed fellow operative"—Cutter raised a sarcastic brow—"I want you the fuck out of my sight."

With that, he turned away and slunk back to his desk on the far side of the adjacent conference room.

One-Mile had had enough—and he knew how to fix this.

He whirled around, in search of Logan. But when he entered the boss's office, it wasn't the younger Edgington he found. Instead, a completely unfamiliar man stood there. He was somewhere around thirty, had some awesome ink and a don't-fuck-with-me vibe.

Logan hustled up behind him, bitching about some computer virus or another.

"Stone, this is Pierce," Logan said to the other guy.

One-Mile looked the stranger up and down. Were they hiring him? He looked badass enough to fit with the crew. More importantly, he didn't look like a snitch, a douche, or another Boy Scout.

He nodded toward Stone. "I prefer One-Mile."

Logan sighed. "One-Mile, then. He's our resident sniper. Rather than his given name, he prefers to be known by his longest kill shot. God save me from big egos."

It had nothing to do with his ego and everything to do with hating his father, but he didn't owe anyone that explanation.

Stone stuck out his hand. "Hey."

"Good to meet you." One-Mile shook it.

"Stone Sutter is a computer hacker extraordinaire. Jack Cole and the boys at Oracle are letting us borrow him to isolate a virus on the server, so don't open any email attachments."

"Not a problem," he told Logan. "I'd like to speak to you."

"What's up?"

"I can't work with Bryant. I quit." Now that he'd delivered his news, he was free to find Cutter and beat the ever-loving fuck out of him.

Before he could escape Logan's office, the former SEAL shut him down. "Nope. You can't. I've got a contract. You signed. We paid the bonus, and you cashed the check. End of conversation."

One-Mile halted. Fucking Logan throwing legalities in his face. Even worse, the bastard was right.

Naturally, Cutter chose that moment to stick his head in the door, glaring daggers. "Fucking douche."

He barely managed to refrain from violence. "The feeling is mutual."

"I told you no drama, so give it a rest, you two." Logan rolled his eyes. "If I can work with my older brother, you can get along enough to get your shit done."

Bryant raked a hand over his military-short hair and shook his head at Logan. "I will never trust him enough to be on an operational team with him again. If he wants to quit, I say good riddance."

Logan slammed a fist on his desk. "Cutter, I don't give a shit that Pierce slept with your girlfriend."

"One-Mile," he corrected through clenched teeth.

"Whatever." Logan waved a hand through the air.

"No! It's not whatever," Cutter insisted. "I can't work with Brea's rapist."

What? Had the dickhead convinced himself that the only way Brea would have ever been underneath him was unwillingly?

I got news for you, buddy, and it's all bad...

"I had her consent."

"You manipulated her so that she had no choice but to say yes." Cutter clenched his fists.

One-Mile glared at the cockroach, arms crossed over his chest. "If you wanted her that badly, you should have claimed her sometime between junior high and July. You had plenty of time. But it took you too long to find your dick. That's not my problem. She's mine now."

Cutter narrowed fierce eyes his way, glowering as if he'd lost his mind. "She's not even speaking to you, asshat."

He shrugged it off. "Misunderstanding."

"No, reality. Something you're clearly not familiar with. And if she fucking winds up pregnant—"

"That's enough," Logan shouted. "I don't care if you beat the hell out of one another after hours, but stop bringing your personal shit to work. If you can't, I'll lock you in a room together until you learn to get along or one of you kills the other. I don't care which at this point. Be professional and do your damn jobs."

Silence fell in the wake of Logan's verbal beatdown. Cutter swore and stomped away.

Despite Stone watching with rapt interest, One-Mile felt a stupid urge to explain, probably because if he was stuck in this job and his bosses despised him, the rest of his two years here would really suck. "I didn't rape her."

"Since she had to choose between saving her boyfriend's life and sleeping with you, I'd say you coerced her. It doesn't get much lower than that in my book. Now get the fuck out."

Goddamn it to hell. They'd bought into Cutter's version of events without talking to him. Even when he hadn't done anything wrong, he got labeled the bad guy. Whatever. He could set them straight, but he really didn't give two shits about their opinion of him as a human being.

"Roger that." One-Mile sent Logan a mock salute, nodded Stone's way, then marched the hell out, making a beeline for the coffeemaker.

Before he could pour his first jolt of liquid caffeine, the elder Edgington peeked his head around the corner. "I need you in my office."

One-Mile rolled his eyes. "One minute."

"Now." Hunter disappeared around the corner.

One-Mile sighed. Somehow, this place had already become asshole central, and Hunter looked like he had even more attitude than Logan. He definitely needed java to deal with this.

After his mug was full of steaming fortification, he dragged his ass to the elder Edgington's digs. Trees Scott slouched in one of the two office chairs yet somehow still towered over everyone.

"What's up?" he asked, staring at the other two.

"Shut the door," Hunter barked.

Frowning, One-Mile complied, then when his boss gestured him to put his ass into the empty chair, he planted it beside Trees.

Hunter pressed his fingertips together, face taut. His voice dipped to something just above a murmur. "We have a mole."

"What?" One-Mile couldn't have heard that right. Fuck, if they accused him...

Hunter nodded. "Yeah. Someone inside this office. We've autopsied the most recent Mexico mission, trying to figure out what the fuck went wrong. Both of you thought on your feet and kept the whole thing from turning into a death trap. But I don't have to tell you how close it was. Somehow, the Tierra Caliente thugs not only knew we were coming in but when and where, too. Trees, if you hadn't hauled Zy out of there when something felt wrong—"

"We'd be dead," said the tall man.

"Exactly. Same with you and Bryant." Hunter nodded his way. "Logan, Joaquin, and I all talked to the colonel about this. We're in agreement that someone on the inside must have fed the cartel information, so we're trusting you two—and no one else—to help us figure out who."

Being on the good guys' team was an interesting turn of events.

One-Mile leaned in. "Uncle Sam hired us. No chance it was someone closer to Washington DC?"

Hunter shook his head. "We didn't tell them our exact plans. Sure, they knew we were going in, but not when, where, or how. Only our guys had those details."

So unless the cartel had guessed their multiple locations really fucking well—and what were the odds of that?—someone he worked with was a traitor.

The thought turned One-Mile's blood to ice. "What's the plan?"

"First, I have to take a step back and give you two a history lesson." Hunter sighed. "About eighteen months ago, Arnold Waxman, a wealthy doctor from Atlanta, hired the colonel to infiltrate the Guerrero region in Mexico and find his daughter, Kendra. She had traveled there with a group of doctors to give medial aid to the poor. They got caught in the crossfire when a couple of factions within the Tierra Caliente cartel started warring and they were taken hostage. Waxman paid the ransom, but Kendra wasn't released. That's when Logan, Dad, and I stepped in and discovered that another rival splinter gang, headed by Emilo Montilla, had overrun the first and taken the hostages. We located them, got in, then extracted Kendra, along with the rest of the survivors."

This was all news to One-Mile. But something must have gone to shit since because it definitely hadn't been their last trip to Guerrero. "Then what?"

"While Kendra was in captivity, she made friends with Valeria Montilla, Emilo's wife. She begged us to smuggle her out with the medical workers. She was pregnant and feared what would happen to her child if she stayed."

One-Mile let out a low whistle. "I know our friendly neighborhood drug lord didn't take that well."

"No."

"So we went to Guerrero a couple of months back…why?"

"Valeria hired us to rescue her sister. Emilo had been keeping her as bait."

"But everything went south," Trees pointed out. "Our mission failed, and we nearly died."

Hunter nodded. "Because of the mole."

"So we're going back in to retrieve Valeria's sister?"

The boss shook his head. "That's not a good idea until we figure out who within our organization turned against us. This mission is purely a screen to smoke out our rat. So you two will land in Acapulco and set up surveillance equipment together in a predetermined location. Trees, from there you'll drive out of the city and head inland to Taxco, where you'll set up surveillance in another location. Pierce, you'll head up the coast to Petalán."

"We're splitting up?" Trees raised a brow. "That's risky as fuck in a place like that."

"It's the fastest way to figure out who's selling us out." One-Mile shrugged. "If we don't, it's only a matter of time before we're caught unaware again. At least we'll be going into this with our eyes wide open." He turned back to Hunter. "So what are you telling everyone around here?"

"Each of the other three operatives will get a different cover story. We'll know who our mole is based on which location Tierra Caliente raids."

As ideas went, it wasn't foolproof. But they didn't have a lot of options, and he understood the rationale.

"We've only got a few suspects. Maybe we can discern our mole without all the cloak-and-dagger bullshit."

"And just so we're clear, Zy would never sell us out," Trees vowed.

How sweet. The tall dude was sticking up for his bestie. Based on what, a pinkie swear?

Still, Zy's family was loaded. He seemed less likely to betray his peers...but it wasn't impossible.

"Trees, I know you're convinced Zy is innocent," Hunter acknowledged, "but we can't assume anything. We have to rule everyone out before we know for sure what we're dealing with."

One-Mile considered the other two possibilities. Josiah Grant was former CIA, so he was more likely to have the international connections needed to stab his fellow operatives in the back. But was that really the surly loner's speed?

That left Cutter. The asshole had a hero complex...but was it possible appearances were deceiving? Just because he couldn't think of a reason Bryant would sell them out didn't mean he wouldn't. On the other hand, no matter how badly he wanted Cutter to be guilty, that didn't actually make him the culprit.

"When are we leaving?" he asked Hunter.

"Tonight."

Son of a bitch. Of all the terrible timing...

One-Mile bit back a groan. "Mission duration?"

With any luck, he'd be back in a few days, and his absence would only be a momentary setback with Brea. Hell, maybe this was for the best. She'd asked for space, and if he stayed in the same zip code, he'd be tempted to corner her, strip her naked, and remind her how good they were together.

"Couple of days, tops. You should head out before you and Cutter are tempted to commit murder on company property."

"Sounds like more fun than fucking with a cartel," Trees quipped.

Amen. But he didn't get that choice. Besides, if he killed Cutter, Brea would never forgive him. "I'm in."

"Listen, you can't tell anyone you're leaving or where you're going. Logan, Joaquin, and I will circulate your various locations after you've set up the surveillance equipment."

One-Mile rose. "Got it."

"Roger that." Trees stood, too.

"Both of you report here at twenty-one hundred. I'll be waiting with further instructions. That gives you about twelve hours to get your shit in order…just in case this doesn't go as planned."

Wednesday, August 20
Acapulco

Coastal Mexico in August was more humid than the ass crack of hell.

Trees downed the last of his beer as the sun set over the little seaside restaurant attached to their shithole motel in Acapulco. The few tourists vacationing here looked happy to disappear into their tequila. One-Mile shoveled in the last of his fish and scanned the area. Nothing out of the ordinary…but the back of his neck tingled and felt tight.

Like someone was watching.

He played it casual and glanced at his watch. "We should go. It will be easier to find our location before the sun sets."

Trees tossed a few bills on the table, then hoisted the duffel at his side as he stood. "Yep. Might as well get this shit over with."

One of the three remaining EM Security operatives—One-Mile didn't know which—had been told he and Trees were meeting a member of a rival faction tomorrow here in Acapulco who could help them bust inside Montilla's compound and free Valeria's sister. The second of the three operatives had been advised of a rendezvous in Taxco on Friday, while the last had been spoon-fed the bullshit about a clandestine meet-up in Petalán on Saturday night.

One-Mile was braced for trouble, but he had no idea when or where it would appear. The setup was making him twitchy.

He heaved a sigh as he paid his own bill and got to his feet. "Got the map?"

"Yep." Trees headed off the restaurant's terrace, toward the parking lot where they'd left their rental. "You been thinking about who's guilty?"

"Hard not to." But every one of the suspects had pros and cons.

"Any conclusions?"

"No." At least none he felt like sharing.

Trees eyed him. "You'd like Cutter to be guilty."

On some level, sure. But it would crush Brea. "I'd prefer not to have a traitor in our ranks at all."

"Same. I'm telling you, man. It's not Zy."

"We'll find out, I guess."

"The truth is, I can't picture any of these guys betraying us."

Maybe Trees just didn't want to. But One-Mile knew good men could be capable of bad things, given the right circumstances.

"And Joaquin felt the same," Trees added. "So did the colonel."

"Hmm." It was nice to know the elder Edgington believed in the motley crew he'd assembled shortly before his retirement...but that didn't change the fact they were in Mexico to hunt the snake slithering in their midst.

"Hey, when we're done with the first setup, do you want to head to the strip? Catch some pretty girls jiggling to some terrible music?"

That wasn't his speed. Besides, with every step he took, his dread kept sharpening. If he was feeling uneasy in broad daylight in the middle of a tourist area, visiting the city's seedy underbelly well after dark would only make him paranoid.

But another scan of the parking lot proved it devoid of people.

"Nah. Let's get the fuck out of here. I'm going to head north early in the morning, so I'd like to go to bed early."

"Fair enough." Trees nodded as they reached the car. "Hey, mind putting this in the trunk while I tie my shoe?"

One-Mile took the heavy duffel from the tall guy. "No sweat."

Trees popped the trunk with the fob and bent to his laces when One-Mile caught sight of a quintet of heavily armed men emerging from vehicles and behind trees at the perimeter of the parking lot and spreading out to surround them. They had the hardened look of cartel soldiers.

His blood ran cold. *Fuck.*

"Get in the car!" he shouted at Trees as he tossed the equipment into the gaping trunk and slammed it closed.

Trees whirled and caught sight of the foot soldiers charging at them, then dived into the front seat. One-Mile sprinted for the passenger door, weapon drawn, as Trees hit the button on the fob to unlock it, then shoved the key in the ignition. He turned the car over as One-Mile popped off a shot, hitting one thug square between the eyes just before he grabbed at the door handle—

Then someone tackled him from behind and forced him down to the gravel, trapping him under a heavy weight that smelled like sweat, testosterone, and gunpowder.

Blood roaring, One-Mile struggled for leverage so he could get off his belly and fight back. He'd learned to defend himself on the streets, goddamn it. He could get himself out of a scrape. But the bruiser on top of him had obviously learned to fight dirty, too, and countered every one of his moves.

He wasn't getting free from this.

"Go!" he managed to scream at Trees as the asshole sitting on top of him pounded his fingers into the crumbling asphalt and wrenched the weapon from his stinging hand.

His fellow operative hesitated for a split second, and he could feel Trees' indecision. Then the car peeled out and began to speed away. The other foot soldiers shot at the little white rental, but One-Mile watched it shudder out of the lot and jostle down the road, both glad Trees had gotten away...and terrified of what happened next.

"Not so tough without your backup now," the foot soldier spat, snorting and panting in his ear. "Are you, Walker?"

Oh, fuck. They knew who he was.

He was as good as dead.

At least Trees had gotten away. There was a chance—albeit a slim one—that his bosses could mount a rescue. The more likely scenario was that they'd recover his body. Someday...maybe. At least they'd know for sure that someone in their ranks was a backstabbing bastard who deserved to be purged.

"Fuck you." What the hell else could he say?

The pungent weight crushing his ribs laughed. "You will, no doubt, change your tune when you see what we have in store for you... But for now, it is best if you sleep."

The fat foot soldier on his back twisted to straddle him, then grabbed him by the hair before slamming his head against the pavement a few times. His skull exploded in pain. Blackness swam at the edges of his vision.

His last thought was of Brea. He wished like hell he had a few more stolen seconds alone with her. At least then he could tell her that he'd fallen hard for her.

CHAPTER EIGHT

Monday, September 8
Lafayette, Louisiana

Wringing her hands, Brea paced the too-familiar halls of University Hospital again. The first time she'd come here, it had been a sweltering summer afternoon. The birds had been singing and the flowers in full bloom. Pierce had been with her, patiently holding her hand and bolstering her while doctors tried to repair her father's heart.

Now, the weather had begun to cool. Football season was in full swing. The sky was pitch-black, except for a hazy moon hanging in the sky. The clock on the wall read two thirty-eight a.m., and the city outside the windows was almost eerily still. No one stood beside her, devoting himself to her moral support.

But her father's failing heart was the awful correlation.

She wished Pierce were here now. Since she'd started pacing the emergency room, she had talked herself out of calling him more than once. During her father's first episode this summer, his steadying force had been her bedrock. Without him now, she felt like she was in free fall. But it would be selfish to reach out to him after weeks of silence. After all, she was the one who had told him she needed space. He'd more than respected her wishes. Why should he come after she'd ignored him for so long?

"Brea!"

She whirled around to find Cutter jogging toward her. She dashed into his arms, grateful she was no longer alone.

But he wasn't Pierce.

At the thought, guilt filled her. Her best friend had come running after a mere phone call, despite the ridiculous hour, and she was grateful. She pushed thoughts of Pierce aside.

"Thank you for being here," she said against his chest. "I-I know it's late. I know you have to work—"

"Shh." He brushed her hair off her face and cradled her cheeks in his palms, forcing her gaze to his. "None of that matters. Tell me what happened. What have the doctors said?"

"I'm still waiting for news. I don't really know much. I was so tired that I went to bed after dinner. An unfamiliar crashing noise woke me up a little after midnight. I ran down the hall and found Daddy on the floor, struggling to breathe. I think he panicked and tried to call 911 but fell out of bed reaching for the phone. I couldn't lift him. He was in agony. I…" She pressed her hand to her mouth, trying to hold in useless tears, but the vision of her father pale and writhing and making inhuman sounds of pain haunted her. "I called an ambulance. I didn't know what else to do. I'm worried he's had another heart attack. He's barely recovered from the last surgery…"

"I know." Cutter held her tighter. "But don't lose hope. He's young. He's already dropped some weight and started exercising. You're putting good food in his system, and the repairs he's had on his heart will help the blood flow. I know you're praying."

"Of course." But she heard the squeak of fear in her voice, felt its burn singeing her veins. She wasn't ready to lose her father.

"Then you're doing all you can. Come sit down, Bre-bee. You look exhausted."

She'd just been tired lately. Not surprising. She had a history of being anemic, and she'd slacked off on taking her iron. "Don't worry about me. I just…have no idea what I'll do if Daddy isn't all right."

"You'll cross the bridge if you're pushed off of it, okay? In the meantime, have you called Tom? He should know that he'll probably need to take over for your father again."

"I was waiting until I knew something definitive. And until it wasn't the middle of the night. There's really nothing he can do now."

"Fair enough." He curled an arm around her. "Do you want some coffee?"

She shook her head. "I walked past the machine earlier. It needs a good cleaning. The smell of it turned my stomach."

Cutter led her over to a padded bench and sat her down. "I doubt you'd find anything appetizing right now."

"No," she confirmed, casting her worried glance to the double doors beyond the waiting area. "I don't know what's taking so long. I've been here nearly two hours. The paperwork kept me busy for a while, but…"

"You want information. I understand. But they'll fill you in once they have answers. For now, no news is good news."

She nodded, trying hard to believe that. "Talk to me about something else. Anything else. I need my mind off this or I'll just keep imagining the worst-case scenarios."

"Yeah. Um…" But Cutter shook his head blankly.

"You never said whether you're coming to the fall market at the church on Friday evening. We could still use a few volunteers to help us set up and break down."

He hesitated a few seconds too long. "I don't know. Brea, I need to tell you—"

"Ms. Bell?"

She turned to find a familiar woman in green scrubs. Her face looked grim. "Dr. Gale. I didn't realize you'd come in. How's Daddy?"

"That's why the attending physician called me. Your father is going to need more bypass work."

Her jaw dropped. Her heart fell. It wasn't the worst possible news…but it was close. "Why?"

"Back in July, the insurance company chose only to bypass the left anterior descending artery. They merely cleared us to stent the others with blockages, despite my recommendation otherwise. Since then, a blood clot has formed in his right coronary artery. We've just completed all the tests to confirm. Time is of the essence, so we're prepping now."

"You're doing the surgery this morning?" Her head told her that waiting any amount of time with a blood clot in Daddy's heart was incredibly dangerous. But all she could think about was her father going under anesthesia again for a risky procedure he might not survive.

What if she never got to say goodbye?

Dr. Gale's face softened as she took Brea's hand. "We don't have a choice."

Cutter slipped a supporting arm around her. "We understand. I know you'll keep us advised. When will you get started and how long do you expect the surgery to last?"

The surgeon glanced at the clock on the wall. "We'll be starting in the next thirty minutes. The surgery should last three to four hours, depending on complications. As soon as we know more, someone will speak with you."

"Thank you, Doctor," Brea managed to mumble, but she felt her legs crumpling beneath her as her head swirled in a dizzy spin.

"Whoa." Cutter caught her and helped her back to the bench, sitting her on his lap. "Are you okay, Bre-Bee?"

"Overwhelmed," she managed to say. "I can't believe this is happening again."

"You should call Mrs. Collins."

"I can't wake Jennifer up in the middle of the night."

Cutter gave her that patient expression he often flashed when he had to explain something she should already know. "You should. She's your father's…girlfriend, for lack of a better word."

He'd suggested that before, but she'd never seen any evidence of that.

"I…" She shook her head. "No."

He cleared his throat. "Yes. A few weeks back, when you went to that concert in New Orleans with the girls from the salon and stayed the night?"

"I remember."

Cutter was not about to say what she thought he would. *Please. Please…*

"You're going to make me say that she spent the night, are you?"

"She wouldn't." Brea shook her head in disbelief. "And Daddy wouldn't—"

"Yeah, he would. He's a man. They're both widowed. I'm sure they're lonely. I think they care about one another. It's not like they randomly hooked up after a swipe right on Tinder."

She winced. Cutter was right…but they were talking about her father. Having a sex life. She'd always viewed him as perfect, above reproach. She'd idolized him, worshipped him. To find out he was only human seemed both obvious and foolishly crushing.

Then again, she knew how tempting the flesh could be. Every single night, she held her finger over the screen of her iPhone, aching to press the button and call Pierce. She'd missed his gruff smile, his scent, his guttural grunts as he filled her, his unexpected tenderness, the rasp in his voice when he called her pretty girl…

"Hey." Cutter snapped his fingers. "Where did you go?"

Should she tell him everything? Brea had agonized over this a million times in the last month—and still had no answer. At first, she hadn't confessed her feelings for Pierce to Cutter because he'd been too angry to listen, and she'd been so sure that she and Pierce would never last. But as the days passed and the rugged sniper haunted her, as her body hungered and she'd begun to crave just having him near…

She realized she cared about him. Very much. And he'd given her way more space than she'd wanted or believed he would ever grant her.

It hurt.

But maybe now wasn't the time to mention it. She needed to stay focused on her father, and she sensed something weighing on Cutter, too.

"Thinking. Sorry." She tried to smile, despite the nagging worry about Daddy's health plaguing her.

Would the sunrise bring shining new hope for his recovery or cast a glaring light on her harsh new reality without him?

Cutter was right; she needed to be optimistic. The trick right now, when hope seemed razor thin, was to stay distracted. "You were saying something before Dr. Gale talked to us. You'll be someplace on Friday, other than the church's fall market?"

Cutter's face tightened. "I don't know if now is the time to talk about this."

"If it will keep me from fixating on my father, please."

He looked away with a grimace, then sighed. "I may be in Mexico come Friday. Walker went there almost three weeks ago on a mission. He was taken at gunpoint in a parking lot by a cartel. We might finally have a lead on his location. If it pans out, we'll be bugging out to extract him ASAP."

As soon as his words registered, Brea's heart—and her world—stopped. Panic ensued. Pierce had been abducted? The big, seemingly invincible warrior with the one-mile kill shot had been overpowered and taken prisoner? No. She couldn't picture it. Didn't want to. Couldn't stand it.

She heaved in a breath made more ragged by the crushing pain spreading through her chest. It wracked her system. Tears stung her eyes. Any calm she'd found since before Cutter entered the emergency room vanished.

"Oh, my... A-a cartel? Is he even..." She couldn't bring herself to finish that sentence. She could barely breathe past her distress.

He had to be alive. She *needed* him to be alive.

She squeezed her eyes shut. *Please, God, let him be all right.*

But what were the odds that an organization fueled by illegal drugs, money, and greed would keep a hostage alive for weeks?

"I don't know. We're hoping." But Cutter sounded grim. "The information we've collected is sketchy, and with every passing hour it's getting older. But it's more than we had to go on yesterday."

Brea clung to hope. She had to. If she let herself imagine where Pierce was and what he was enduring, she would melt down. "Why didn't you tell me sooner? I didn't know he was in danger. I didn't have any idea. I would have prayed for him or..."

Something. She would have done something. Honestly, anything. But what could a small-town hairdresser really do to save the man she cared for way more than she ought to from a cartel?

"I didn't want to bring him up after...you know, everything that happened. You did your best to save me, and you betrayed yourself to do it. I hate how much pain it caused you."

She shook her head. "It wasn't like that. He—"

"Don't." Cutter held up his hands. "Don't try to make me feel better. I don't deserve it."

The guilt was still eating him alive. "Don't ever think you're unworthy. There's no reason for that. And I don't regret a thing."

Brea didn't say more. Cutter wasn't ready to hear that some part of her heart belonged to Pierce and probably always would.

Cutter closed his eyes with a sigh. "As much as I hate to admit it, as much as I hate who he is and what he's done, he's saved my life twice. My bosses are absolutely losing their shit over this. I have to go. I have to help."

Even though he despised Pierce, Cutter insisted on being a part of his rescue. Because he was a good man.

"Please. Promise me you'll do whatever you can. Whatever you have to..." She grabbed Cutter's hands. "Bring him home."

He nodded. "I know how you feel about brutality and senseless death. Even if Walker's record is hardly spotless, you would never want more violence or wish anyone dead."

All of that was true...but hardly her rationale. She missed Pierce fiercely. Needed him. And she was sickeningly, painfully worried about him. Maybe she hadn't pictured a life with him—except occasionally, late at night when she missed him like mad. But it nearly killed her to imagine a world without him.

"Let me know as soon as you have any word. And you keep safe, you hear?"

"Yes, ma'am." He managed a smile for her. "Now call Mrs. Collins. I really think she'd want to be here."

It took all her will, but Brea managed to block out her terror and focus on mundane but important tasks. It turned out that Cutter was right. Jennifer didn't hesitate to jump out of bed, toss on her clothes, and drive through the black night. Tears sheened her eyes when she raced through the doors. The woman sobbed. Brea joined her as they clung together through the long wait for news.

But as the sun rose, Dr. Gale emerged from the operating room, looking both exhausted and triumphant, to tell the exhausted trio that her father had come through the surgery successfully. He was in recovery, had already regained consciousness, and was asking to see her.

Brea held back sobs as she thanked God for the miracle. Daddy would always have to watch his diet and weight, not to mention his cholesterol, but she was so grateful to Him for hearing her prayers and sparing her father.

But inside, she was quietly frantic with unrelenting worry—and shamefully ready to beg Him for one more favor. So as she was escorted back to her father's bedside, she closed her eyes and asked the Lord above for one more good deed.

Please, God, bring Pierce back to me whole and alive...

Thursday, September 11
Guerrero, Mexico—middle of nowhere

One-Mile had no idea what day it was or how long he'd been out. He pried open one swollen eye. He saw only bare concrete walls—thick and uninterrupted—without a window in sight. No surprise that he was alone.

He'd figured out a while back that he was being held underground. He knew that because the few times he'd been dragged outside, it had still been hot as hell, but the air on his skin now was almost chilly. Despite that, a wringing sweat covered his body. He trembled. His stomach cramped. His head felt as if it might explode.

Fuck, he needed to make some decisions.

He eyed the door. Sure, he should probably check it. But why? The damn thing had been bolted up tight each of the other four thousand five hundred ninety-two times he'd searched for some way to escape. No sense wasting more energy he might need to simply stay alive.

How much longer before someone came back and stuck a needle in his arm? He both craved and dreaded it. At least afterward he wouldn't feel the stabbing pain in his jaw or the throbbing of his knee. He wouldn't care that his back was in ribbons or that he could barely feel his fingers. No, once whatever shit they pumped his veins full of hit his system, he would fade off for...who knew how long? He'd awaken at some point, hungry, dehydrated, sweating, and wondering what fucking day it was.

Then someone would come in with a meal and a needle...and the cycle would start all over.

Unless they decided to "interrogate" him again. That was always a fab time. But no one had raised a whip or crowbar to him in a few highs. Unfortunately, that wasn't good news. If Emilo Montilla and his gang of assholes had given up on him divulging any useful information about Valeria's whereabouts, that made him expendable. Then they wouldn't bother beating him again. They'd just give him a double tap to the brain and toss his body into a shallow grave. He'd be buried somewhere in the goddamn desert on foreign soil. No one would ever know what the fuck had happened to him.

Would anyone even care?

Brea Bell—maybe. She alone might mourn.

Not that she loved him. He'd kissed her, even though she belonged to a teammate, because he couldn't stand not knowing the flavor of her mouth. He'd touched her because he hadn't possessed the self-control to leave her innocent. He'd worked his cock inside her again and again because he hadn't been able to tolerate an inch of space between them. Because he wanted her to be his.

Because he was pretty fucking sure he'd stupidly fallen in love with her.

Brea was gentle, kind. She would mourn him, if for no other reason than she believed in God, cherished the sanctity of life, and had the purest soul he'd ever had the privilege of knowing.

Of all his regrets—and he had plenty—he hated that he hadn't called her before he'd left on this mission and admitted exactly how he felt.

Now it was too late.

For a minute, he was tempted to pray to her God, but he didn't. He didn't really deserve God's mercy. Brea didn't know about his past, but God did…and that was probably why he'd end up dying in the middle of nowhere before they threw a little dirt on him and left him to become coyote shit.

On that cheerful note, he slumped back on the cot and closed his eyes, shivering against the chills and withdrawals. His sandpaper tongue stuck to the roof of his mouth. He swore he felt his ribs against his spine. And fuck, he needed to pee.

The next person who came into this room, he'd kill. Not that it would get him anywhere. Even without a weapon, he'd already offed a handful of them—until they'd started shackling his hands, bashing his kneecaps, and swinging fists at his jaw. They'd slowed him down, sure.

But unless he was dead, they couldn't stop him.

On his left, One-Mile heard the click of the lock. He swiveled his head, opened the one eye he could, and lay deceptively still, waiting to see who came through the door. That would tell him how much effort he'd need to exert to trip the thug du jour and stomp his larynx until the gunman suffocated.

But it wasn't some armed-to-the-teeth asshole who entered the room but a delicate Hispanic beauty who looked twenty, max. Her entire body trembled as, tray in hand, she cleared the door. Immediately, it shut—and locked—behind her. She jolted at the sound.

"Who are you?" The raspy slur of his voice barely sounded human.

She didn't look at him. Fuck, he probably should have saved his breath. Besides Montilla, only a handful of people in this shithole spoke English, and his Spanish sucked.

As she set the tray on the nearby table, she shook so hard the dishes rattled. She finally met his stare. Her brown eyes were wide and full of terror. "My name is Laila, Señor Walker. Emilo is my…um—how do you say?—my brother-in-law."

So she was Valeria's sister? The one the EM team had tried to rescue during their first mission, before they'd been ambushed?

"I am sorry," she rushed on. "I have not used my English in too long."

The guys who brought his meals usually had a face as attractive as a pug's ass and a wide sadistic streak, so sending in a pretty, unarmed female was definitely a new tactic.

He didn't trust it, but he played along. "Are you going to untie me so I can eat or feed me yourself?"

"I have been sent to feed you, see to your bath, and"—she swallowed hard—"any other comforts you may desire."

Her answer rolled around in his brain. Translation: drugging, starving, and beating him hadn't worked, so they were going to force this frightened woman to sex him up so he'd get happy enough to betray his bosses back home?

One-Mile nearly snorted at that bullshit. He would have—just before he set her straight—if he wasn't one-hundred percent sure Montilla and his thugs were listening in.

Instead, he played along...for now. "What do you have under that lid?"

Laila lifted the dome. "Water. Cold beer. Tortilla soup, refried beans, homemade flan..."

More than he'd eaten in one sitting since he'd been taken captive. And the food actually looked fresh for a change.

On the far side of the tray, he also caught sight of the needle with the drugs. "That my after-dinner cocktail?"

A guilty flush stole up her cheeks. "That is up to you."

Somehow, One-Mile didn't think she meant they'd pump him full of shit if he wanted it. But if he proved uncooperative... "I see. How about we eat first?"

"As you wish."

With a gentle hand, she helped him stand, then guided him to the room's lone chair. Patiently, she stood over him and fed a straw through his swollen lips, past his sore-ass jaw, and waited until he'd managed to swallow half the bottle. He eschewed the beer, slurped the soup down as she guided it—one slow spoonful at a time—into his barely open mouth, then fed him a few beans before finishing with some flan.

Since that was the most he'd eaten in weeks—or was it months now?—it didn't take much for him to get his fill. But consuming everything took a long damn time. He did his best to stay patient and use the time to figure out how he could benefit from this change of circumstance. Short of threatening a female half his size and trying to use her as a shield to fight his way out, he wasn't seeing it. Besides, Emilo wouldn't have sent her in here if she wasn't expendable.

Gently, Laila wiped his mouth with a napkin, then helped him to his feet. "Would you care for a shower now?"

"And a toilet?"

"Of course." She looked up at a camera in the corner of the room. Another internal door buzzed open, and she led him inside. It locked shut behind them. "I am allowed to untie your hands in this room."

He held them out and scanned the place. Sure, he'd been here before, but the memories were always hazy since the trips had come after the needle. But his captors had made certain there was nothing he could use as a weapon and no way to escape.

Slowly, she unwound the bindings from his hands. Blood rushed in, tingling and painful, as full circulation returned. Vaguely, he wondered…if he managed to find some way out of this hell, would he ever fully recover?

Why fucking care? It was unlikely he'd ever escape, so torturing himself with this train of thought was pointless.

For the first few days in captivity, he'd hoped the Edgingtons and Joaquin Muñoz would bust in here with the rest of the EM crew and save his sorry ass. But no. First, they probably had no idea where he was. Hell, he didn't, except that he was a long way from Acapulco. And second, why would they? It was no secret how much Cutter hated him. He'd thought for a while that maybe Logan liked him and Hunter trusted him somewhat…but they more or less thought he'd raped Brea, too. Why would they save him when it was easier to replace him?

When he'd been taken, Trees had driven away as quickly as possible—as he should have. But he hadn't fired a shot or come back with reinforcements. Zy was too busy chasing Tessa's skirt to care about much else these days. And Josiah…who knew where the guy fell? They didn't talk much.

One thing One-Mile did know? No one was coming to his rescue. He was going to have to work with Laila.

She allowed him a few minutes alone in the toilet, then started the shower while he washed his hands and brushed his teeth with the toothbrush she had helpfully provided.

When he'd finished, he pivoted to face her, assuming she'd step out while he washed himself.

Instead, she began disrobing.

He watched with a frown. This must be the "whatever he desired" portion of the evening.

No thanks.

One-Mile stayed her with a hand on her shoulder. "You don't have to get naked for me."

Relief stamped itself all over her face—but she kept stripping. "Yes, I do..."

Silently, he studied her as she peeled her dress from her body and draped it over a nearby counter. She'd worn nothing underneath. Shadows shrouded the feminine hollows of her body. Light clung to her curves. She was a beautiful woman...and she didn't do a damn thing for him.

Her breasts bobbed gently as she approached and helped him pull his shirt over his head. The movement hurt his back like a bitch. The wounds had finally scabbed over, but they'd likely leave scars—if he lived long enough for them to heal.

Then she reached for the button of his jeans.

One-Mile gripped her wrists to stop her. "Laila..."

"Shh." She pushed his hands away and continued on. "Let me. Please."

Her eyes begged. Since he didn't have much choice, he relented with a nod.

One-Mile stood motionless while Laila shoved his dirty, blood-stained jeans down his legs. He braced against the wall as he stepped out, now as naked as she was.

Then she took his hand and led him under the hot spray. He hissed and grimaced as the water pelted his healing skin. She merely pressed her body against his with a whisper. "The shower is the only place they cannot hear us."

So the girl wanted to escape. She had a plan and something to say to him. He was on board for that. It was a long shot…but any shot was more than he'd had ten minutes ago.

Smiling, he pulled her close, then bent to murmur in her ear. "Now what?"

"I want to be gone from here. I convinced Emilo that, if they let me see to you, I could seduce information from you."

One-Mile pretended to caress his way down her arm before he planted his hand on her hip. "I'm not telling you anything."

"I did not expect you to. I-I have begun sleeping with one of my brother-in-law's thugs, and I have been able to use his phone while he sleeps to sneak coded messages to my sister through a message board. I told her where we are and that Emilo is keeping you hostage. She said she would pass the information to the men who rescued her. Last night, she wrote back to say that a rescue mission is in place."

His heart started revving. He wanted to grill her. Hell, he was even half tempted to shake her by the shoulders and demand to know if she was telling the truth. But she glanced at the camera in the corner, then brushed her lips up his chest. Yeah, they were watching. So he caressed his way down her ass and nuzzled her neck. "When?"

She sent him a come-hither smile and sidled closer. "Tonight. About an hour."

That damn organ in his chest started chugging even harder. "Got a plan?"

There had to be a few dozen gunmen here, not to mention Emilo himself, who was fucking evil with the whip. Unless the Edgingtons and Muñoz were dropping in with some of Uncle Sam's boys, they were going to be incredibly outnumbered.

Her flirtation suddenly looked far more like a grimace. "You should pretend to attack me. I will scream. Emilo's men will come to my rescue…I think."

"You don't sound too sure."

"I am worth nothing to them. But Emilo wants Valeria back."

"Because he loves his wife?"

Laila scoffed. "No. He does not want her back as a lover. Why should he when he has so many whores willing to take his cock and his money? He flaunted them in my sister's face while she lived with him. He is a pig."

One-Mile didn't disagree. In fact, Laila had phrased things much nicer than he was inclined to.

"But he suspected Valeria was pregnant when she escaped, and he refuses to let his child go."

"What will he do if he manages to find her and the kid?"

"Punish her, make an example of her. He will kill her. She knows too much about his operations, and he fears she is already telling your government."

Probably.

"The child... If she gave birth to a son, Emilo will groom him to take his place in the organization. Perhaps if he is ruthless enough, he will survive. If she gave birth to a daughter, she will be raised a princess, then married off to another drug pusher who can increase Emilo's standing in the cartel. After that, she will have a miserable existence of sexual servitude and fear."

Laila was a realist, if nothing else.

He fisted his hands in her hair and sent her what the watching goons would interpret as a leer. "And you think Emilo is keeping you alive and well so he can use you as leverage against your sister?"

"Yes."

"You understand that if I attack you and they come to your rescue, we'll be separated. They'll beat the shit out of me, and I won't be in any position to help you."

She nodded, dragging her palms down his chest with what probably appeared to be a seductive scratch of her nails. "But quarters are cramped here, so they will take you outside to do it."

Where the rescue party could actually reach him...provided Emilo and his men didn't kill him first.

As plans went, it sucked. And it was a long shot. But any chance at freedom was better than no chance at all. "All right. What's your idea?"

She gave him a blank stare. "I have not thought beyond that."

One-Mile wasn't surprised. She was barely more than a girl. She wasn't a soldier, much less a tactician.

He reached for the bottle of shampoo and lathered his hair, while Laila grabbed the bar of soap and gave him a thorough scrub. "Any suggestions on how we kill the next forty-five minutes? Just a guess, but you don't want to fuck any more than I do."

"Emilo allowed one of his underlings to first rape me when I was fourteen. Sex is not something I do for enjoyment."

Every time she spoke, he hated Montilla and his violent band of assholes even more. "If I can do anything to make sure you get out alive, I will."

"Thank you." Her lips trembled.

He nodded. "How about you play along?"

"Of course. I am willing to try anything."

Yeah, he was, too—even getting the shit beat out of him again.

They lingered in the shower, pretending flirtation and sexual interest. Finally, he cut off the spray, dried them off with a towel, then carried Laila back to the cot, faking some sweet nothings in her ear.

Together, they fell into a naked heap on the cot with a forced laugh. He reached for the beer. She drank it while he held her on his lap, caressing her back and thighs.

"You're feeling drunk, aren't you?" he suggested in a low, almost unrecognizable mumble.

She pretended a giddy smile. "Maybe a little. Why does it matter? Are you thinking of taking advantage of me? I am far too small to fight off a big man like you."

Did that turn some guys on? Disgusting. "I have something else in mind. You're not going to fight me, are you?"

"Should I?" She batted her lashes. Fear gleamed in her eyes.

His gut cramped. They were both risking their lives. He didn't have any choice except to keep playing his part and push until the bad guys barged in to shut him down.

One-Mile dragged Laila closer, then reached behind her to grab the needle off the tray. "Someone else besides me should be high on this shit. And if I stick this into your veins, it won't be in me."

Her dark eyes flared, and he saw the exact moment she wondered if she'd made a mistake in trusting him. "That is enough to kill me."

"Oh, well," he quipped as he grabbed her arm. "Better you than me."

Then her fighting turned real—or if it wasn't, it was damn convincing. One-Mile didn't point out that if he'd really wanted to pump her full of drugs, he would have already done it, and she couldn't possibly have escaped him. Instead, he let her beat against him and empty the syringe into the air during the scuffle. After he ducked her attempt to punch him, she tried to knee him in the balls and kick his shins. He growled and snarled and pushed her against the wall, shaking her hard enough to jar her teeth as he growled empty threats her way.

She screamed. The tears came. She sent a pleading stare at the security camera. He let that last a few good seconds before he picked her up, tossed her on the cot, then climbed on top of her.

Shouldn't be long now…

Right on cue, a group of underlings with automatic weapons and attitude lifted him off of her and hauled him to his feet, shouting things in Spanish he didn't understand. Then again, he didn't need to know the words to grasp that they wanted the pleasure of killing him.

Laila wrapped herself in the blanket on his cot and glared at him with accusing eyes as the goons prodded him into his filthy jeans, up the stairs, and out into the breezy desert night. Emilo Montilla was waiting, whip in one hand, crowbar in the other as they clapped him into the shackles drilled deep into the concrete wall of the bunker.

Fuck, this was going to hurt.

"You have been a pain in my ass. It is time we reminded you that you should play nice because *I* am in charge. But I will spare you if you tell me where to find my wife."

"Are you just stupid or is your memory that bad? I've already said a hundred times that I'm not telling you a fucking thing."

Emilo snarled, then opened his back again with a single lash of the whip. Fire burst across One-Mile's skin. He hissed and arched, but nothing stopped the agony until the drug lord backhanded the side of his face with the crowbar.

An instant after pain exploded in his head, One-Mile's world went black. If he ever opened his eyes again, he hoped he would be anywhere but here.

CHAPTER NINE

A blast jolted him back to consciousness with a gasp. Gunfire. Pops of it resounded all around him, along with scuffling and shouting. One-Mile lifted his cheek from the wall and tried to open his eyes. A floodlight beamed down into his face, blinding him. He flinched but couldn't escape.

What was happening, some fucking apocalypse? Maybe that meant the end was coming so his fuck ton of pain would finally stop.

Every bit of his body hurt as if someone had set him on fire. His jaw throbbed. His back sizzled. Something warm and liquid ran down his arms. He couldn't fucking move. With his remaining strength, he tried to rise from his knees, which felt as if someone had driven stakes through them. But he was shackled. He smelled blood.

He was pretty sure it was his own.

"Over here!"

The voice was male. American. Familiar. One-Mile's head hurt too damn much to place it. Friend or foe?

Did it matter anymore? Either way, he was going to die.

He slumped forward, pressing his overheated cheek against the cool wall, and closed his eyes.

A pair of amber eyes haunted him.

Brea.

"Find 'em?" asked that familiar voice again, this time closer. "Toss them to me." No sooner did a metal clink fill his ears than the man shouted, "Fuck!"

More gunfire filled the air with a rapid *rat-tat-tat*. One-Mile lifted a lid to find a shadow standing over him, clutching an automatic weapon, wearing an angel-of-death glower, and spraying bullets into the darkness beyond.

"Get him now. We've got to get the hell out of here!" another American voice called, even more familiar. "I'll cover you."

An Edgington?

"On it!" said the first man as he blocked the blinding light and jerked at his imprisoning shackles.

One-Mile squinted up to see who had come to his rescue.

Cutter.

What the fuck?

"We're going to get you out of here," Bryant vowed grimly.

Why? Sure, they were teammates, but why would Brea's boyfriend rescue *him*?

"Can't move. Leave me."

"I promised Brea I'd bring you home, and I'm going to live up to my word."

Suddenly, his wrists were free. He tried to steady himself and use the wall to stagger upright. But agony gouged his knees. And his left shoulder. Dizziness turned his pounding head around and upside down.

One-Mile slumped to the ground.

Was this where he'd die, face down in the mud, when he'd been on the verge of safety?

Fuck no. Not if Brea wanted him back. For her, he'd fight.

One-Mile planted a hand in the mud and grimaced as he mustered the last of his strength to climb to his knees, then cling to the wall and stumble to his feet.

Cutter was right there. "Let's go. You're in no fucking shape to walk." He shoved the automatic in One-Mile's hands. "Keep our backs clear."

Before he could figure out what Bryant had in mind, Cutter hoisted him onto his back. Then Logan was beside them, taking down Montilla's lackies and thugs, clearing a path forward.

More goons gave chase. Every fucking bone in One-Mile's body hurt, but the opportunity for some payback was too good to pass up. He saw one of Montilla's heavies grab Laila by the hair and toss her to the ground.

Fuck that. She'd suffered enough.

His hands were shaking. Seeing double would totally affect his aim, but he'd seen Laila's expression. She'd rather be dead than stay another minute in this hellhole.

But One-Mile didn't intend to miss.

He pulled the trigger. The kickback was a bitch, but the thug jerked and stumbled. Laila screamed.

The asshole fell to the ground.

Josiah was there to scoop her up and wrap her protectively against his chest. Hunter, weapon in hand, flanked his back, signaling everyone with a wave of his arm to get the hell out now.

The team made a mad dash into the desert for freedom. Cutter's every pounding footfall against the hard soil jarred him. He clutched the weapon and, through sheer will, watched as the floodlight he'd once been pinned under grew fainter and fainter in the distance.

He heard the whir of chopper blades nearby. Another undertow of dizziness threatened to pull him under. His strength gave out.

With suddenly limp fingers, he let go of the weapon. It clattered to the dirt.

Hunter scooped it up again, barking instructions. The cacophony scrambled his head; he couldn't hear a word. But Cutter flung him down inside the cockpit. One-Mile caught a glimpse of the rivets in the domed top before his vision blurred over and blackness closed in.

His last conscious thought was that he hoped he'd regain consciousness, and that he'd be looking into a pair of soft amber eyes if he did.

Friday, September 12
Louisiana

WHEN HER PHONE chirped with the ringtone she had assigned Cutter, Brea lurched up in bed. She glanced at the digital clock as she grabbed her cell off the nightstand. Three thirty-four a.m. At that hour, she didn't bother with hello. "Did you find Pierce?"

"Yeah." Cutter's voice sounded rough, grim. "It's not good, Brebee."

She shut her eyes as dread washed over her. She was almost afraid to ask what the cartel had done to Pierce. He'd been so big and vital, so larger-than-life. She couldn't imagine him any other way. Brea didn't want to harbor hate in her heart, but it festered and snarled for these savage people who pushed drugs on children and destroyed a man fighting for right.

But she dredged for her courage and asked what she was afraid to hear. "Is he still alive?"

"For now."

"Where is he?"

"New Orleans, at Tulane Medical Center. The entire team went in to retrieve Walker. We're all a little banged up, but we'll be walking out this afternoon. If he makes it the next twenty-four hours, he'll be down for a while."

Brea bit her lip, but nothing held in her tears. The arm she curled around herself didn't give her any comfort. She'd prayed and worried constantly since she'd learned he had been taken prisoner, but during the days and weeks before, when she hadn't reached out, contacted him, begged God to save him… Those ate at her. The guilt consumed her.

"I'm coming there."

But how could she do that? Her dad was recovering from another successful bypass surgery, which should keep his heart functioning for years to come, God willing. But he hadn't been home long. He still needed nearly round-the-clock care. She owed it to him to make sure he got his meds and ate healthy meals, to see to his responsibilities at the church and his comfort…

"Why?"

Cutter wanted to know the reason she'd traipse across the state to show mercy to her rapist. Brea wasn't wasting the time or energy to cut through his pigheadedness now. He wasn't ready to hear that she'd fallen for Pierce. He might be her best friend...but he didn't always understand her heart.

"He saved your life. For that alone, I'll be eternally grateful. And he has no one else." She defaulted to arguments he would understand. "And I show everyone Christian charity. It's not my place to judge who deserves it and who doesn't."

"But I know you." He sighed. "You won't want to see another human being nearly beaten to death."

Cutter's description made her catch her breath. She had to go to Pierce. Her father was getting stronger every day. If the remorse she felt for not reaching out to Pierce since she'd last seen him ate her up, how much worse would her regret be if he didn't pull through? Devastating. She needed to tell him that he'd touched her heart, that she would never forget him, and if God deemed it necessary, she would mourn him, bury him, and find some way to say goodbye.

"Please don't treat me like I'm fragile. He's endured this ordeal and fighting through all the resulting pain. It's nothing for me to come to him, hold his hand, and pray."

Cutter hesitated. "All right. Some of the others are heading up to Lafayette soon, but I'll wait for you here."

"I'll...call Jennifer. Hopefully, she'll be willing to come watch over Daddy."

"I have no doubt she will," he said wryly. "Ring me from the road. It'll be dark for most of your drive."

"I will."

Brea hesitated ending the call. Once she did, she would be severing the only line of information between her and Pierce. That scared her. The thought of him enduring such agony made her physically ache.

So often, she swallowed back tears in times of tumult or tragedy because she had to be the stalwart one. She almost always filled the role of someone's prayer partner, helpmate, or rock. Today, she couldn't hold in her sobs.

"Bre-bee…"

She sniffled and tried to quiet her tears. Between her father's relapse and Pierce's shocking captivity, she felt as if she'd been weepy all week. Knowing the man she'd fallen for might die was simply too much.

"I'll be fine. I promise." She hated lying to Cutter.

"You don't have to come here. Really."

"I do." She *needed* to be with Pierce. "I'll see you soon. Bye."

Brea ended the conversation before he tried to talk her out of coming again.

In under twenty minutes, she called Mrs. Collins, dressed, threw a few things in a bag—just in case—promised to call later, and hopped in her car. As she pulled out of the driveway, she waved at the widow who'd vowed to take excellent care of her father.

Then she sped down the road.

Brea hated driving in the middle of the night. Some of Louisiana's highways were a little narrow and a tad scary. A lot of it was over water, and she always had visions of accidentally driving off a bridge and into a swamp to become gator food. But now, she refused to let any of those fears stop her.

She would reach Pierce before dawn.

By the time she hit Lafayette's southern outskirts, her phone was ringing. She and Cutter chatted off and on for the next two hours. No change in Pierce's condition that Cutter knew of. He was in ICU. They were running tests. What he'd heard so far didn't sound promising.

"I need to prepare you," Cutter insisted. "His face is almost unrecognizable. But that's nothing compared to his back, which may have significant scarring. Those were the injuries I could see. I'm still waiting to hear about the rest. He's in surgery now. I don't know what for since none of us are family…"

Every muscle in Brea's body tightened as she tried to hold herself together. "Thanks for the update. How are you?"

"I'm fine. A few stitches aren't going to stop me for long."

"I'm grateful you're safe and relatively unharmed."

She ended the call, pleading the need to focus on the road. Just over an hour and a stop for coffee at a twenty-four-hour drive-thru later, she made it to Tulane Medical Center. Immediately, she tore into the parking garage, slung her compact into the first available spot, grabbed her phone, and ran as fast as her tired body would take her.

When she found her best friend in the emergency room's waiting area, her first two thoughts were that it looked like a larger, more crowded version of University's in Lafayette. The second was that Cutter, Hunter, and Joaquin all sat clustered together, seemingly big and out of place and obviously exhausted. She hadn't thought to bring them coffee and breakfast muffins or any of the other "nice" things she usually delivered in times of crisis. But she couldn't spare any regret as she dashed over to them.

"Any news?"

Hunter's and Joaquin's confusion showed as Cutter stood slowly, looking disheveled and weary, then wrapped his arms around her. "Other than he's out of surgery, no."

"No idea what they repaired? Or where they're taking him next? Or his long-term prognosis?"

"We're not family." And Hunter sounded bitter about that. "Logan has medical power of attorney documents back at the office. Once he gets there…"

Brea understood a patient's right to privacy, but right now Pierce needed people who cared about him. He needed her watching over him, holding his hand, advocating for him. He didn't need to be fighting for his life alone. "I'll be right back."

It took some polite asking, a bit of cajoling, and a whopping lie she didn't regret at all to convince his surgeon and the nurse in charge that Pierce had no one he considered family except her. Once they were on board, she finally got the lowdown on his condition and resulting surgery. What they told her was incredibly frightening to hear. It was beyond hard not to lose her composure. She also got permission for the others to see Pierce as soon as he came out of recovery. Suddenly, Hunter, Joaquin, and Cutter were really glad she'd come.

"The surgeon said he had broken ribs, which he can't do anything about. But Pierce had a punctured lung and some swelling of the brain, along with a broken jaw, sprained knees, and a dislocated shoulder. They also say he's going through some sort of detox."

"I think those fuckers addicted him to drugs," Hunter groused. "Pardon my language."

Brea shook her head. She had the urge to call those animals something even worse. "Speaking of...what happened to them?"

Their downturned expressions grew darker. "Emilo Montilla, the slimy bastard, got away. We took out a number of his cohorts. The *polícia* were arriving to arrest even more as we pulled out. We also rescued a woman named Laila in the compound, who was instrumental in helping us arrange the rescue mission."

Brea didn't know anything about her or why she'd helped Pierce, but if she had contributed to saving his life, Brea wanted to shake the woman's hand.

"But Montilla seems to have disappeared somewhere into the desert. Poof..." Joaquin tossed his hands in the air.

That wasn't good news. She knew without being told that cartels were full of dangerous people with long memories. What were the odds they could give up on Pierce simply because his fellow operatives had rescued him and hauled him back to the States?

"How long until he's out of recovery?" Cutter asked. "Before they know what kind of permanent damage he'll sustain?"

She shook her head, resisting the pull of fresh tears. She shifted with nervous energy instead. "I'm hoping it's not much longer. The surgeon called the operation a success, but he has no idea at this point how much Pierce will eventually recover. The next twenty-four hours are critical, so I'm going to stay."

Cutter frowned. "In a motel?"

"Yes. I'll find one later."

He hesitated, then glanced Hunter's way, who nodded. "I'll stay with you."

"You don't have to. I appreciate you wanting to protect me, but I can do this." She needed to.

"I know." He sighed. "I forget sometimes how damn grown you are. I still remember being sixteen and scaring off the bullies in your third-grade class who pulled on your pigtails."

She managed a wobbly smile. "You did. But the only thing that scares me right now is Pierce's condition."

"That's why I'm going to stay. I can be as strong as you need me to be."

"You always are." She squeezed his hand in thanks.

Hunter and Joaquin stood, then the elder Edgington brother spoke. "We're going to head home for a spell. I'd like to see Kata and my son, get some decent sleep. Then I'll be back…"

"Your wife called me earlier, too, and said she'd like to see her brother." Joaquin pointed at himself. "And my wife is worried sick. Bailey wants me home."

"Go on," Cutter said. "If there's any change, I'll call you."

"You're a bigger man than me," Hunter said.

Brea wanted to correct him. Cutter had never been her boyfriend and, contrary to popular sentiment, Pierce hadn't raped her. But Joaquin quickly shook Cutter's hand, then nodded her way, before he lifted the duffel at his feet and headed out. Hunter did the same.

She sighed. Their opinions weren't important. Right now, she needed to focus all her energy on Pierce and his recovery.

But the hours waiting for news dragged on. She refused breakfast, choosing instead to pace and pray and worry how she would cope if the worst happened. For possibly the first time in her life, Cutter was unable to soothe or console her.

Finally, at ten a.m., a nurse sought them out. "Ms. Bell? Your fiancé is out of recovery and back in his room. He's not conscious yet, but visiting hours have begun, so you're welcome to sit with him."

Relief filled her. She snatched her purse up from her abandoned seat. "Thank you. I'll follow you."

Cutter fell in behind her. "Fiancé?"

She shot him a glare over her shoulder and silently shushed him. Later, she'd take the time and energy to explain that was the only way the hospital staff had been willing to bend the rules. Now was about laying eyes on Pierce.

But nothing could have prepared Brea for the sight of him lying so bruised, half-starved, and lifeless in the sterile hospital bed. Both his eyes were black and swollen shut. Another massive hematoma covered the side of his head, which flared with a goose-egg-size knot and had been shaved to reveal an ugly, multicolored wound. The respirator covering his nose and mouth were the least of her concerns once she saw the stitches in various places on his scalp and the drain taking fluid from his brain to a bag near the bed. Bandages pinned his right arm in place and more surrounded both legs.

The sight of him so broken took Brea to her knees. "Pierce..."

Cutter was right there to pick her up and help her into the chair he rolled to One-Mile's bedside. He stood beside her, palming his face. "Jesus..."

"He's in bad shape," the nurse said. "If it had taken you and your friends even another hour to get him medical attention..."

The shake of the older woman's head said what Brea could see with her own two eyes. He would have died.

Brea pressed a hand over her mouth to silence her fear, anger, and grief. They wouldn't help him now. Only her love and her positive thoughts might.

It had been almost a month since she'd asked Pierce for space, but not a day had gone by that he hadn't crowded into her thoughts. Now she was ashamed for avoiding him, for assuming they had all the time in the world for her to sort out her feelings, for being too afraid of everyone else's reactions to open her heart to him.

That stopped now.

"What can I do?" she asked.

The nurse shrugged. "Sit with him. Hold his hand. Talk to him."

"Even though he can't hear me?"

"On some level, I think he can. He'll feel you. If there's a TV show he likes, play it. If there's a book he enjoys, read it to him. Pray for him."

"I will. Thank you."

It struck Brea that she knew Pierce on an almost painfully intimate level as a man—his scent, his kiss, his growl when he found pleasure— but she knew almost nothing about him as a person. She didn't know his TV preferences or reading habits. Did he have any food allergies? Weird quirks? She'd never asked about his past, his hopes, his concerns. They'd never discussed his politics, his religion, or his beliefs.

That realization left her feeling ashamed and distressed. She hadn't taken the time to learn him before allowing their incendiary chemical attraction to overwhelm her good sense. And now she might never have the chance to learn the real, true Pierce Walker.

Something else to mourn.

She reached for his big hand. It, too, was bruised. And battered. But she held it between hers and closed her eyes, feeling tears burn down her cheeks. "You're not alone anymore. I'm here."

No response. Not that she'd expected one. But she'd wanted it. She'd wanted the miracle. Some foolish part of her had hoped that she could heal him with her caring and her touch.

Cutter dropped a hand on her shoulder. "Don't lose faith."

He was right. This was the real world. The miracle would be Pierce surviving.

She met his glance. "I'll keep praying."

"I've never known anyone with a bigger heart. I don't know everything he did to you—"

"Don't." She couldn't talk about that night with Cutter. "Not now."

He held up his hands. "I won't. But your capacity to forgive is humbling."

Pierce had done nothing that required forgiveness, and she didn't want to waste the energy defending him now when he needed her more. "It isn't."

Because she hadn't forgiven herself for being human, for being weak in the face of temptation. But in some ways, she'd cast Pierce into the role of her personal Satan. It had been so easy to believe he'd lured her with his attention, his masculinity, his sexuality. He might have seduced her...but she had let him. And deep down, she'd blamed him. He had taken her breath away. He had overwhelmed her.

It had been so unfair. Pierce hadn't done anything except be himself. Acknowledging that painful truth made her want to cry. She needed to accept the blame for her own actions—and not let well-meaning people like Cutter and Daddy tell her she was too good to be at fault.

She would also have to decide what—if anything—came next for her and Pierce.

But the days of turning her back on him simply because she didn't have the strength to confront her own moral fragility were over.

"Would you mind leaving me alone with him?"

Cutter hesitated. "Are you sure?"

That she was ready to handle this, no. But she needed to. "Yes."

"All right. I'll, um, get us a motel room and wait there until I hear from you."

She nodded absently, then scanned him. "Are you okay to drive?"

"Yeah. And I'll be one-hundred percent after some food, a shower, and a nap."

"Thank you." She fished her car keys out of her purse and handed them over. "I'll call you when I'm ready to leave."

"All right." He pressed a kiss to the top of her head. "Bye."

"Bye," she called after him. As the sound of his footfalls grew fainter, she took Pierce's hand again and let her tears fall. "I came as quickly as I could. Oh, Pierce… My gosh. I can't even imagine how much you've suffered. You're probably not aware I'm here, and it's not much, but I'll stay by your side. I'll hold your hand. Together, we'll do everything we can to make sure you pull through."

Hours passed. She prayed and prayed. Nurses came in to check his vitals, draw blood, and change his sheets. She flipped channels on the TV until she found a sports station she hoped he might like. The shadows coming through the windows lengthened. She'd nodded off in her chair once or twice but awakened with his hand still in hers.

Early in the evening, the doctor came by to check on him. He glanced at Pierce's chart, studied his progress, then ordered more tests. As the orderlies took him away, she squeezed his hand, then glanced at the clock. It was nearly six in the evening. She hadn't eaten all day.

After a quick call to Cutter, he picked her up and took her to a nearby diner, where she devoured everything on her plate. At the motel room, she took a shower, then fell onto one of the two beds for a long nap. Cutter grumbled when she asked him to take her back to the hospital alone, but he did it.

When she arrived, it was late. The hospital was noticeably quieter. She was grateful the doctor had given her permission to stay as long as she liked.

She turned off the sports channel and turned on some of her favorite music, setting the device on the table close to Pierce. "I don't know how you feel about Coldplay, but if we're going to get along, you have to at least be willing to tolerate them."

Silence, except for Chris Martin's vocals.

She sat and stared.

Nothing.

Dang it, she had to stop hoping for the miracle.

"It feels strange not to have been at the church's market tonight. It's one of my favorite things to organize every year. I usually find a lot of Christmas presents there, you know. Well, you don't know, but I do." When she tried to imagine big, bad Pierce wandering around all the little handcrafted items that interested and fascinated her, she smiled. "It might not be your thing. But if we're going to get along, you might have to tolerate that, too."

She took his hand and squeezed it again. "When you wake up—not if, because I'm determined you will—we have a lot to talk about. And the first thing I want to tell you is how much I missed you."

Tears stung her eyes and trembled on her lashes.

As they began to fall, he twitched in her grip...almost as if he was trying to squeeze her hand in return.

Her heart leapt to her throat. She watched him, blinking, holding her breath, almost afraid to hope. "Pierce?"

He turned his head toward her voice and tried to open his eyes. "Brea..."

———— ·—×—· ————

Wednesday, October 15

One-Mile glanced at his phone. It was after seven in the evening. Brea was usually here by now. He'd memorized her schedule—hell, her every move—in the weeks since he'd been released from the hospital.

He texted her. She didn't answer.

Fuck.

A solid dozen of his worst what-if scenarios—everything from a car accident to violence to her quitting him—rolled through his head. Panic crowded in. He sucked in a rough breath to cool his anxiety. Brea was a good driver. The likelihood of anyone shooting up the small-town salon where she worked was slim. And she would never turn her back on anyone without a word, much less the man for whom she'd been a savior for the last month.

After he'd awakened in the hospital in New Orleans, Brea had maintained her vigil at his bedside for the next two days. Cutter stayed glued to her, but by unspoken agreement, they'd kept the peace, in part for her. The other part... Well, he'd saved Bryant's life in the past, and now the Boy Scout had saved his.

They were square.

Everyone had encouraged him to talk about his time in Mexico. His bosses and his team claimed they'd come to visit, but he knew the drill. They mostly wanted tactical information—how many men, what kind of operation, who were the key players. Brea had simply encouraged him to share his experiences with her. One-Mile had declined. First, he hadn't seen much that would be helpful. Second, he didn't want to traumatize Brea any more than she already was.

Since his release nearly a month ago, his condition had improved day over day. He and Brea had settled into a rhythm. She came every night after work to puree him some dinner, tidy up his house, and do an occasional load of laundry. They talked—at least as much as he could with his jaw wired shut—mostly about his physical therapy and doctor's appointments, his frustration with lingering headaches, short-term memory losses, and periodic exhaustion. She empathized, always doing her best to maintain a cheerful front and positive outlook. Yes, he knew how far he had come in just over a month. But he was impatient to be one-hundred-percent healed.

When he could get her to talk about something other than him, Brea admitted how much she worried about her father's heart condition and fretted about organizing activities at the church. He sensed she had something else on her mind, but the few times he'd asked, she'd given him a false smile and changed the subject.

He had no fucking doubt he was in love with her...but he was clueless about where he stood. Trying to express himself beyond the super-ficial when he couldn't really enunciate was somewhere between grating and I-want-to-punch-a-fucking-wall frustrating. For multiple reasons, it was hard to ask why she'd stayed by his side and done everything to help him over the last month. Because she had feelings for him? Or because she just felt sorry for him?

The idea of being her pity project made him sick.

So did the knowledge that she was still with Cutter.

During her bedside vigil in New Orleans, he'd figured out that she spent her days with him…and her nights in a nearby motel room with Bryant. If he'd had any doubt before that the two had "taken their rela-tionship to the next level," he didn't anymore. Sure, Brea might have refused to fuck her boyfriend while giving most of her waking atten-tion to the guy who had popped her cherry. But realistically, if the tables had been turned, One-Mile would have been all over Brea every chance he got. He couldn't be in the room with that woman and not crave her. But he would have wanted to remind her that, no matter how much attention she paid to another man, she belonged to him.

He glanced at his phone again. Seven-fifteen. He tried to quell his rising panic. Hair took a while to color and curl and whatever else she did, right? She wouldn't have put this much care and compassion into helping him recover if he didn't mean *something* to her. Or was he desperate enough to bullshit himself?

Fuck if he knew. He had never had more than the standard ten-minute haircut. And he'd never tried to have a real relationship with a woman. Until he could fucking talk, he still couldn't.

Eight days. That's how much longer his jaw would be wired shut. That's how long he had to wait before he could open his mouth well enough to tell Brea how he felt, kiss her senseless…and hope she recip-rocated.

He hoped like hell that she loved him—at least a little—too.

A gentle knock sounded at the door. Brea.

Thank fuck.

Excitement replaced anxiety. His heart started revving, just like it did every time he saw her.

Usually, she let herself in the house. Early in his convalescence, it had taken every bit of strength he possessed simply to get out of bed. Walking downstairs to open the door had been almost impossible and wiped him out for hours. So he'd given her a key. Tonight, despite nagging fatigue and needing a shower he feared would sap him even more, he let her in himself.

"Hey." He settled for greeting her with a nod, but he'd give anything to lay his lips over hers, get her underneath him, and convince her to ditch Cutter.

She sent him a wry smile and an eye roll as she stepped into the foyer. "Sorry I'm late, and I couldn't text you back while I was driving. My last appointment was a mess. Mrs. Goodwin thinks her husband is having an affair, and nothing I said would convince her that hair extensions weren't the answer to her marital woes."

It wasn't funny…but it kind of was. "You did them?"

"No. That takes *hours*, and I didn't have the product there. So I colored and curled her…and listened to her talk about buying new lingerie. She scheduled the extensions for next week."

"Eat something?" He shut the door behind her.

With a wrinkle of her nose, she shook her head. "My stomach is unsettled again today. Just…not hungry. What about you? Yogurt? Soup? Smoothie? Did that protein powder you ordered come in?"

He'd love to take her out to dinner, where they could eat together, talk, hold hands, and eye-fuck as they counted the seconds until they were alone. But he kept running into the limitations of his body…and the unspoken hesitation he kept feeling from her.

"Yeah. Surprise me." The short answers his broken jaw forced him to give were pissing him off, too.

"Okay. Any laundry?"

"I did it." At the surprise in her expression, he scowled. "You aren't my maid."

"No, but that's a lot for you to tackle. You should be resting. I'm here to help…"

He fucking didn't want her pity. "I got it."

When she reared back, he cursed. He must have been growlier than normal. But he felt like a volcano building and building. Every day he woke up, he ran face-first into all the things he still couldn't do—talk normally, pump serious iron, sleep without nightmares, resume his job, lay his heart on the line and tell Brea how he felt. And without that last part, sex wasn't happening. He wanted it. Ached for it. Two months was a long time without it, and she was right in front of him every day, somehow looking prettier and more womanly every time he set eyes on her. He thought about her, masturbated to fantasies of her.

He couldn't keep going like this.

"Sorry. I pushed today. I'm tired."

Her face softened as she set her purse down, gave his arm a gentle squeeze, then headed to his kitchen. Once there, she threw some juice, a protein drink, and vegetables into his blender. "And you're frustrated. I know you're used to being able to do anything and everything."

He retrieved the protein powder and set it on the counter beside her. Her hair smelled like some flowery fragrance he didn't have a name for, but it turned him the fuck on. "Yeah. Day felt long."

She paused while opening the canister and turned with wide eyes. "Oh, that's right. It was your first day without the home nurse. What was his name?"

One-Mile nodded, glad she'd remembered so he didn't have to explain while he felt like a cross between a ventriloquist and a drooler. "Stewart."

"Not too hard, I hope," she said as she scooped powder into the blender.

"No. Just more computer work."

Brea tried not to laugh. "I know how much you love that…"

"Not."

"Did you start making a dent in that Netflix list yet?"

One-Mile didn't have the heart to tell her no. She had painstakingly compiled that queue shortly after he'd been discharged from the hospital. He'd watched a few documentaries…but didn't remember much between the naps and the pain meds. In the past two weeks, he'd focused most of his effort and waking hours on rebuilding his strength and stamina.

So he'd started an exercise regimen, first walking, then running on his treadmill. Push-ups, pull-ups, biceps and triceps curls, planks—he pushed his body to the limit of the doctor's advice...and a little bit beyond—working harder every day. He'd also talked Josiah and Trees into giving him rides to the shooting range. He wanted to go back to work, so he had to stay sharp.

After all, he had a vendetta to settle.

"Got busy."

"Did you nap?"

"No." He'd resisted the urge, because once he resumed work, the bad guys weren't going to let him curl up with a blankie in the corner and check out for a couple of hours. And if he got tired enough, maybe he'd finally sleep a whole fucking night without waking up in a cold sweat.

She narrowed her eyes at him. "Did you work out again?"

Last Friday, she'd had a midday cancellation and dropped by to check on him, only to find him in his home gym pulling up on the bar attached to the door. She'd taken one look at him shirtless and dripping in sweat, swallowed hard, then blessed him out.

"Want me to lie to you?"

"Never." She sighed and started the blender. "If I thought it would do any good, I'd give you a tongue lashing."

"It won't." But he knew what he'd like her to do with that tongue.

She checked the consistency of his dinner, then, seemingly satisfied, poured it into the big plastic cup with its accompanying straw and handed it to him. "Is there anything the home nurse helped you with that you can't do yourself?"

"A shower."

Brea stilled before her stare drifted back to him. She studied him— up his legs, his abs, his chest...all the way to his face. Vaguely, One-Mile wondered whether she'd noticed behind his denim that he was hard as hell for her.

He sent her a lazy smile. "That a problem? You've already seen it all."

"Um...no problem."

Her breathless reply gave him hope. Despite his injuries, the passing of nearly two months, and however Cutter had fucking touched her, he still got to Brea. She hadn't forgotten the night she'd spent in his bed. It was all over her face.

"How can I help?" she asked.

Such a deliciously open-ended question. He almost hated to take advantage of her sweetness. He felt a teensy bit bad about trying to tempt her to cheat on her boyfriend again.

But not enough to stop.

He shrugged. "Pretty much everything. If I lose my balance and hit my head…"

"Oh…" She paled as if that possibility hadn't occurred to her. "That would be horrible."

"The neurologist said another concussion this soon could take me back to square one."

That was the truth. Not being able to shower without help…not so much. He'd been doing that for nearly three weeks. But if it took showing some skin to break down the walls between them, he was all for flashing her a full monty.

"O-okay." She nodded like she was working up her courage. "You drink your dinner. I'll, um…"

Busy yourself so you don't think too hard about seeing me naked? "You'll what?"

After a comically long moment, she sent him a stilted smile. "Find you some clean clothes. Maybe I'll change your sheets while I'm up there, too."

Perfect. "I'll be there in a few."

With a nod, she disappeared upstairs. Yeah, he felt a little guilty for stretching the truth. But he couldn't stand the bland politeness between them. If he wanted to know how she felt about him, he had to bust them out of it.

He also wondered how she would react to a body covered with a whole new litany of scars. His hair had grown back enough to disguise the ones on his scalp and the last of the yellowish bruising flaring from his temple, over his jaw. The bruising on his shoulder had almost healed. The tube they'd shoved between his ribs to help reinflate his lung was long gone, replaced by a red, puckered reminder. His back was still a network of scabs and discolorations. He'd never been anyone's definition of pretty, not with eyes like black holes, a long nose, and an aggressive jaw. Now he probably looked downright scary.

But so far Brea didn't seem afraid. He was calling that a win.

He did his best to slurp down dinner, then tiptoed upstairs. He found her in his bedroom being industrious and leaned against the doorjamb to watch her bend to tuck his sheets in place. Goddamn, she looked juicy, her hips seemingly a little rounder, her ass a little riper.

Fuck, he'd do anything to lay her across his mattress and muss up everything she'd just arranged.

"Need help?" he asked.

She turned, clearly startled. "No. Almost done."

One-Mile waited patiently while he enjoyed the view. She kept stealing clandestine glances at him. Did she want to know what he was thinking? Was she imagining him naked? Probably not, but a guy could dream.

Less than a minute later, she stood and squared her shoulders. Her face said she still worried about his condition, so she was trying to be completely appropriate and platonic.

Good luck with that, pretty girl.

"Where do we start? I'm assuming you can undress yourself?"

"Yep. Grab a towel from the linen closet in the hall and meet me in the bathroom."

Brea almost looked relieved he'd given her something else to do besides watch him strip. "Sure."

He winked her way, then headed to the bathroom and started the spray. Then he slid out of every stitch he'd worn—with the door wide open.

"I assume the blue one is okay. I—" She stopped in the doorway, blinking furiously as she stared at him. Her cheeks turned pink, her stare glued itself to his body, and her nipples went hard. "Oh, my goodness."

He just smiled. "Sorry for the, um…reaction. You do this to me."

Her gaze shifted down to his cock, standing tall and desperately ready to spend quality time with her.

Brea pressed her hand to her chest. "I…"

Clearly, she didn't know what to say. "You?"

"Ah…wanted to know if you need shampoo."

"Nope. But it might be a good idea for you to hold my hand while I climb in. You know, so I don't lose my balance on the wet tile."

"Right." Her voice trembled, but she still didn't move, just swallowed.

She was reluctant to touch him.

He backed off. "But if this is too much for you—"

"No," she assured him in a rush, then approached, hand outstretched. Her cheeks had gone red. "I just didn't expect to see you this…exposed."

She'd thought he'd be somehow less naked?

Wiping the smile off his face, he stepped into the walk-in shower, then released her hand. The hot water sluiced down his body, washing away grime and sweat. He groaned.

"Are you okay?" she asked. "Does something hurt?"

Brea was a carer. She worried about people, often more than herself. As he reached for the shampoo, he really looked at her face. The dark smudges he saw under her eyes worried him. He didn't remember seeing them before.

"Fine," he assured. "I'm better every day. What about you? Tired?"

"I am. I don't know why, just feeling run down lately. Suddenly, I want to nap all the time. It's got to be the change in seasons and the fact we've had such gloomy skies this week."

Maybe, but he didn't like it. As soon as he finished showering, he'd stop yanking her chain and take care of her for a change.

"Have you been sleeping?" she asked, changing the subject.

He lathered his hair, then grabbed the soap to scrub up his body.

Brea was still watching.

"Not much." Now that he was almost healed and getting good calories, he wasn't constantly exhausted. That was great during the day. At night? The fitful hours sucked.

"Are you still having nightmares?"

"Yeah." He turned his back on her, not eager to continue this conversational thread.

He'd been around other soldiers enough to know the symptoms of

PTSD. He was a month out from his captivity. If the anxiety and bad dreams didn't ease soon, that therapist his bosses at EM Security Management had forced him to start videoconferencing with would put a label on him that might persuade everyone to bar him from action.

One-Mile wasn't having that shit.

"Do you want to talk about them?"

"No."

"Pierce..."

As he managed his final rinse, his half-formed plan to soap up his hard cock and stroke it for her went down the drain with the suds.

Fuck, he hated that the mood between them was dead.

"Don't worry." He cut off the water.

She handed him the towel. "Of course I'm going to worry. If I didn't, why else would I come see you every day?"

"Why do you?" he asked, wrapping the terry cloth around his waist.

A pretty flush that had nothing to do with the warm, humid bathroom rushed back to her cheeks. "Because you matter."

"To who? My bosses? The guys I work with?" He stepped from the shower, challenging her. "Or to you?"

She frowned. "Of course you matter to me. Now sit so I can put this ointment on your back."

One-Mile wanted to press her for more, but it was too many words to speak with his jaw wired shut. For now, he had to settle for the fact that he mattered to her in some way. He could build from that.

Instead, he bit back a surly growl and yanked the prescription tube from a nearby drawer, then handed it to her and lowered himself onto the closed lid of the commode.

Seconds later, she set the tube down on the adjacent counter and began to spread the thick antibiotic ointment across his back, focused on where Montilla's whip had opened his flesh repeatedly over his twenty-two days of hell. Her fingers glided over his skin in a delicate brush that made him shudder in pleasure.

God, he'd love to have her hands all over him...

"Your wounds are looking a lot better," she remarked. "The scabs are really healing over."

He grunted. He couldn't see his back, but he'd believe her.

"Do you have any vitamin E oil?"

Why would he? "No."

"I'll bring some tomorrow. It helps with scarring."

Honestly, he didn't care about that much, except the damage done to his ink, but… "Will you put it on for me?"

"Of course."

"I'd like that."

She lifted her hands off him and washed them in the nearby sink. "I laid some clothes out for you on your bed in case you were too tired. Can you manage from here?"

He nodded.

"I'll meet you downstairs."

"Thanks."

Thirty seconds later, he'd tossed on the sweats and T-shirt she'd folded nicely on his well-made bed he'd give anything to share with her tonight. Just being in the same room with her made him feel calmer, more centered. Whole.

Jesus, he sounded like a lovesick schmuck—and he didn't fucking care.

After finding a pair of tube socks, he slid into those and padded down the stairs. He stopped halfway down when he spotted Brea on his sofa, head propped up on her open palm, eyes closed.

She was asleep.

On soft footfalls, he made his way to her and sat. She awoke with a start as he pulled her onto his lap and curled her head onto his shoulder.

"W-what are you doing?"

"Showing you that you matter to me, too. Rest."

The starch left her body, and she melted against him, eyes closing again. "Just for a minute."

"Sure." He dropped a kiss onto her forehead.

She sighed, then her breathing evened out.

Suddenly, he was the happiest he'd been in what seemed like an eternity.

Without really trying, Brea had become his everything.

As she curled her legs against his side and cuddled closer, he started scheming ways to keep her with him forever.

CHAPTER TEN

Thursday, October 23

Less than thirty minutes after her last client left the salon, Brea rushed toward Pierce's front door, feeling almost giddy.

Today, his jaw had been unwired. Tonight, they would finally be able to talk.

For weeks, she'd purposely kept their conversations short since speaking had been both hard and frustrating for him. But as she'd left his house yesterday, his smoldering stare had promised he would have a lot to say tonight. So did she.

Brea couldn't wait.

She'd fallen in love with Pierce Walker. After their night together, she'd already been halfway there. But now? There was no denying her stalwart warrior held her whole heart in the palms of his big hands.

Looking back, she suspected she'd been head over heels from the start. Now she had the courage to admit it.

What happened next? She didn't know, but surely God had a plan. The gospel of John said, "A new commandment I give to you, that you love one another..." So whatever He had in store, she would follow her heart.

It wouldn't be easy. Cutter still disliked Pierce. Her father knew nothing about him except as Cutter's injured teammate who had needed her Christian charity. She and Pierce were from different worlds, and they were still getting to know each other. But she refused to lose faith. After all, Joseph and Job hadn't when presented with incredible trials. By comparison, this was nothing.

She and Pierce could make something work, right?

Brea hoped so…and prayed he felt something for her, too. Because her heart kept yearning for the fairy tale.

What if he didn't love her in return? Yes, he'd given her a hundred signs that he cared. He'd even admitted he'd never felt about a woman the way he felt about her. Had he meant that as romantically as it sounded?

He's not the marrying kind.

Cutter's assertion blazed through her memory. If her best friend was right, what did that make her to Pierce, simply a friend with benefits? Had she, in her naiveté, confused his desire for love?

Tonight, she'd find out.

As she stepped onto Pierce's porch, she fluffed her hair and double-checked her lipstick in her little compact's mirror. She'd chosen a berry shade that was a bit vampier than her usual nude pink. She'd taken extra care with the rest of her makeup, too.

After she tucked the compact away, she knocked softly and waited. When he didn't answer, she used her key to unlock the door. It was the first time since he'd come home from the hospital she'd hesitated to let herself into his personal space. Now that he was healed, he wouldn't need her every night. Would he even want to see her half so often?

As she tiptoed in, music filled his great room. Not his usual hard rock with screaming vocals, but a sexy R and B tune. Soft candles lit the space. And a profusion of white, pink, and red rose petals had been scattered in a trail across the dark hardwood floors.

Goodness, what was he up to?

"Pierce?"

"In here."

She followed the petals and the sound of his voice to find him standing in his dining room, wearing a blinding white dress shirt and

distressed jeans. Light and shadows loved the angles of his sharp jaw
—no longer wired shut—almost as much as she did. He looked so
swoon-worthy, she got a little dizzy.

"You like it?" He gestured to the table beside him.

Until he pointed it out, she hadn't pried her gaze off him long
enough to realize he had set it, much less elegantly.

Had he planned dinner to say thank you for helping him? To
seduce her back into his bed now that he had healed enough for sex?
Or did the gesture mean everything she hoped? "It's very nice."

"I hope you're hungry because I'm going to feed you for a change."
He pulled out her chair. As she brushed past him to sit, he blocked her
with his big body. "Wait. It's been so damn long. Are you going to let
me kiss you, pretty girl?"

Brea didn't have to ask if he wanted to. His expression said he was
desperate to get his mouth on hers.

That still doesn't make it love…

Despite that, she gave him the only answer she could. "Yes."

"Thank fuck." He took her face in his hands and bent to devour her
mouth.

Her wildly racing heart stopped for an agonizing moment, then
thudded furiously again. Eagerly, she pressed herself against him,
barely noticing when her purse fell to the floor.

The rational part of her insisted they should talk first. But when
Pierce sank inside her mouth, desire muted logic and muzzled her
worries. She stopped caring about anything in that moment except
being as close as possible to this man.

Suddenly, he pulled away with a groan.

She blinked up at him. "What's wrong?"

"Nothing. I promised to feed you, so I'm going to." He stepped
aside and helped her into the chair. "And we can finally talk."

She was dying to know what he had on his mind, but his health
came first. "Tell me what the doctors said."

"One second." He dashed into the kitchen and, with two mitts, took
a pair of plates out of the oven. He set one before her. The other he
dropped in front of his chair beside her, then eased into his seat.

Her eyes widened. "Lasagna, asparagus, and garlic bread? You remembered?"

"That they're some of your favorites, yeah."

"Thank you." Her heart fluttered. "That's incredibly thoughtful."

"It's not homemade since I can't cook for shit, but I asked around and heard this place had the best Italian food in town."

"It smells amazing." But after his kiss, her body was pinging with life. Food was the last thing on her mind.

"It's a small way to thank you. You came here to take care of me every day for nearly six weeks, even though you'd worked on your feet all day and your father is still recovering. Even though you were burning your candle at both ends and you were tired..."

Of course Pierce had noticed. Under his gruff exterior, he was kind. Brea tried not to be disappointed that he had planned this dinner merely to show his gratitude. He'd probably feel guilty if he knew her urge to nap often lasted all day. Or that, lately, her stomach rolled from the moment she got out of bed until long into the afternoon. But telling him served no purpose.

Tonight, she felt well enough to eat the yummy, cheesy pasta he had thoughtfully brought her, so she would. She'd push aside her stupid fantasies of a future with Pierce, too.

And now that he didn't need her anymore, when she left tonight she'd take a giant step back out of his life.

"My pleasure." She managed a smile.

"You were there for me every day," he finished. "That means more to me than I can tell you. So thanks."

"There was no place else I would have wanted to be." It was true. She swallowed back the rest of her feelings. He didn't want them.

Pierce reached across the space between them to cup her cheek. "Being with you every day was *my* pleasure, pretty girl. Believe me."

She got lost in his eyes as tears stung her own. She was so utterly in love. And if he kept looking at her like that, she was going to stupidly blurt it out.

"Let's, um...get to eating, huh?" He sounded surprisingly rattled.

"Sure." She forced herself to bite into the tender pasta. The flavors burst on her tongue in a tangy surprise. "Oh, my gosh. This is really good."

"I'm glad." He shoveled in a forkful of chicken in a white wine sauce. "Hmm. I missed real food."

"No doubt." She took another bite and did her best to simply enjoy her time with him. Soon, she wouldn't see him much at all. "So tell me. What did your doctors say?"

"The neurologist went over my latest scan and gave me a clean bill of health. It's hardly a shocker that I'm supposed to avoid more head trauma. But otherwise, he released me. The orthopedic surgeon studied the last films she took of my shoulder and knees. All good. I started exercising a little earlier than she'd recommended, but it actually ended up helping me build back my strength. It wasn't my first rodeo with the shoulder, so I knew how not to pull it out of whack again. She wants to see me in another month but told me I can go ahead and resume normal activity, including work."

Brea could see the relief on his face. She'd been worried his injuries were so extensive he'd be unable to come back, and he must have had moments of doubt, too. "That's great. Just make sure you take it easy for a while."

"I'll try." He leaned forward and studied her. "But it's not an easy job."

"I know." And she did from being around Cutter. What they did was dangerous and unpredictable. Just yesterday, her best friend had been sent to Dallas at the last minute to bodyguard an up-and-coming clothing designer with a stalker. Every time he left, she worried. She could only imagine how she would feel once Pierce resumed missions again. "And I know you're a tough guy, but you're only human."

"Don't tell the bad guys that." Pierce winked. "But the best appointment was with the oral surgeon. It feels great to have my jaw back."

"I can tell you're thrilled."

"Hell yeah. He's still stunned I didn't lose any teeth, which made the process easier." He smiled. "And no one can shut me up now."

"No one wants to."

He raised a black brow. Just like that, reality splashed cold water on her. Cutter would love to shut him up. Every time she turned around, he still seemed determined to come between them. He was convinced Pierce was no good for her.

She was so happy when they were alone together. Here, in his house, she and Pierce had shared some wonderful times just making small talk, performing domestic tasks, and curling up on the sofa. She sometimes pretended they could spend their lives that way. But the reminder that, even if Pierce ever fell for her, one of the most important people in her world would never approve ate her up.

And Cutter wasn't their only obstacle. Whatever he thought, he would convey to her father. Since Daddy had always trusted Cutter's judgment implicitly, once her best friend said that Pierce didn't deserve her, getting Daddy to hear her side of things would be difficult at best. Convincing him she was right would be even more challenging. Daddy didn't mean to be old-fashioned...but he was. Just like Cutter. Neither believed she was incapable of taking care of herself; they just didn't think she should have to.

"Well, I want to hear whatever you have to say," she corrected.

He gestured to her plate. "There's a lot. Hurry and get back to eating."

"I'm doing my best without making a mess," she pointed out, then sipped from her water glass.

"Shit. I got a bottle of wine. I forgot to open it..." He stood.

She laid her hand over his. "Don't. I have to drive. I'm good with water."

He sat with a sigh and reached for his own glass of *agua*. "You sure? I wanted everything to be perfect."

For what?

"It is. The music, the rose petals, the food." She gave him the best smile she could. "You didn't have to thank me for helping you, but this is very sweet."

"Just sweet?"

Their gazes connected. In his black eyes, she suddenly saw a lot more than gratitude. Everything inside her trembled. "Were you trying to make it romantic?"

"If you've got any doubts, pretty girl, I should have tried harder."

So he hadn't done all this merely to thank her? Pleasure rushed Brea. Her smile widened. Was it even a little bit possible that he loved her, too?

"How?" she breathed.

He leaned closer. "Maybe I should have been nicer."

"If you had, I would have wondered who you were and what you'd done with the real Pierce."

"Fair enough. Maybe I should have cooked your food myself."

"Even though you can't?"

"I didn't say it was a great idea."

She laughed. "Feeding me an inedible dinner wouldn't have done much to impress me."

"Yeah, screw it." He leaned closer. "Maybe I should have just kissed you longer."

Her breath caught. "Maybe you should have."

Pierce's eyes turned impossibly darker.

No, that wasn't love…but it sure felt like it.

Then he hooked his big hand behind her neck, tilted his head, and brought her in for a crushing kiss. The desire that had been simmering under the surface collided with the feelings she'd been hoarding in her heart. Together, they made her body ache for his touch, his caring, his possession.

As he slipped inside her mouth, his tongue sliding intimately against her own, she flashed with heat. She had missed this man desperately. Not seeing him for a month after their night together had been torture. She'd been so relieved when he'd been rescued, but even over the last long weeks of his recovery, during his lowest points and surliest moods, she'd begun to ache for him again in ways she knew many would call shameful. But the need was unrelenting and inescapable. She wanted him more than the first time. More than even yesterday.

Suddenly, he lifted free, heaving hot, harsh breaths. "Fuck."

Before she could even question why he'd stopped kissing her, he lifted her from her seat, strode to the other end of the table, then laid her across the cool, hard surface.

"I want you, pretty girl. I want to make love to you. I want to do this right." He swallowed as he gripped her thighs, parted them, and stepped in between. "But I don't know how much more I can stand not being inside you. It's felt like an eternity."

"It's felt even longer than that." She didn't mean to utter her thoughts aloud, but she couldn't help it. Having Pierce so close rattled her.

"I've missed you so fucking much. I need you." He shoved her skirt up to her hips and stopped. Stared. Swallowed before he brushed his thumb up her sex, barely covered by sheer, pink silk panties. "Oh, Brea…"

Her womb clenched. Blood rushed between her legs. Moisture spilled to all the parts he caressed.

Her brain shut down.

With a whimper, she pushed her hips up to him in a desperate plea for more.

Their first night together, she'd been torn between what was right and what she'd wanted until the pleasure he'd dazzled her with silenced her misgivings. Tonight, she refused to think about anything except being close to him and feeling the ecstasy he heaped on her. Because her body burned for the satisfaction it seemed only he could give her. Because his captivity had reminded her that no one was guaranteed a tomorrow. Because she'd fallen in love with him and wanted to show him how she felt…even if she never spoke the words.

"God, I've missed you. You have the prettiest pussy," he whispered thickly as he bent to her. "Swollen, juicy…"

Pierce fastened his mouth over her, teeth nipping into the pad of her sex, tongue flattening against her clit as if her panties didn't exist. No, this still wasn't love, but need roared through her. She gripped the edge of the table to steady herself against the electrifying desire rolling through her.

"Pierce!"

"Say yes. Say you want me. Say you can't wait."

She didn't even hesitate. "Yes. I want you. Now."

With deft fingers, he unbuttoned his dress shirt and shrugged out of it. Then, with one hand, he draped it over the back of the nearby chair. With the other, he tugged her sweater up her abdomen. "Take it off."

Brea wanted it gone, too.

As she struggled to peel the V-neck over her head, Pierce shoved his big fingers under the elastic waistband of her underwear and yanked them down. The second he pulled them free and tossed them aside, he began petting her again where she ached most.

Finally, she wrestled off her sweater, but it didn't bring her any relief. Heat assailed her. Her feverish skin felt tight. If he didn't do something besides stoke this blaze, she would combust.

"Your tits look so fucking luscious," he rasped, his stare glued to her lace-clad breasts.

Under the black fire of his stare, her ache grew. Her nipples tightened and tingled. As if he now had mastery over her body, she arched, offering him her breasts. She parted her legs, giving him her sex.

"Brea. Baby…" His thumb delved between her slick folds to center on her sensitive bud. "I've dreamed of this. Why don't you remind me how pretty you look when you come?"

Everything was happening so quickly. Fierce need clawed its way past her remaining good-girl decorum, stomping all over her worry that he'd never return her feelings.

Maybe they didn't need to talk with words right now. Under this heady rise of ecstasy, she felt his caring in every touch.

As her heart gonged in her ears, her orgasm climbed in a hot rush, then crescendoed in a sharp slide up before peaking with a stunning shock of ecstasy. He unraveled her, and she imploded, bucking under him and keening until her throat burned.

"Yes." He panted, chest heaving. "Fuck."

Brea hated that word…except when he said it. Then, somehow, it ignited her. Because he was forbidden? Because when he said the word, it sounded like both an expletive and a need? Yes, and when he wrapped his raspy voice around that one blunt syllable, it sounded like praise. Like a benediction.

"I imagined you constantly," he went on. "After you said you needed space, I tried to tell myself that you couldn't have been as sexy as I remembered. But I was so fucking wrong." He brushed a kiss across her lips. "Memories of you got me through Mexico. You're everything to me."

Shock and hope sparked inside her. "Pierce, you mean so much—"

He grabbed a fistful of her hair and seized her mouth before she could finish. Brea didn't object, simply gave in to his urgency and opened herself to him, helpless to stop this new rise of desire.

Pierce tangled their tongues and slid deeper into her mouth, kissing her senseless—while managing to unfasten the clasps of her bra at her back. When the last hook gave way, he tore the garment from her body, took her breasts in his rough hands, and sucked desperately at her nipples. The pull multiplied the desire building again between her legs.

She wanted it. Craved him. But her breasts felt too tender. "Ouch."

He frowned. "Too rough?"

"A little."

"Tell me. Always tell me. I don't ever want to do anything in bed except make you feel good."

He eased off, licking, flicking, teasing. It drove Brea insane. The orgasm he'd given her so recently had somehow only left her achier and needier. Without him inside her, she felt hollow. Empty. Bereft.

She needed him to make her whole.

Brea wriggled to sit up as he kept at her nipples like a man too starved to stop. But she persisted, nudging and shoving, until she finally got a breath of space in between them.

Then she tore into the fly of his jeans, ripping the button free and yanking down his zipper.

"Oh, pretty girl. Fuck… I can't wait anymore."

He shoved his pants down, nudged her to her back again, then aligned his crest at her opening. "Tell me this is mine."

"It's yours," she gasped.

"Tell me you're mine."

She met his stare. "I'm yours."

"And no one else's," he growled. "Don't you ever fucking forget that."

Brea nodded. It was all she could manage before he gripped her hips in his big hands and impaled her with his cock.

She gasped, back arching, as she went from clenching and empty to blessedly bursting full in seconds. "Just yours."

"Yes." He clutched her with rough fingers and pushed in deeper, setting a million nerve endings inside her on fire.

"More…"

Pierce hissed, teeth bared, as he set a steady rhythm. Her breasts bounced with every thrust. Her toes curled. Her clit swelled. But it wasn't enough.

She wrapped straining fingers around his thick, bunching shoulders. "Please. I need—"

"Me to fuck you harder?"

"Yes!" Even the promise had her body revving and tightening.

"Oh. I'm fucking dying"—he banged his way inside her with more force, prodding a spot that had her eyes flaring and her desire soaring —"to be inside this sweet, tight cunt and remind you that… You. Belong. To. Me."

"I do," she panted. "I always have."

He crushed her lips beneath his for a feverish press, then wrenched back with a gasp. Their stares collided. She fell into those twin black holes. There was no escape, especially when he grabbed her hair in one fist and pressed her closer. "From now on, no one else fucks you."

"Only you," she blurted as her tension gathered and her blood rushed. "Only ever you."

Pierce shoved himself deeper, then halted as he pushed his face against hers with a growl. "Ever?"

Her heart and her breath both ceased in that moment. "Just you."

"Why?"

She needed him to thrust inside her again too much to filter. "I'm in love with you."

His whole face softened as he withdrew, then plunged home again. "Oh, Brea… Baby. My pretty girl. I fucking love you so much. I've wanted to tell you…"

His words and his touch sent her heart soaring. "Really?"

Brea didn't get a chance to say more before he seized her mouth and slammed deep, filling her again and again. Breathless, clawing, desperate, she rocked under him, pressed against him, let herself be full of him. Her need rose to dizzying heights. She cried out, called his name. Legs wrapped around him, her nails in his back, she urged him on, more aroused by every growl and harsh breath he panted in her ear.

He grew impossibly harder inside her. His strokes lengthened, deepened. His fiery stare riveted her every bit as much as his insistent cock.

"You going to come for me again?" he asked.

"I'm close..." The ache swirled and churned just behind her clit, almost there.

He ground his pelvis against her, providing the extra friction she needed to completely unravel.

"Yes... Pierce!"

"Oh, fuck. That pussy. Baby!"

The force of his impaling cock sent her higher, robbing her of breath and thought. Vaguely, she was aware of the table shaking as his every thrust inched it across the hardwood floors. Then his body stiffened, his back bowed, and he gave a hoarse shout of ecstasy. A sudden gush of warmth filled her.

They'd forgotten a condom again.

She needed to see her doctor about birth control, because right or wrong, sin or not, she wasn't giving up the pleasure she shared with Pierce Walker. He owned her—heart and body.

And he loved her.

Rough breaths and damp skin aside, she smiled up at him. "That was better than dinner."

He smiled in return. "Way better. Want to finish the pasta now or..."

When he nodded toward the stairs, she didn't hesitate. "Definitely or."

"Hmm, you're perfect." Pierce kissed her, then eased free of her body before helping her off the table.

Brea stood on unsteady feet. "I'll put the food back in the oven."

"Great. I'll start the shower."

"Shower?"

His grin widened. "I want to clean you up before I dirty you again."

She bit her lip shyly. He had a wonderfully filthy mind. "That sounds good."

"I'm going for awesome. You can tell me later if I get there." He cradled her face in his hands. "I don't ever want to give you a reason to go to bed with anyone else."

She blushed. He must know she wouldn't. But his expression said otherwise.

Then again, she'd given him too many reasons to think she was still romantically involved with Cutter. She needed to sit him down and set him straight.

Promise me you won't ever tell him we're not a couple. That will be like waving a red cape in a bull's face.

"Don't keep me waiting." Pierce kissed her, then dashed up the stairs.

Brea covered their dishes, then schlepped them into the oven. Back in the dining room, she picked up their clothes and left them folded on the table. Then she headed up the stairs.

She heard the water running, but he hadn't turned on any lights. She stopped halfway down the shadowy hall. The air pinged with tension. "Pierce?"

Brea felt his body heat behind her an instant before he pressed himself into her back and plastered her, front first, against the wall.

He nuzzled his face in her neck. "You're still naked."

His breath made her shiver. Her own turned choppy. "Yes."

"Good. I like you that way." Pierce took her hands and tangled their fingers together. She had no idea what he was doing until he pressed her palms flat against the wall. "Keep them here." Then he shoved his feet between hers and nudged them apart. "I want you splayed out and helpless. You can't stop me from kissing your neck or playing with your pussy. I can rub against you, put my scent all over you, slide my dick inside you again."

And he could. Already she could feel him hard and prodding her backside.

A thick ache of desire she would have sworn moments ago would be impossible to feel replaced her languid satisfaction. "You're a very bad man."

"Who gets off defiling this very good girl."

As his lips trailed across her shoulder, his palms roamed down her ribs, curled in with her waist, then curved out to follow the shape of her hips. His fingers skimmed back and forth, dangerously close to where she ached.

"Pierce..."

"Pretty girl?"

"You're torturing me." Her head fell back to his shoulder, exposing her throat.

He took advantage of the vulnerable space she'd ceded, dragging his lips up her neck to whisper hotly in her ear. "You want me again?"

It was as if all Pierce had to do was touch her and her body went up in flames.

"Yes."

"Not until I can fuck you properly. I want you in my bed, all spread out—waiting and panting and mine."

When he took her hand and led her to the bathroom, she frowned. "You're mean."

"Poor baby..." He shot her a dark smile. "Don't worry. I won't make you wait more than an hour or two."

"What?" she screeched in protest, every inch of her skin already sizzling and tingling for him again.

He laughed as he eased her into the wide walk-in shower. As the warm water cascaded down her body, she moaned with a whole different kind of pleasure, then tilted her head back and let the spray drench her. When she opened her eyes, she found Pierce staring as if he'd never seen any sight sexier in his life.

Brea felt confident, like a vixen who could wrap her big man around her little finger. "Come here. Don't you want to be wet like me?"

"That's a dangerous question."

"Is it?" She raised a brow at him. "What are you going to do?"

His laugh was anything but reassuring. "You can't even begin to guess. I've had weeks to dream up the filthiest ways imaginable to make you scream. My list is long and obscene."

She shivered. If anyone had asked her before meeting Pierce what her sex life would be like ideally one day, she would have said things like loving, pleasant, considerate, and sensitive. But the need he inspired in her was carnal, almost animal. She couldn't *not* want him.

"Want to give me some hints?"

"When I'm enjoying tormenting you this much? No."

He reached for the bottle of shower gel on the nearby shelf and squirted a healthy dollop into his palm, then lathered up his hands. The stare he pinned her with then made her breath catch.

He soaped her shoulders, then he caressed his way back to cover her breasts. He paid gentle attention to her nipples until she dragged in a shuddering breath before he trailed his fingers down her abdomen. "Spread your legs so I can put my hands on your pussy."

That shouldn't turn her on as much as it did. But Brea was done questioning why she enjoyed him talking so dirty to her. Instead, she parted her thighs.

He covered her sensitive sex with one big palm, rubbing and working, circling and pressing until her breath turned more uneven. Her ache gathered and grew. Her knees nearly gave out as she melted into the wall.

Then Pierce swiped the shower head from its mechanism and set the spray against her throbbing flesh.

Brea let out a needy whimper and clutched his shoulders in a silent plea while he rinsed her good and clean with a smug smile.

That wasn't all right with her.

She grabbed the bottle of soap off the shelf, lathered up her hands, and rubbed him all over with a leisurely touch, starting at his chest and slowly working her way down toward the thick stalk of his cock. When she reached it, she skimmed around his erection, focused on his thighs, paid special attention to the scars at his knees, even soaped between his toes with her fingers.

When she glanced up, he'd gathered up the suds sliding down his body and was stroking himself, eyes flaring at the sight of her on her knees.

That gave her an idea.

She leaned to one side, letting the shower spray wash away the lather coating his body. Then she pressed kisses up his flank, to his hip, over to those notches low on either side of his hair-roughened abs. When he closed his eyes with a groan, she moved in.

And licked the swollen purple crest of his hard cock.

"Brea..." He sucked in a rough gasp and slid his fingers in her hair, nudging past her lips and onto her tongue. "Yes, pretty girl. Holy fucking shit..."

His girth stretched her lips and strained her jaw. But he tasted clean, if slightly salty. He smelled like soap and musk and him. She didn't know what she was doing, but there was something both intimate and primal about having the most private part of Pierce's body in her mouth. She'd never imagined she would like oral sex. Well, she'd loved it when he'd gone down on her, but this... It was heady, almost powerful, knowing how much she could affect him.

He let out a shuddering groan, then slowly pulled free. "Okay, you've persuaded me. We'll fuck now."

Brea laughed. He didn't mean that to be funny, and maybe she should have considered it downright crude. But she knew what Pierce meant. She felt it, too. He wanted to connect with her, be inside her.

She needed that so much.

"Glad you're seeing things my way."

Together, they dried off, sharing a towel and kisses before making their way to the bedroom. He flicked on the bedside lamp, bathing the room in a muted golden glow. Without a word, she took his hands, then lay back on the bed, bringing him down with her.

Pierce poised himself over her, cock in hand, crest pressed against her opening. "Did you mean it?"

"What?"

"That you love me?"

She'd never imagined this big warrior, who'd survived a cartel's torture, would look so afraid of her answer.

With a soft smile, she caressed his cheek and said the words with her eyes before they fell from her lips. "Yes."

His sigh of relief sent his whole body forward, onto her, into her. "Brea. My pretty girl…"

She exhaled, feeling complete as he filled her. "Did you mean it?"

Elbows braced on either side of her face, he cradled her cheeks as he worked a slow rhythm in and out of her pussy. "Yeah. You have no idea…"

Then they stopped talking with words and started communicating with their bodies.

By unspoken agreement, it was a long, slow avowal of their feelings. She'd never imagined Pierce could be so gentle, yet his touch held just as much passion. Brea soaked in all his attention and caring. She needed this. After tonight, she didn't know how she would do without it. They still had so many obstacles to navigate, but she tried not to let that daunt her. No, she didn't know when or how they would overcome their hurdles. She was only determined that they would.

Her need rose swiftly, a barely banked fire that he blazed back to life with his touch, his kisses, the sound of her name on his lips. Together, they climaxed, clinging to one another through lingering caresses and shuddering moans.

Then he curled his body around hers as if he'd never held anything more precious in his life. And she cried—for how much he'd suffered, for how renewed she felt in his arms, for how bumpy their road ahead would probably be.

"You okay?" he murmured, skimming her cheek with his knuckles.

"I will be. It's a lot. I'm used to being there for everyone else and only letting go of my emotions when I'm alone. But when I'm with you, I feel so safe and adored. And all my feelings just spill out."

His dark eyes swam with unshed tears. "I've never loved anyone in my life until you."

"No other woman?"

"No one, period. I've never said those three words to anyone but you."

"Except your parents."

Pierce stiffened. "My mother died when I was a baby."

They had that in common, and her heart went out to him. "I'm sorry. I didn't know. I know how that feels, though. Weren't you close to your dad?"

He hesitated a long time, choosing instead to kiss her face, brush his lips over hers, caress the hair from her forehead. Anything except answer her question.

"Pierce?"

He sighed and shifted. She could still feel him inside her, slowly softening, but he pressed in as if he didn't want to leave. "Pierce Senior died when I was fifteen. Since my father was a horrible human being, I'm glad he's gone. I hated him."

"You don't mean that."

"Yeah, I do. It's why I killed him."

The shock of his words had barely registered when his phone chimed with a siren-like peal.

"Fuck," he muttered, then eased free from her. He was gentle about that...not so gentle when he kicked the half-open bedroom door on his way down the stairs to retrieve the device.

Her brain was still replaying his words. Every part of her turned to ice.

Had he really just confessed to killing his father as a teenager out of hate?

Yes.

Why? She'd known he killed for a living, but he ended bad guys to make the world a better place, right? He didn't shoot anyone for sport.

But did that really make it okay? According to the way she'd been raised, no.

She'd conveniently swept his profession under the rug because she'd convinced herself she knew his heart. Even now, she was desperate to believe he had a compelling reason for taking his father's life...

Or had Cutter warned her away from One-Mile precisely because he was the sort of man who didn't need one?

Pierce had defied—no, laughed in the face of—multiple commandments. He had taken the Lord's name in vain and committed murder. Since he believed she belonged to Cutter, he didn't mind committing "adultery," either. And he definitely hadn't honored his father.

Still, she hated to think that Pierce was a bad man.

Because her heart would never let her fall for someone unworthy? Or because her devotion had made her blind to his faults?

Brea darted to her feet, grabbed the bath towel they'd shared, then ran down the stairs to her clothes, only to find Pierce standing beside the dining room table stark naked with the phone pressed to his ear.

"I'm in." He paused. "Yes, I'm sure. When and where?" He listened and nodded. "On my way."

He ended the call, then turned to her with regret, as if he had something unpleasant to say. As if he hadn't terrified and confused the devil out of her moments ago. "I have to leave."

"Where?" But deep down, she knew. She'd been through this with Cutter.

He palmed her shoulders. "I'm sorry. It's work."

A completely new fear ripped through her—that he'd come back bent and broken again. Or worse, in a pine box. "Already? You just got medically cleared today."

Pierce sighed grimly. "Emilo Montilla appeared in the US, not far from where his wife and her sister are staying in a safe house. We have to stop him." He turned and headed for the stairs, then paused.

When he cupped her face, she flinched.

He swore. "I dropped a lot on you about me and my dad. I swear there's an explanation. I'll tell you the whole ugly story when I get back. You'll understand."

But what kind of explanation would make what he'd done all right?

"I promise, Brea. For now...I love you. Please be here when I get home." He brushed a kiss over her frozen lips. "And say you'll move in with me."

Look for part two of One-Mile and Brea's story, *Wicked Ever After*.
Releasing April 7!

What's next for One-Mile and Brea?
Find out in the exciting conclusion of their epic duet…

WICKED EVER AFTER
One-Mile and Brea, Part Two
Wicked & Devoted, Book 2
By Shayla Black
April 7, 2020!

He's dangerous. She's his—even if he scares her. But once he unravels her secrets, he'll do whatever it takes to claim her for good.

Sniper Pierce "One-Mile" Walker nearly had everything he ever wanted—until a fateful mission stripped it all away. Now an outcast, he's forced to watch the off-limits beauty who stole his heart slip through his fingers. Left with nothing but revenge, he's determined to defeat evil and win her back. But when he learns she's planning a future without him, he vows he'll break every rule and defy all odds to make her his again—forever.

Brea Bell was always a good girl…until Pierce Walker. Despite everyone's warnings, she gave the rough warrior her body—and her heart. When she receives news that shatters her world, he devastates her by walking away. Terrified of losing all she's ever known, Brea tucks away her dreams and commits to a "safe" future. Then Pierce appears in the dead of night, challenging and seducing her. Brea isn't sure she can trust him…but she also can't say no.

Angry and betrayed, he leaves to pursue vengeance, while her sins are exposed to the world, forcing her to fight painful battles. Can Brea and Pierce conquer the dangers that threaten their happily ever after…or will fate wrench them apart forever?

EXCERPT

CHAPTER ONE

Thursday, October 23
Louisiana

Standing naked and numb, in the middle of the empty dining room, Brea Bell blinked. What had just happened?

She felt flattened. Her world had been shaken, turned inside out, upended every which way.

Pierce Walker did that to her.

While her body had still been glowing from the pleasure he'd heaped on her, everything had begun falling apart.

Now he was gone.

The second he had answered the unexpected ring of his phone, her lover had been replaced by pure warrior. Within minutes, he'd dressed, grabbed his bag, and disappeared on a dangerous mission to tangle with the drug lord who had nearly killed him mere weeks ago.

He'd left her terrified for his safety—and burning with so many questions.

She'd known he made his living as a sniper but killed bad guys and terrorists while keeping his fellow operatives safe. At least that's what she'd told herself.

I'm glad my father is gone. I hated him. It's why I killed him.

Until Pierce had uttered those words, she would never have thought him capable of murdering his father in cold blood. How could anyone kill their own flesh and blood? Brea couldn't fathom it, but Pierce had.

And he'd expressed no remorse.

Say you'll move in with me.

His soft, shocking demand just before he'd slipped out the door still rang in her ears. How did Pierce think she could do that without imploding her entire life? And how could she commit to any sort of future with him when she didn't know whether to believe he was the steadfast protector she'd come to know…or concede she'd fallen for a bad-boy fantasy who was good with his body?

Brea couldn't stay here. She needed to go home. She had to think.

Trembling, she dressed, then defaulted to familiar domestic tasks that calmed her mind. Soon, she'd silenced the music, boxed and stored their food in the refrigerator, and cleared the table. She also made Pierce's bed, trying not to remember just how good it had felt to be underneath him on these very sheets.

Some headstrong part of her wanted to linger, as if the secret to understanding him hid under his roof and she could absorb his truths if she simply remained. But that was her hopeful heart talking.

She had to start using her head.

As she retrieved her purse from the floor, she tucked the half-spilled contents back inside, then glanced at her phone. It was nearly midnight, and her father had texted to ask when she was coming home two hours ago.

On my way.

As soon as her reply was delivered, she darkened the device. Tears threatened to fall, but she stifled them. Once she was in her room, where no one would disturb her, she could start unpacking everything alone.

Brea flipped off lights all over Pierce's house and contemplated leaving his key on the table. But that would be a cowardly way to end their…whatever this was. She owed it to them both to hear his story. Then she'd decide if giving in to her heart and including him in her future were in her best interest.

How ironic. She'd knocked on Pierce's door a few hours ago, hoping they had a chance at a new beginning together. After tonight, she wasn't sure there'd be any coming back.

The silence as she headed back to Sunset through the inky night felt heavy. The old her would have called Cutter and asked for his advice. But she already knew what he'd say. She didn't want any opinions now except her own.

When she pulled into her driveway, the house looked dark, except for the light Daddy kept on above the stove whenever she was late. Bless him…

Her fingers fumbled as she unlocked the door. She dead-bolted it behind her, then dashed to her room. In the dark, she dropped her purse on the desk to her left and shut herself inside before she fell across her bed and let her thoughts run free.

Who was this man, deep down, she'd given herself to? What had she done?

She'd fallen in love. She'd let herself believe she and Pierce could forge something lasting, despite their chasm of differences.

She might have made a colossal mistake.

Brea grasped now why people called it heartache. Hers bled with wrenching uncertainty and pain. Sobs followed.

Behind her, the lamp on her nightstand suddenly flicked on.

She sat up with a gasp. Her father stood not two feet away, watching her with a disappointed stare.

"Brea." He never yelled. He never had to. His ability to emote, which made him so good behind the pulpit, also made him an amazingly effective parent.

She wiped the tears from her cheeks. "Daddy, what are you doing up? Do you need something?"

With a heavy sigh, he sat beside her and took her hand. "Just to talk to you. You've been the best daughter a man could have asked for, and I know you're a grown woman…"

Brea heard the "but" in his voice. Since she was a pleaser, the worst possible punishment had always been enduring her father's disapproval. "Daddy…"

"Let me finish. I know where you've been and what you've been doing." He frowned.

He'd found out about Pierce? Figured out they'd had sex?

Her heart stopped. "I can explain."

But what could she say to reassure him that wouldn't be a lie?

"You may think I'm naive or out of touch, and I realize almost no one saves themselves for marriage anymore."

She knew where this was going, and it wasn't fair. "Then why are you lecturing me? You're not waiting. I know about you and Jennifer Collins."

"I never said I was perfect. But there's a big difference. Jennifer and

I have both been married. We lost our spouses because it was His will —my wife shortly after childbirth, her husband in war. We spent months getting to know each other. We started as friends. We've taken our relationship very slowly. We waited three years to take the step you have with this man you've known for...how long?"

By comparison, her answer would make her sound rash. "Not three years."

"Not even three months. I know your generation has a 'hookup' mentality, but—"

"It's not like that."

"All right," he conceded. "But the fact that I haven't met him—that he hasn't done me the courtesy or you the honor of even showing his face—concerns me."

Of course Daddy would see it that way. "I didn't think I needed your permission to date someone. I'm an adult."

"You are, but I'm concerned. You haven't acted like yourself in weeks. You've been quiet. Secretive. Sometimes even evasive. I've been worried something was troubling you. So I asked Cutter. He expressed concern about your attachment to this fellow operative, whom he categorized as savage and unprincipled. Dangerous. And not good enough for you."

She wasn't sure what to think about Pierce right now, but she couldn't not defend him. "You don't know him, Daddy. Cutter is biased after they argued during a mission."

"Maybe. But do you know what this man does for a living?"

Her father was gentle. He condemned violence. Though Cutter and Pierce worked on the same team, her friend got a pass because he rescued hostages and often provided first-response medical attention to people in need. He protected those afflicted by war.

Pierce just killed.

"Yes."

And how would Daddy react if he ever found out Pierce not only executed others but had killed his own father?

"Then you understand why, in my eyes, he seems like a taker of virtue and lives. Brea, you falling for someone like this... It's not you."

"He's more than his job. And he saved Cutter's life."

"I'm grateful for that, but I fear he's twisted your naive heart to his advantage." He squeezed her hand. "Sweetheart, I'm not blaming you. I'm not surprised you weren't worldly or strong enough to resist. I just want you to open your eyes."

Brea reared back. Not worldly enough was fair. But strong? "I've taken care of you through two surgeries while keeping your church activities rolling, handling your parishioners, and still doing my own job. I've always tried to make you proud. But if he's a mistake, Daddy, he's mine to make. I'll handle it."

"I know you've had a lot on your plate. And of course I'm proud of you. Like I said, I've been blessed with the best daughter I could have asked for. But this man—"

"Stop. I've resisted every other temptation. Maybe I didn't resist him because I'm not meant to."

He pressed his hands together, almost as if he prayed for her. "Has he ever discussed marriage?"

"No."

He'd talked about moving in… Something she couldn't do without bringing shame to her father, her church, and her upbringing.

Brea knew these were antiquated concepts to most people her age. Nearly everyone she'd met in cosmetology school thought she was nuts. They'd shunned her because she didn't want to drink at bars, swipe right, or spend her Saturday nights in bed with a stranger. She'd been okay with that—mostly because she'd never been tempted.

Pierce had changed everything.

If he had asked her yesterday to move in, she would have been hard-pressed not to say yes—even knowing she would have had to ask her father for forgiveness and her community for understanding. But for a man she *really* believed in, she would have risked everything.

She didn't know if Pierce was truly that man.

Despite her doubts, her heart didn't want to let him go. Most of her drive home, she'd tried to negotiate with herself and rationalize some way in which him killing his own father was okay. Other than self-defense, Brea couldn't think of a scenario.

"Is that why you were crying?"

It was tempting to tell Daddy what he wanted to hear, but

compounding a sin with a lie wasn't right. "No. I was crying because I don't know if he and I can work it out."

"I'm sorry if he breaks your heart. Anything that hurts you hurts me. But I hope you'll make the best choice for your future." He took her shoulders in his grip. "If that's not with him, I promise you *will* heal. And someday, you'll find a man who loves you and wants to honor you with vows and his ring."

She understood what he was trying to say. But Pierce hadn't grown up a preacher's kid or steeped in a church. For most people her age, without her upbringing, moving in together was a vast commitment. He probably thought he'd shown her his devotion.

"I want to get married someday. Right now, I'm just trying to figure things out."

His face softened. "I know. And we all make mistakes. It's God's way of teaching us what we need to know. Your red eyes tell me this lesson has been hard for you."

"I hear the cautions you and Cutter are giving me, but my heart wants to believe he's the one."

His smile was full of understanding. "First love is like a fever. It sweeps through your whole body, and you feel so weak in the face of something so strong." He hesitated. "When I was seventeen, I knew what I wanted to be when I grew up. I'd already heard God's calling. But...so many of my friends had girlfriends. And they were having sex. It was fine, I told myself. Resisting temptation was a trial from God, so I stayed strong. Until I met a girl while working my summer job. We had a lot of fun dating in May. By the end of June, I suspected I was in love. Then things got heated. Over Fourth of July, her parents went on vacation and left her behind." He shrugged. "I was weak, and it wasn't my finest moment. I wasn't her first lover, but that didn't matter to me. I loved her. My parents found out what I'd done and they did something amazing for me."

"What?"

"They challenged me not to see her for a month."

Brea frowned. "Why?"

"My father told me that if it was truly love, then a month would change nothing. I would still be in love with her and she would be waiting for me. It was either that or they would take my car keys until school started in September."

"What happened?"

"I chose her and gave them my car keys. I thought walking to work in the heat and missing out on time with my friends would be a small hardship because she would be by my side. As it turned out, not so much. She wasn't as interested in being with me when I couldn't take her places. And by August, she'd found someone else and left me brokenhearted. I spent a miserable month wishing I'd taken my parents' alternative."

Brea understood. That girl clearly hadn't loved him at all.

"So I'm going to ask the same of you."

"Daddy, I'm twenty-two. I paid for my car. I'm not giving it up. Besides, I couldn't get to work without it."

He held up a hand. "That's not what I meant. I'm merely challenging you not to see him for a month so you can figure out how you feel. If he really loves you, he'll wait."

But Daddy's tone made it clear he was convinced Pierce would move on. Brea didn't know what to say.

"By the way, I met your mother four years later. I knew instantly she was the one. We both agreed to explore the sexual part of our relationship after we were married. My wedding night was one of the best of my life because I knew we'd made the right decision. I won't lie; that was a long wait, but so worth it."

Daddy was brilliant at persuading people to look at a situation through his lens. And he often made great points.

"I need to sleep on everything you've said." And she needed to hear what Pierce had to say before she could determine if she needed to fight for him...or let him go.

"Of course. We'll catch up on Saturday. I'm doing my first full day back in the office tomorrow, so I'm expecting a lot of crazy."

"Okay. Let's talk then."

He kissed her forehead. "No matter what, I love you."

"I love you, too."

"Just promise me you'll make decisions that add to *your* happiness before worrying about anyone else's."

"I will."

———— ·—·—· ————

The following morning, Brea rolled over, stretched, and opened her eyes. Last night when she'd laid her head down, she would have sworn she was far too upset to do anything but toss and turn all night. Instead, the minute her head had hit the pillow, she'd all but fallen into a coma.

She glanced at her bedside clock. Eight thirty? Her first appointment was in an hour. Yikes!

Tossing off her covers, she sat up and bounded out of bed.

Instantly, a crash of nausea dropped her to her knees. She clutched her stomach and barely managed to crawl to the toilet before she lost the contents of her stomach.

Ugh. She must have picked up the stomach flu from one of her clients.

Early in her career as a hairdresser, she'd learned the hard way that the public was germ-filled. She'd been sicker that first year than she'd ever been.

When she'd finished retching, Brea flushed the toilet and lay back on the blessedly cold tile. She was going to have to call into work, darn it. After all the disruptions to her schedule these past few months, she really hated to lose the cash flow—or, potentially, her hard-earned clientele. But it wasn't like she could coif people while she was vomiting.

Brea took some deep breaths, trying to calm her rolling stomach. But the smell of her citrus-vanilla bath beads on the nearby tub stung her nose and revived her urge to throw up.

Seconds later, nausea forced her to pitch her head over the toilet again.

When she'd finished, she pinched her nose closed and picked up the offending box, dragging it—and herself—to the garage, where she dumped the bath beads in the trash to go out with Monday's pickup. The second she let herself back in the house, she sagged against the doorway with a groan.

What the heck was going on? She'd loved that scent since one of her middle school friends had given her those bath beads as a birthday gift. She had repurchased them over and over because they always brought her comfort and pleasure. So why had the smell suddenly made her sick? Well, sicker.

Scents had nothing to do with the stomach flu...

Instantly, a more terrifying reason for her smell sensitivity crowded her brain.

She raced across the house and grabbed her phone from its charger. The first thing she saw was a message from Pierce.

`Made it to location. No sign of the asshole yet. May be here a few days. I'll call when I can. See you when I get home.`

Her relief that he was safe—at least for now—warred with her indecision about their future. But she shoved it aside to launch the app on which she charted her periods.

According to this, she hadn't had one since early August. November was a week away.

That couldn't be right. She couldn't possibly have missed *two* periods.

But she feared her memory wasn't faulty.

August, September, and October had been a whirlwind of craziness —Cutter's hostage standoff, Daddy's relapse and second surgery, Pierce's capture and recovery, keeping the church going, her business flowing... She vaguely remembered thinking earlier this month that she'd missed a period, but she hadn't been shocked, given all the stress she'd been under.

She hadn't really believed that in one night Pierce had gotten her pregnant.

But it was possible. She was tired all the time. Her breasts were tender. She was weepy. She craved sex. The signs were there; she simply hadn't put them together.

Brea sagged back to her bed, staring at the ceiling, and gaped. If she was pregnant...what was she going to do? If Daddy had been disappointed last night, he would be crushed by this news. And what would she tell Pierce? He'd asked her to be his live-in girlfriend, not have his children.

And what kind of father would he, a man who took lives, make?

Don't get ahead of yourself. One thing at a time.

First, she had to find out what she was dealing with.

Thanking goodness Daddy was already at the church, she brushed her teeth and called in sick to work. The receptionist, bless her, promised to contact all her clients and reschedule. Then Brea dragged on some sweatpants and a hoodie, mustered up her courage, shoved down more nausea, and drove to the drugstore.

As she sat in the parking lot at the little pharmacy around the corner, Mrs. Simmons, her first-grade teacher, walked out of the sliding double doors and waved her way. She watched Mr. Laiusta, one of her dad's parishioners, hop out of his car two spots down. Two guys she'd gone to high school with emerged, sodas and chips in hand, and eyed her through her windshield.

She couldn't possibly walk into that store and buy a pregnancy test. Someone would see her. And everyone in town would know her secret by the end of the day.

Swallowing down another wave of sickness, she backed out and drove to Lafayette. She was familiar with the drugstore near the hospital; she'd had some of Daddy's medicines filled there after he'd been discharged. No one at that location would know her. No one would care.

Even so, when she arrived, she braided her long hair, wound it on top of her head, then plucked of one Daddy's discarded ball caps from her backseat and pulled it low over her eyes.

It took her less than five minutes to purchase a pregnancy test. The bored forty-something woman behind the register didn't blink, just counted out her change and looked to the next customer in line.

Bag in hand, Brea froze in indecision near the door. Drive the twenty minutes home to take the test? What if Daddy's first day back at the church had proven overwhelming and he cut his day short to come home? Or what if she messed this test up and needed another one?

She couldn't risk it. Besides, she didn't want to wait any longer than necessary to learn the truth.

Head down, she slinked to the back of the store and found the ladies' room. Thankfully, it was a restroom for one. She shut and locked the door, then tore into the box and scanned the instructions.

As she washed her hands, they shook. Then she sat on the toilet with the test strip.

A wave of nausea swamped her again—a combination of her nerves and the sharp scent of the antiseptic cleanser. She swallowed back another urge to vomit as she finished administering the test. Then she set the strip on her plastic bag strewn across the counter and bent to wash her hands again.

She had to wait three minutes. It would be the longest one hundred eighty seconds of her life.

But as soon as she rinsed the soap and dried her hands, she glanced at the test strip.

Less than a minute had passed, and the result window was already displaying two solid pink lines.

Pregnant.

On a gut level, Brea had expected it, but she still found herself stunned. She looked at herself in the drugstore's grimy, water-splotched mirror. "What am I going to do?"

Her reflection had no reply.

She broke down and sobbed.

Everything in her life was about to change.

Why hadn't she insisted on a condom? Why hadn't he ever used one?

Maybe he just hadn't cared. After all, he wasn't the one pregnant now… He didn't have to pick up the pieces or face his community or raise his child alone.

The handle jiggled, then a light tap sounded at the door. "Someone in there?"

"Just a minute," she answered automatically, then gathered up the bag, box, and test before throwing them all in the garbage. Then she swiped away her tears, tried to plaster on a fake smile, and opened the door.

As she walked out, a woman with a baby on her shoulder and a diaper bag in hand gave her a little smile. "Thanks."

Then the door closed. Brea was alone, with the rest of her life stretching out, endless and terrifying, in front of her.

What was she going to do?

She slid her hand over her still-flat belly and exhaled. Apparently, she was going to have a baby.

But without hurting her father, jeopardizing her career, and tearing apart her community, how? And how would Pierce feel about this?

Mechanically, Brea eased into her car and headed back to Sunset. Traffic was light. She didn't remember the drive.

When she reached home, she parked and ran into the house. She tore off her clothes and slid back into her pajamas. The house was so quiet. She felt utterly alone—shocked and scared. Eventually, she'd have to get up and face her problems like an adult, and she knew her tears were pointless. But right now she needed to shed them, just like she needed reassurance that somehow, someway, everything would be all right.

She needed Cutter.

He was in Dallas, working. Normally, she would never call while he was on the job. But he alone would hear and understand her like no one else.

Brea grabbed her phone from the purse she'd discarded at the foot of her bed and dialed her best friend. Before he even answered, more tears sprang to her eyes.

"Hey, Bre-bee."

"C-Cutter, hi. I hate to call you...but I could use an ear."

"What's wrong?"

"This is probably a bad time, and I'm sorry. Really. But I don't know where else to turn."

"Slow down. It's okay. Tell me what's going on."

"I woke up this morning and I felt horrible. I didn't know what was wrong and then I... Ugh. I'm talking too much. But I'm afraid to just blurt everything. You're going to be mad. Everyone will be shocked. Daddy will be disappointed. I just"—her breaths came so quick and shallow that she feared hyperventilating—"don't know how to say this but...I think I'm pregnant."

"What?" he growled. "Have you seen a doctor?"

"No. I bought a test at a drugstore in Lafayette and took it in their bathroom. I'm still in shock. B-but I'm shaking and I can't stop crying. I don't know what to do."

"Make an appointment today. Find out for sure. If you're right, this isn't going to go away."

"I can't see Dr. Rawson. The first thing he'll do is tell my dad. I know he's not supposed to but..." She shook her head and tried to think of solutions instead of continuing to dump problems on him. "What about that clinic near your apartment?"

"Fine. Call there. But you need to see a doctor before you make any decisions. I'll go with you if you want. I'm home in a week. I promise not to confront Walker until then. But if you're right—"

"You can't say or do anything to him."

"The hell I can't."

"He doesn't know yet. He left on a mission last night, and I don't know when he'll be back. He's gone after the guy who held him captive in Mexico, so I don't even know if he'll return in one piece. I'm worried." She clutched the phone. "You have to promise me—"

"That when he shows his ugly face I won't kill him? I can't promise that."

"Cutter, you aren't helping."

"All right." His voice took a gentle turn. "I promise we'll figure this out. I'll take care of you. I always have. I always will. And I hate to do this to you now, but I have to go."

"Are you in a situation?"

"Client meeting."

She winced. "I'm sorry."

"No, I'm glad you called me. As soon as I'm free, we'll talk, okay?"

"Thanks."

The sudden silence in her ear told her that Cutter had ended the call. The sound was lonely and terrifying. And when she darkened her own device and tossed it on the bed, she lowered her head in her hands and started to cry again.

WICKED & DEVOTED WORLD

Welcome to the new Wicked & Devoted world! So thrilled you've joined me on this adventure. There's lots more to come!

So far, you've read a little about a lot of characters. Some of them still haven't had their stories. Others have. Below is a guide in case you'd like to read more about those you may have missed in other books:

WICKED LOVERS

Wicked Ties

Jack Cole (and Morgan O'Malley)

She didn't know what she wanted…until he made her beg for it.

Surrender to Me

Hunter Edgington (and Katalina Muñoz)

A secret fantasy. An uncontrollable obsession. A forever love?

Belong to Me

Logan Edgington (and Tara Jacobs)

He's got everything under control until he falls for his first love…again.

Wicked All the Way

Caleb Edgington (and Carlotta Muñoz Buckley)

Could their second chance be their first real love?

His to Take

Joaquin Muñoz (and Bailey Benson)

Giving in to her dark stranger might be the most delicious danger of all…

Falling in Deeper

Stone Sutter (and Lily Taylor)

Will her terrifying past threaten their passionate future?

DEVOTED LOVERS

Devoted to Pleasure

Cutter Bryant (and Shealyn West)

A bodyguard should never fall for his client…but she's too tempting to refuse.

Devoted to Wicked

Cage Bryant (and Karis Quinn)

Will the one-night stand she tried to forget seduce her into a second chance?

Devoted to Love

Josiah Grant (and Magnolia West)

He was sent to guard her body…but he's determined to steal her heart.

As the **WICKED & DEVOTED** world continues to collide and explode, you'll see more titles with other characters you've met here and (hopefully) love. So stay tuned for books about:

Zyron (Chase Garrett)

Trees (Forest Scott)

And more!

I have *so* much in store for you on this wild, wicked ride. Happy reading!

Shayla

LET'S GET TO KNOW EACH OTHER!

Shayla Black is the *New York Times* and *USA Today* bestselling author of nearly eighty novels. For twenty years, she's written contemporary, erotic, paranormal, and historical romances via traditional, independent, foreign, and audio publishers. Her books have sold millions of copies and been published in a dozen languages.

Raised an only child, Shayla occupied herself with lots of daydreaming, much to the chagrin of her teachers. In college, she found her love for reading and realized that she could have a career publishing the stories spinning in her imagination. Though she graduated with a degree in Marketing/Advertising and embarked on a stint in corporate America to pay the bills, her heart has always been with her characters. She's thrilled that she's been living her dream as a full-time author for the past eleven years.

Shayla currently lives in North Texas with her wonderfully supportive husband and daughter, as well as two spoiled tabbies. In her "free" time, she enjoys reality TV, reading, and listening to an eclectic blend of music.

TELL ME MORE ABOUT YOU.

Connect with me via the links below. The VIP Readers newsletter has exclusive news and excerpts. You can also become one of my Facebook Book Beauties and enjoy live, interactive #WineWednesday video chats full of fun, book chatter, and more! See you soon!

Connect with me online:
Website: http://shaylablack.com
VIP Reader Newsletter: http://shayla.link/nwsltr
Facebook Author Page: http://shayla.link/FBPage
Facebook Book Beauties Chat Group: http://shayla.link/FBChat
Instagram: https://instagram.com/ShaylaBlack/
Book+Main: http://shayla.link/books+main
Twitter: http://twitter.com/Shayla_Black
Amazon Author Page: http://shayla.link/AmazonFollow

BookBub: http://shayla.link/BookBub
Goodreads: http://shayla.link/goodreads
YouTube: http://shayla.link/youtube

If you enjoyed this book, please review it and recommend it to others. It means the world!

Join the

Shayla**BLACK**

NEW YORK TIMES AND USA TODAY BESTSELLING AUTHOR

Book Beauties
Facebook Group
http://shayla.link/FBChat

Join me for live,
interactive video chats
every #WineWednesday.
Be there for breaking
Shayla news, fun,
positive community,
giveaways, and more!

VIP Readers
NEWSLETTER
at ShaylaBlack.com

Be among the first to get
your greedy hands on
Shayla Black news, juicy
excerpts, cool VIP
giveaways–and more!

OTHER BOOKS BY SHAYLA BLACK

"Wicked All Night" (novella)

"Forever Wicked" (novella)

Theirs to Cherish

His to Take

"Pure Wicked" (novella)

Wicked for You

Falling in Deeper

"Dirty Wicked" (novella)

"A Very Wicked Christmas" (short)

Holding on Tighter

THE DEVOTED LOVERS (Complete Series)

Devoted to Pleasure

"Devoted to Wicked" (novella)

Devoted to Love

THE PERFECT GENTLEMEN (Complete Series)

(by Shayla Black and Lexi Blake)

Scandal Never Sleeps

Seduction in Session

Big Easy Temptation

Smoke and Sin

At the Pleasure of the President

MASTERS OF MÉNAGE

(by Shayla Black and Lexi Blake)

Their Virgin Captive

Their Virgin's Secret

Their Virgin Concubine

Their Virgin Princess

Their Virgin Hostage

Their Virgin Secretary

Their Virgin Mistress

Coming Soon:

Their Virgin Bride (TBD)

DOMS OF HER LIFE
(by Shayla Black, Jenna Jacob, and Isabella LaPearl)
Raine Falling Collection (Complete)

One Dom To Love

The Young And The Submissive

The Bold and The Dominant

The Edge of Dominance

Heavenly Rising Collection

The Choice

The Chase

Coming Soon:

The Commitment (Late 2020/Early 2021)

FORBIDDEN CONFESSIONS (Sexy Shorts)

Seducing the Innocent

Seducing the Bride

STANDALONE TITLES

Naughty Little Secret

Watch Me

Dangerous Boys And Their Toy

"Her Fantasy Men" (Four Play Anthology)

A Perfect Match

THE MISADVENTURES SERIES

Misadventures of a Backup Bride

Misadventures with My Ex

SEXY CAPERS (Complete Series)

Bound And Determined

Strip Search

"Arresting Desire" (Hot In Handcuffs Anthology)

HISTORICAL ROMANCE

(as Shelley Bradley)

The Lady And The Dragon

One Wicked Night

Strictly Seduction

Strictly Forbidden

BROTHERS IN ARMS (Complete Medieval Trilogy)

His Lady Bride

His Stolen Bride

His Rebel Bride

PARANORMAL ROMANCE

THE DOOMSDAY BRETHREN

Tempt Me With Darkness

"Fated" (e-novella)

Seduce Me In Shadow

Possess Me At Midnight

"Mated" – Haunted By Your Touch Anthology

Entice Me At Twilight

Embrace Me At Dawn

CPSIA information can be obtained
at www.ICGtesting.com
Printed in the USA
LVHW042041090320
649445LV00009B/1384

9 781936 596591